P.O.W.E.R.S.
Road to Psion

T.C. Pulley

Copyright © 2019 T.C. Pulley
All rights reserved.
ISBN: 9781689262606

DEDICATION

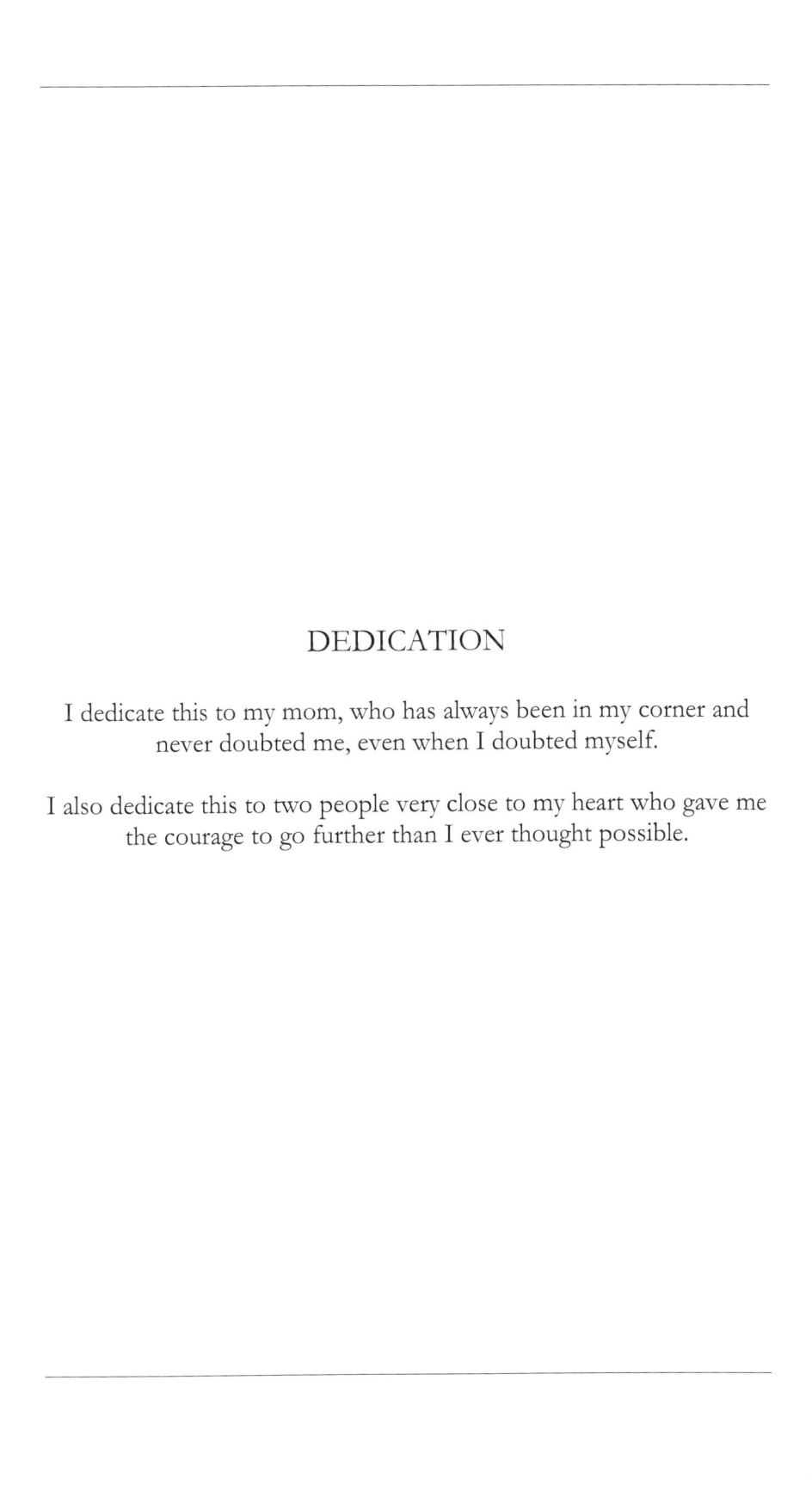

I dedicate this to my mom, who has always been in my corner and never doubted me, even when I doubted myself.

I also dedicate this to two people very close to my heart who gave me the courage to go further than I ever thought possible.

Table of Contents

Prologue .... Pg. 1

Chapter 1: Sek, 1994 to 2015 .... Pg. 9

Chapter 2: James, 1998 to 2014 .... Pg. 13

Chapter 3: Amanda, 2006 to 2007 .... Pg. 18

Chapter 4: Amanda, 2007 to 2010 .... Pg. 24

Chapter 5: Crow and Amanda, 2010 .... Pg. 32

Chapter 6: Crow, Amanda, and Hugo, 2012 .... Pg. 37

Chapter 7: Crow, 2012 .... Pg 51

Chapter 8: Crow's Return, 2012 to 2016 .... Pg. 64

Chapter 9: James' Departure, 2016 .... Pg. 73

Chapter 10: Sek's Awakening, 2016 .... Pg. 78

Chapter 11: Sek's Misadventure, 2016 .... Pg. 89

Chapter 12: Sek and James, 2016 .... Pg. 103

Chapter 13: First Meetings, May 13, 2016 .... Pg. 118

Chapter 14: Preparations .... Pg. 129

Chapter 15: The Trap .... Pg. 141

Chapter 16: The Chase .... Pg. 154

Chapter 17: To Psion .... Pg. 168

Chapter 18: Settling In .... Pg. 178

Chapter 19: One Hour .... Pg. 190

Chapter 20: Junior Team .... Pg. 200

Chapter 21: Equipment in R&D .... Pg. 213

Chapter 22: Breaking In .... Pg. 221

Chapter 23: The Bayou Brothers .... Pg. 228

Chapter 24: Into the Lab.. Pg. 238

Chapter 25: Debrief and Decompress....................................... Pg. 249

Chapter 26: The Prayer Garden... Pg. 258

Chapter 27: The Whistling Man... Pg. 264

Acknowledgement

I would like to thank my editor Martha E. Hermerding who not only helped uncover the diamond in the rough, but also taught me a thing or two along the way.

I would also like to thank those who inspired James and Sek for the laughs and the jokes along the way that made this more than just another story.

Prologue

July 4, 1950 – 4:45 AM

    Deep within the Cheyenne Mountain Complex, Robert Stonegate, the warden of the highest security prison the citizens of the United States knew nothing about, was making his way to his specialized interrogation room. Dangerous thoughts raced through his mind and he vowed that today his point would be made. To the people confined within the Cheyenne Mountain Parahuman Detention Center, Stonegate was the harbinger of death, standing six feet tall with his dark hair buzzed in the typical military cut and his cold, steel gray eyes focused on his destination ahead. Weaker men would cringe and moan at his very shadow, but the man he was going to deal with so early in the morning was no ordinary man. No matter how much he had been put through, he had refused to break, but Stonegate was not concerned. After all, everyone had their limits, and when he met his, it would be at the toe of the boot of the man every parahuman in existence feared.

    "Oh, Sammy boy, I hope you got a good night's sleep. You're going to need it," he called out as he stopped just beyond the door. A dangerous smirk curled at the corner of his mouth as he opened the door and began, "Samuel Irons, aka Uncle Sam. You –"

    His words died in the back of his throat as his gaze fell on broken metal scraps, damaged tools, and his beloved "Pain Chair" twisted and destroyed in the middle of the room. The prisoner meant to be secured was nowhere to be found, and Robert grit his teeth. Keeping a calm exterior, he raised his balled fist and slammed it into the frame of the door, bending the metal beneath the force of the blow. Seething hatred reflected in his cold eyes as he said the name of the one man he suspected to be behind it, "Iron Mountain."

Just then an alarm began to howl throughout the facility, and instinctively Robert Stonegate unhooked his faithful baton from its secured holster on his hip. With a press of a button, it extended to its full length, and with another click, there was a hum before a current of electricity coursed wildly through it, and the customized brand at the top started to glow with heat. Every prisoner had felt the fire of the electric hot metal as it burned his initials into their flesh, marking them as his. He left the room and walked back from where he came muttering, "Let the games begin."

July 4th, 1950 – 5:03 AM

The containment cells deeper into the mountain were alive with chaos. The only light was the faint red glow of the emergency lighting running the length of the floor on each side, and weak, battered prisoners stumbled out of their cells to cluster in the middle of the hall. Each wore a muted gray jumpsuit with the letters CMPDC with a series of numbers beneath it embroidered across the breast. They ranged from men to women, young to old, and across all nationalities. Each prisoner was worn, beaten down, and tired except for the two brothers systematically going from cell-to-cell making sure everyone was out.

The first was a man in his mid-forties with bright blue eyes and curled hair so blonde it almost looked white. He stood at about five-foot ten, and even though he had an average stature, the muscles peeking out from his jumpsuit made it clear he had strength to spare. He was Uncle Sam: The inspiration behind the classic U.S. military recruitment poster.

The second man stood at eight feet tall. Where Uncle Sam had a fair complexion that had been tanned by hard work in the sun serving his country, his brother's skin was metallic, the color of a naval ship hull. In fact, there were tracks and deck rivets running up the length of his arms that disappeared under his sleeves. He raised his head to get a better look at his brother, and the words DE-173 could be seen across his left collarbone. His trademark naval haircut was made of the same deck steel a few shades darker than the rest of his body. What would have been the whites of his eyes was a lighter shade of gray, and his pupils were as dark as the rest, but his irises were so pale a gray that the fierce blue they had once been almost shone through. This was the man known as Iron Mountain.

Together, they rallied their comrades and initiated the next step of their escape plan.

July 4th, 1950 – 5:43 AM

Overcoming numerous obstacles and suffering a few losses of their own, the group following Iron Mountain and Uncle Sam made it to the last room just beyond their escape: hanger bay fourteen. However, upon trying to open the doors, they realized that those who had broken from their group to hack into the system had not succeeded. While fear and regret began to overcome a few of the escapees, Iron Mountain, Uncle Sam, and another prisoner – an old man with inhuman physical strength – went to force open the hulking doors. The second they gained access into the bay, soldiers descended on them.

Many of the parahumans called upon their unnatural abilities to stand against the hellfire of bullets that rained down upon them and pushed their enemies back so the weaker prisoners could move safely along the sidewall of the hanger. Iron Mountain and Uncle Sam did everything within their power to keep the enemy focused on the two of them, but as more and more soldiers filed in, others had to take up arms. Destruction was unavoidable and so too were casualties on both sides. The downtrodden prisoners persisted and pushed forward until they were able to take on the final stand of soldiers at the end of the bay.

A few more fell to the gunfire of the soldiers, and it was the death of a small child that changed the course of battle. Up to that point, the prisoners had merely been trying to get to freedom, but now they were taking it, heaven help whoever stood in their way. They easily dispatched the men who stood before them and blocked the path behind them, buying as much time as they could. Their group, which had started out together sixty-one strong, had now dwindled to thirty-five, but they would not be stopped by regret. Instead, they pushed on in memory of those who had fallen.

But when they made it out to the landing dock, it was empty.

July 4th, 1950 – 6:17 AM

Iron Mountain and Uncle Sam stepped out ahead of their group, scanning the sky for the ship that was supposed to be waiting for them piloted by fellow prisoner Roswell. There was nothing that could hint why he was not there, and the brothers looked at each other at a loss for what to do next. A sense of doom began to fall over the prisoners who had just tasted the outside air for the first time in so long. Feeling their chance at freedom slipping from their fingers, the group rallied around their leaders just as a strange humming sound could be heard through the air. The wind around them began to fluctuate and the humming grew to be almost deafening.

That was when a large, circular object whizzed around one of the surrounding ridges of the mountain to hover just outside of the docking airspace. Strange glowing lights flashed from it sporadically, and a green hue seemed to be emitted from the energy source powering it. It was nearly as large as a football field around with portions of the outer haul removed in a spotty array. Its movements were jerky and made sounds that were suspiciously similar to the backfiring of a car. It wobbled over the dock and nearly struck the side of the mountain before finally coming to a halt overhead. There were a few clicks before a modulated voice rang out, "Did someone call for a rescue?"

Roswell had gotten to his ship safely, but his three team members sacrificed themselves so the others could have a chance. While he struggled to work with a ship that was three-fourths dismantled, they were finally able to beam up everyone except for Uncle Sam, Iron Mountain, a sickly-looking woman, and the very old man who helped them force open the doors to the hanger bay. Just as the frail woman was about to step into the beam, there was a loud crash behind them and the four spun to see a large, metal door on an upper level that was two stories high fly clean off its hinges. As the hunk of metal tumbled down the stairs, they could tell that it had been hit with enough force to bend it in half, and a lone figure stepped out of the shadow of the doorway.

It was Uncle Sam who spoke his name first, "Stonegate."

July 4th, 1950 – 6:32 AM

The only man who could single handedly strike fear into the hearts of enemy and ally alike stopped at the top of the staircase, and the group below noticed that he was dragging something behind him. He looked down the bridge of his nose and called out that they seemed to have forgotten something. That was when he turned to lift the thing he had been dragging over his head, and the group below realized in horror that it was the unmoving body of one of the parahumans they had sent to hack into the systems. After hefting the body overhead, he flung it over the railing with little effort, and the body plummeted down the two-story drop. Iron Mountain leapt into action and managed to catch the poor soul before crashing to the ground on his knees. However, he was too late. The young man, just shy of his twentieth birthday, was already dead with a sickening burn mark in the middle of his forehead and a bloody gash on the side of his face.

Iron Mountain cradled the body of the fallen boy as Uncle Sam and the older man moved to stand at his sides. Robert vaulted over the rail and landed in a three-point stance as the ground beneath him indented slightly. He straightened up and wiped some blood from his uniform as he snapped his baton out at his side. Fueled with rage, Uncle Sam stared Stonegate down as he called out, "Where's your honor, Robert?! This is not the same man I served beside!!"

"The man you served with died when a parahuman murdered his wife and unborn child!" Stonegate said. "The war is over Samuel Irons, and you're no longer the Nation's favorite son. The U.S. Army deemed you a danger if left to your own devices, and that's why they sent you here. You are no soldier. Now you're just prisoner two-seven-three of the Cheyenne Mountain Parahuman Detention Center. In other words, I own you and every other pathetic insect you're trying to spirit away on that ship there. You made quite the valiant effort, but it's time you gave up. Game over." He raised his right hand. It was glowing with a bright blue aura.

The old man to rushed forward and delivered a decisive blow that sent Robert Stonegate skidding a few feet back. Yet, whereas most people would have been knocked unconscious from the force of the impact, Stonegate merely spit out a mouthful of blood and responded swiftly. The old man was the next to fall at Robert's hands, and when the soldier took a step toward the brothers, the frail woman took action.

With a flex, a slight radioactive glow began to envelop her and her energy pulsed in the air. A new alarm began to sound, warning them that various nuclear power sources and other explosive materials were on the verge of melting down. Stonegate knew he had met his match, and he pointed at them as he roared, "You think this is the end? Even if you manage to kill me, there will be others. I didn't do this alone, Irons! Even the government knows the scourge you parahumans hold over the human race and there will be many more to take my place and snuff you all out of existence!"

"And just like every other oppressive regime, there will be those who stand against it," Iron Mountain answered. "You and yours can keep at us, but a younger, more powerful generation will rise up and break your chains of slavery."

Before anything else could be said, the ground beneath him burst open from an explosion, and Robert Stonegate disappeared in a cloud of smoke and flames to the depths below. The expenditure of power weakened the frail woman, and Iron Mountain scooped her up into his arms and gently aided her in entering the ship while his brother cradled the old man in his final moments on Earth. When the woman was safe inside the ship and the old man had passed into the world beyond, the brothers met once more and looked over the dock. Iron Mountain could tell there was something else bothering his brother and it was more than just what had happened.

"There are still planes and jets that are operational and even with Reactor blowing most of the power cells we could still be followed," Uncle Sam noted. "I doubt they left much arsenal on Roswell's ship either,"

"You're going to stay."

"I have to."

"How exactly do you plan to take on an entire army by yourself?" Iron Mountain asked in defeat. Once Uncle Sam had his mind made up, there would be no changing it.

"The same way I did in Germany," was his simple answer as he walked over to where the floor had exploded. After peeling off a sheet of metal large enough to shield him and punching a strip in place for him to hold it, Uncle Sam picked up a gun from an armory station. He turned back, and the brothers shared wishes to keep safe, knowing that it could be the last time they saw each other. Then, Uncle Sam waded back into the facility to make sure the group would not be followed, and Iron Mountain was pulled into the ship. The UFO sputtered and shot off, leaving the facility that had held untold horrors for all behind.

Thus, the founding members of P.O.W.E.R.S (Parahuman Organism World Emancipation and Rescue Society) escaped the Cheyenne Mountain Parahuman Detention Center. Many of the world governments attempted to find their base of operations, and when that failed, to find out more about its members individually, but all they could ascertain was that P.O.W.E.R.S.' mission was to rescue endangered or oppressed parahumans, protect innocents, and fight for parahuman rights in a world that considered them nothing more than dangerous freaks.

As time went on, legends grew from the actions of Iron Mountain and Uncle Sam, setting wheels in motion for a younger generation to pick up their struggle and spur it forth with a new point of view and dream for the future ahead.

Chapter 1: Sek, 1994 to 2015

Born in Salisbury, England, Arthur Seckel was an inquisitive child. He began destroying VCRs with toast, cassette players with coins, and later graduated to gearboxes. It was apparent from early on that he would always be obsessed with how things work. There were multiple occasions his mother and father came home to find one of their many electronics to be in his possession and had to go out to replace it, which was only tedious in the fact that they had to leave the house to get it. Sometimes, they merely sent the help. His mother and father were extremely well off due to their personal business headquartered in whichever expansive house they lived in at that given time, so, as it was, money was of little consequence. Often, those watching young Sek found the destroyed electronics and quickly went out to replace it before it was seen. Sek would tag along, looking over the many devices on the store shelves, his young mind going over the possibilities if he could only get his hands on them. His watchers didn't mind even though there were many times they would have to find the small child after he wandered off in these electronic candy stores.

There was one particular caretaker who took notice of the tinkering habit and encouraged it. She moved with the family whenever work would take them somewhere new and was as much the children's nanny as she was the cook and maid. A young woman in her mid-thirties with long, golden hair that would make other women turn green with envy; she was soft spoken and gentle, well suited to handle the curious minds of Sek and his younger sister while seamlessly appeasing her employers without trying. Her name was Matilda and she noticed how Sek would focus on things and would often come to work with a new device for him to pick apart and take it home when her day's work was done.

As time wore on, she would bring him more complicated devices and he could learn how they worked and took pleasure in categorizing which pieces were responsible for what jobs. One day when Matilda was busy, Sek found the perfect focus for his attention. After hearing his father growling about burnt toast setting him in a foul mood for the rest of his day, Sek waited until both parents went to work before setting up at the kitchen table. He gathered the tools he deemed necessary for the task and in short order had the device cleanly pulled apart with many of the pieces spread out before him. A few hours passed as he picked through each component carefully and found that not only was one of the heat coils damaged, but there was a circuit that had not been fully connected; most likely a small manufacturing oversight. Sek corrected these problems and with the same careful precision he used when he took it apart, reassembled the toaster. He placed a piece of bread in and was pleased when it came out toasted to the exact setting he had placed it on.

Later that night, he sat his mother and father down to show them what he had done. His father laughed and said, "Well, at least I won't have to eat burnt toast before work anymore."

On the other hand, his mother's interest had been piqued, "So how did you do this?"

"Well, it wasn't difficult to take off the main plates and get into-"

"Did you use tools to do this?" she asked, the tone of her voice taking a curiosity that Sek didn't altogether understand.

"Yeah..." he said slowly and when it was clear that she didn't have anything else to say, continued to tell them what he had done.

Sek noticed that as he went on to explain just what the problem had been, his mother visibly deflated as though she had been expecting some greater explanation than the one he was giving. When he was finished, she sighed and calmly stood.

"That's nice dear. You're learning quite a bit, " she said dismissively as she patted him on the head and then left the room. His father rose as well and took the toast his son had set on the table before him as he followed behind his wife. Sek sank into his seat, taking in his parents less than thrilled response, but was quickly pulled from his thoughts as Matilda appeared with a warm smile and kind word over just how clever he truly was.

She was always there, giving him support, praising how far he had come, and telling him that he only needed to impress himself. Eventually, he learned that he did not need the praise of others to continue with his way of doing things. Especially his parents. He only needed to keep himself amused.

Sek never knew exactly what his parents did, but he didn't care. All he knew was they were well taken care of and he always had Matilda to look after him with each different, expensive house they lived in. During the times when he was on his own, Sek would sink into books and study along with his own self-guided learning, tinkering, and destruction. As he got older, Sek was particularly interested in electricity, how it worked, and what could be done with it. Oftentimes, he would wonder off, so thoroughly left to his own devices that he could experiment. Though they were not always the safest experiments, Sek was able to keep from being injured and often kept his findings to himself. After all, even Matilda wouldn't be happy to learn that he could've been hurt with what he was doing, but he did talk about some things to his little sister, Ava. She was just like him. For the most part she kept to herself, but she was extremely bright for her age and could understand a bit of what Sek had figured out. Sek valued the time he spent with her, and it gave her someone to look up to in the absence of their parents.

Sek flourished into quite the brilliant teenager. When work brought his family to the United States, he found there were even more opportunities in store for him. At sixteen, he was suddenly removed from Europe for the first time and plopped into Ruidoso, New Mexico. There he blossomed socially, finding that being foreign could be used to his advantage, and easily fell into the rhythm of American high school. Of course, being a good-looking youth with cropped brown hair and clear blue eyes had worked wonders for him socially as well. He was 6'3", a bit on the lanky side, and often when he entered a room was a natural center of attention. Sek was quickly taken in by all social groupings, and academically he was strong. Finishing his schooling, he graduated in the top five and earned a place in Eastern New Mexico University with his outstanding test scores to work on Materials Science as an Undergrad.

That was when work called his mother, father, and sister back to England. He thought about returning with them, but the cool rebuttal from his father let him know that he would be best suited to stay. His parents told him to get the education that he had earned and they would see him again when it was finished. It was a wonderful opportunity, but it would leave him alone. Both his sister and nanny would be going back to England. However, both of them reassured him this would be good. He had a brilliant mind that could be put to good use, and this was his chance. He came to graduate summa cum laude and enter graduate school in Boulder, Colorado, working with a doctor famous in the field on piezoelectric ceramics.

Sek could never even have guessed at the horror just waiting around the corner.

Chapter 2: James, 1998 to 2014

    James Vinci never asked for his abilities, but they were there all the same. In the beginning, he would collect images of his favorite video games and movies to pull items from, making them rise from the image and become real. He could only pull out small things at a young age, and they always had a mechanical look when they materialized. It tickled him that he had such abilities, and, frankly, what child wouldn't be thrilled? If there was something he wanted or that he thought was cool so long as it was small, it could be his. Though, it took quite a bit of concentration. His recreations would be gone after he woke up the next morning, but he could easily call them back.

    With each passing attempt, he learned something new. He would learn his limitations and how far he could push himself. It was all a great game when he was younger. It was something he could be proud of.

The adopted son of two career military men, Arnold and Martin Vinci, James talked to his fathers about this ability and asked if it could help them. People would sneer when they walked by, women would whisper in hushed tones when they would see them holding their son's hand, and men would growl in disgust and harsh words when they walked past. As a young child, he couldn't understand why theirs was different than any other family? However, his parents were proud of the job they had done shielding him from the cruelty of the world. As far as their son was concerned, he was loved, and they were teaching him to be a good man, and this concern only reinforced that they had done their job in raising him right.

James' fathers chose to keep his abilities a secret for fear of the same people opposing their union would try to kill their son. They were targets enough as it was, and it didn't seem fair to mark their son in a similar fashion. His fathers knew what the world would do. They knew that people don't understand those who are different, and when people can't understand someone, they tend to let their imagination run wild; they let their fear take control. That was something they could not afford to let happen. Their son was too innocent, too naive and too kind. As his parents, they vowed to never let the world turn him cold. Whenever little James asked his fathers about his adoption, all they would tell him is that it was closed and they had no honest idea of who his biological mother and father were, but they reassured him that he was special and made their lives complete. This always seemed to satisfy him, and he would go about his business happily.

For a long time, they managed to keep their little family strong. They raised their son with a steadfast sense of right and wrong. There was no question of their feelings, and it was easily seen that the family was a loving one. His fathers were high-ranking officers, the heads of many special operations. When they decided that it was time for them to retire and start a new chapter in their lives, their entire squad was in support. In fact, they even threw them a magnificent retirement party to show they could always rely on their comrades to have their back.

It was while James's fathers were out at the party that the unthinkable happened. James was the only one home when three unknown men broke into the house. At first, he didn't know what to do but soon came to the decision to fight against them in defense. But James was not much of a fighter, and there was no way he could have known this was no simple break in. The three men had no intention of stealing anything material from the family. No, their intentions were to take something far more precious.

The sixteen-year-old didn't stand a chance. At first, it only seemed that they wanted to beat him to death. They took great pleasure in tossing James between the three of them while they mocked his pathetic attempts at fighting back. Every punch and kick flared through James' body like fire and knocked the air out of his lungs. James could feel his skin rising with bruises and could hear their laughter ringing in his ears. Finally, one of the thugs threw such a devastating punch to James's jaw that it caused him to temporarily black out.

When James came to, he realized he had been pushed face first in the carpet and there was a weight on each side. Knees pressed into his shoulder blades as they held his arms in place behind him. It was then that his stomach turned itself into a knot as he realized he could feel the carpet on his upper thighs while his jeans were being ripped down his legs.

James attempted to struggle with every ounce of power he had left, and it only succeeded in earning him a swift punch to the back of his head, dazing him again. The same hand that had delivered the punch now gripped the back of his neck and pushed it into the ground, making breathing difficult. James' right arm was released, and it instinctively came to rest beside his head. As hands were placed on either side of James' hips, he closed his eyes tight and tried to block everything out.

He didn't want to hear their taunts. He didn't want to hear them defame his fathers for being gay. He didn't want to hear how he was nothing more than a toy for their pleasure, and he didn't want to hear that he was going to enjoy it like his parents would. He didn't want to hear their disgusting words. He didn't want to feel their fingers biting into his skin as they held him down. He didn't want to feel them moving and positioning him to their liking. He didn't want to smell the stench of their sweat in his nostrils, and he wanted to block out the pain not only from the bruises and surely broken bones, but the pain from every violent thrust that caused his face to skid across the carpet a few inches. Most of all, he didn't want to think of how he had failed his parents. If he had really been their son, he would've fought the three attackers off and not allowed himself to be victimized. He would've been able to make his fathers proud by holding off these bastards all by himself.

James opened his eyes, searching for anything that could possibly give him some sense of hope. It was then that he noticed one of the cases to his games was lying a few feet away. On the cover was a soldier standing with some futuristic armor that could take a barrage of bullets and not have a scratch on it. If he could draw out that armor, he would still be able to make his parents proud. Doing everything he could to ignore the pain pulsating through his every cell, he reached his hand out to the game case, nearly choking in despair when he found that it was just inches out of his reach. Nonetheless, he strained forward, and with many more thrusts from his attacker, he was pushed close enough that the tips of his fingers could graze the corner of the image.

Just as his fingertips would touch the image, black armor would start to ripple and materialize around his arm. He could see it starting to solidify just in time for him to be pulled back enough to break contact and it would disappear. James knew if he could just get it to stick, he would make his parents proud and make the depraved thugs regret ever coming into the house. However, the man on his right noticed him reaching for something and delivered another jarring blow to the boy's head before locking his arm behind his back and shoving a knee further into his shoulder blade. Finally, the pain was too much, and James fell unconscious.

Later that night, his fathers returned home to the horrific scene and found their son battered and beaten. They rushed him to the hospital as quickly as they could, and through the love of their military family who worked together to gather donations, the medical treatments were fully paid for so that the family could focus on the only thing that mattered; trying to mend James's broken body and spirit.

Becoming a recluse at seventeen, James received a camera filled with images of pleasant places and things that would bring out a smile, but his fathers could see that each smile was forced and every laugh was hollow. A dark cloud had hung over him ever since that fateful night.

James kept in practice of pulling things out of the images, and in May of that year he pulled a rope from one of the pictures, attempting suicide. Found lying on the floor of his bedroom by his parents ten minutes after he'd lost consciousness, James was taken to the emergency room.

Upon later inspection, his fathers could not find the rope that he used to hang himself. Overcome with grief and worry, they never left his side. He was held in the hospital until he could physically be released, but his fathers made sure that he went to every mandated therapy appointment. Though they had managed to save his life, they couldn't save the child he had been before the incident. They couldn't seem to get him to understand how proud they were and that he had not failed them that night, and for the first time in his life, they felt completely at a loss to help their son.

Chapter 3: Amanda, 2006 to 2007

The first thing Amanda could remember was being strapped to the table, electricity shooting through her temples. The nine-year-old girl's mind was shattered and broken beyond a normal doctor's capability, and there was no memory of what had caused it. There was no one there to speak for her and no one to claim her. For all anyone knew, the girl was completely and utterly alone, and so she fell into a world of her own making. It was something that she could understand, that she could cope with. Doctors took on the personas of what her mind imagined them to be. Children in the hospital were her comrades. Slowly, she came back to life. Though not quite whole, it was a start. In the beginning, the doctors were patient with her delusions. They played along with her belief that she was in some post-apocalyptic safe haven, saved from whatever horrific event had ravaged the world outside. But as time went on, they grew impatient with her as they did with many of their other patients.

Memories would flicker across her mind. Flashes of faces and echoes of words would drift up from the past. Amanda couldn't place everything that came back, but from what she gathered, she had been happy once until the explosions. Amanda couldn't piece together much of anything after that. She remembered the blasts. She remembered hearing people screaming. Then her world went dark until she woke up at the hospital.

But the hospital was anything but happy. They told her she was special. All their patients were special and they were the only ones who could help them. But they didn't help them at all. She could hear other patients screaming. She could hear them crying. She knew they were in pain. She didn't see the point in the prescribed tortures. Her comrades weren't hurting anyone, so why humiliate them for how they want to live?

One boy close to her age thought he was a rat. The doctors made him eat trash, and when night came, she would hear him crying. Every day they told him the same things: If he would just stop being foolish, he would get better. It was his fault he had to live this way. He was lucky to be under their care. No one else would want to deal with him. No one would want to take care of damaged goods.

The staff was just as cruel. Whenever they got the chance, they would amuse themselves at the expense of the poor beings placed under their care. Sure, Amanda could admit that some of her comrades' behaviors weren't exactly normal, but they weren't hurting anyone. They just wanted to live and stay out of the way.

In the beginning, she held onto the hope that someone would save her. She had memories that once she had a family. Grandpa Sam. Grandma. Uncle Johnny. Surely, they would've been trying to find her. But since no one ever came, she could only guess that they didn't survive the blasts. She really was alone, aside from her comrades. Together, they watched the outside world on a small television one of her friends had somehow snuck into her room. Despite the horror that had ravaged the outside world before, Amanda knew that those who lived outside had recovered. No matter how bad it was out there, they were all in agreement that it would be so much better than where they were now. It was what they all wanted.

That was when they decided they needed to break out. They would work together. They would watch each other's backs and once they got out, they would face the outside world together. They just needed something to protect themselves. One of her friends made paper guns. She could use the guns, even though she only got one shot per gun, but it was better than nothing. She had spent a year in hell, and it as time for her to leave.

The night they decided to leave though, things didn't go as they had planned. One of her comrades didn't make it to the meeting place. He had been found out, but he did manage to draw all the staff and attention away from the other two. Amanda came to the first lock and drew the paper gun her friend had given her. After taking careful aim, she fired, and where nothing would've happened for anyone else, she was special. A bolt of almost pure energy flew from the barrel of the gun and blew the lock clean off the door. She quickly dropped the paper as it simmered into ash. There was one more lock she had to take care of, and then they were outside. It was the first taste of freedom they had in so long, but there was no time to enjoy it. They only paused long enough to catch their breath, and one of the guards grabbed her friend not far from the door. He kept hitting him and hitting him until Amanda shot the guard in the middle of his back. He fell and didn't get back up. She ran back, trying to get her friend, but he wouldn't move. He was breathing, but no matter how hard Amanda tried he wouldn't wake up. Knowing she was running out of time, she left the last gun with him and ran. Running was all Amanda knew to do, and she was good at it.

    At first, she was surrounded by trees. So many trees that she didn't know what way she was going. Instinct was what fueled her, and soon she broke through the trees to find a road. Amanda only stopped long enough to determine which way to go and chose the path that lead to a large city.

    As she went, the medications the doctors had forced her to take started to wear down, and her delusions began to overlay the reality before her. The road would change between the black pavement to rugged and cracked debris as though it had been worn away by more than just time. The plants on either side would go from green and healthy to withered and yellow like they could be dangerous to even touch. As she drew closer to the city even the buildings would shift before her very eyes. The sleek skyscrapers towering over her head would warp and look like patchwork scrap metal welded together and a thick layer of grime smeared the glass that made it impossible to see inside. Even people's appearances would change as she entered the city. Men and women dressed professionally would soon be clothed in mix-matched rags, many with patchwork cloaks hung around their shoulders. Glasses turned to goggles and hats to helmets or welding masks. It only furthered her delusion that anyone who saw her coming would avoid making eye contact and shy away from her as though they knew she didn't belong. She wandered through the strange, ever-changing city meeting no one that would pay any attention to her except for the people who wore strange body armor and had dozens of shiny buttons and clips on their jackets. They had weapons openly displayed on their hips, and Amanda wanted nothing to do with them. Just the sight of them was nearly enough to send her into a panic, and she wouldn't stop running until she was sure she had lost them.

    One week passed in this way. By the end of the second week, she was so exhausted from hunger that she couldn't move anymore let alone run. She collapsed in the back of a dirty alley hidden away from the streets busy with people. Huddled off in a corner under a torn blanket she had scrounged from someone's garbage, Amanda couldn't stop herself from crying. It was her crying that drew him. His footsteps echoed in the otherwise silent alley and she tried to make herself as small as she could as she ducked her head under the blanket, hoping he wouldn't see her. They were the only ones in the alley, and he knelt beside her, placing a gentle hand on the blanket as he moved it back to see her. Then he smiled at her and wiped the tears from her face. His name was Hugo, and instead of taking her back to the dark world of the hospital, he took her back to his apartment.

    It turned out that Hugo was an undercover FBI agent doing work in Indianapolis. He had a coworker he called "special" who told him there was a young child in the area with peculiar abilities. That was how he found her. He could tell that she had been through hell, and he took a few days off from his assignment to get her on the mend. Mostly, Amanda just slept and ate, content that he wasn't going to harm her and allowed her mind to rest for the first time since she could remember. In fact, when she seemed uneasy he would often sit down with her and watch the Wizard of Oz. Though the time did come when he had to go back to work, and the hospital administration had increased their efforts to find her. Hugo sat her down so they could figure out how they would proceed from there.

    "Listen, Amanda. I have to go back on assignment tomorrow. Legally, I can't keep you here. If the police find you, they will return you to the hospital, and there is nothing I can do. If my supervisors find out I've been hiding you, they'll do the same thing," Hugo began. Amanda's dark skin paled, and fear flashed behind her eyes. She was on her feet, frantically pacing back and forth, holding the sides of her head.

"No, I can't go back. Not to the people. I can't go back. Not to the people," she began choking through short breaths and tears formed in her eyes. Memories flickered through her head, and she held her hands tighter against her temples. She could distinctly remember the shock therapy sessions they frequently put her through to make her more compliant. She couldn't go back. Hugo got to his feet and pulled her into a gentle, brotherly hug.

"Shhhh. Calm down, it's going to be ok," he soothed.

She had not spoken a word about the hospital or why she had escaped it, but the terror he could feel through her trembling form told him enough to guess that it was anything but healing. After soothing and coaxing her to breathe normally again, Hugo sat her on the couch and knelt before her.

"I never said I was going to take you back there, Amanda, and I see now, that it's not an option. I'm just telling you what will happen if you get caught. I'm going to fight for custody of you. We have a good chance since in the eyes of the court they lost you in the first place. But you have to work with me in the meantime. You have to stay out of trouble until it's all over. It won't be easy. It's going to take time. But when we're finished, they can't take you from me. Do you understand?"

Amanda was shocked. Her fractured memory was torn apart, and while she could vividly remember the horrors she had endured in the hospital, she could only remember flickers of people in the past that showed the kindness Hugo was extending to her. She was overwhelmed, and all she could offer in response was to hug him. After she had calmed down, Hugo explained that she wasn't a prisoner, but she needed to lay low. The hospital would be sending people out to find her, and until he had legal custody, he couldn't stop them if they did. He could, however, with the help of some trusted friends, divert them and throw them off her trail. She readily agreed to this and for the first few days, Amanda did as she promised. She stayed in his apartment and only went out for short walks when she got restless and needed some air.

But Amanda couldn't ignore her instincts, and the longer she stayed out of the hospital, the stronger they became. One day while she was out walking, she caught sight of plastic sticking out of a trashcan sitting on the curb. She glanced around to see that no one was watching and then quickly swiped it. She made her way down the sidewalk and disappeared into an alley to look over what she had. It was a plastic toy gun that was often used to shoot foam darts, but it looked as though some careless child had damaged the barrel and their parent threw it away. A large grin broke across her face, and she skipped back to Hugo's apartment. After digging around and finding the tools she needed, she set to work on repairing it. It felt natural for her to get it back in working order, and when she was finished, she sat on the floor running her hand over it lost in thought.

It had been a long time since she held a gun, and with the feeling of the grip in her hands, memories started to come back to her. Images of her running at night—no, not running—hunting, came to mind. She could faintly make out the shadow of someone dressed in a long coat and a hat that obscured his face. She couldn't remember much about him, but she could remember the long rifle always slung over his shoulder. She was sure she learned to hunt from him. The mere thought of hunting, tracking down bad guys and bringing them to justice, fueled her instincts, and she couldn't ignore them anymore.

That night she left Hugo's apartment and let her instincts take control.

Chapter 4: Amanda, 2007 to 2010

Amanda's skills were astounding. She could track better than most police dogs, and her intuition was spot on. She couldn't remember what she had been hunting all those years ago, but she knew what she was going to hunt now. Bad people. People that would hurt others. People that were so bad, that they couldn't be redeemed. People that stole more than they needed to get by. People that killed. People who made victims. People like those who had hurt her.

Amanda knew where she could get information when she needed it. She knew where there were people that knew the entire city, including the parts that most pretended didn't exist: the homeless. There were plenty of homeless camps around Indianapolis, and she quickly found them and the places that worked to feed them. At first, they didn't know how to handle the spunky little girl that frequented their tents and usual hang outs, but they soon adopted her as one of their own, and whenever officers came around asking about her, they kept her a secret. She would often bring them back enough bologna sandwiches to feed everyone and curl up there when she needed rest. They found quite a few people for her that were beyond redemption and tarnished the good name of the city she found herself calling home.

In the midst of her newfound purpose, her promise to Hugo drifted to the back of her mind, but she managed to find another piece of her childhood she had long since lost. She found her best friend. It was an overcast day in Military Park near downtown when she heard a group of guys causing some trouble. Assuming they were picking on a smaller kid, Amanda decided to put the jerks in their place. She scrambled up a nearby tree and, making sure the branches could support her weight, leaned out to get a better look.

Instead of some bullies picking on a younger kid, she saw a young Japanese girl dressed in a strange black fighting uniform with her hair pulled back and a wooden sword in her right hand. She looked like she was about fourteen years old, and she was surrounded by a group of seven older boys. The boys made jokes about her, but the girl remained unfazed by their taunts. Realizing that their heckling wasn't getting the reaction they wanted, one of the boys approached her boasting that he could wipe that dirty look off her wonton-looking face.

As soon as he reached out to take the sword away from her, she stepped back, swept the sword toward the back of his legs, and knocked them out from under him. The bully landed unceremoniously on his rear. Before he had a chance to recover, the young woman landed a swift kick to his chest that sent him skidding back to his friends. He coughed and sputtered as he tried to catch his breath.

Shifting into a balanced stance with her sword held out in front of her, she smirked, "Anyone else?"

Her voice clicked in Amanda's head, and memories crashed to the front of her mind: memories from before the hospital; memories from a time when she had been whole, when she had been happy; memories of her adopted sister and her growing up, and of them causing absolute chaos with their shenanigans.

Amanda could barely contain herself as she stood on the branch and called out, "Hey! That's MY Jap-bastard! Save some fun for me, Crow!!"

Before any of them had a chance to react, the young girl leapt from the tree and pounced on the shoulders of the closest boy like a wild animal. The sudden, unexpected attack sent him face first into the ground, and Amanda cracked him in the head with the butt of her gun, knocking him out. Crow looked up in surprise and laughed as she recognized who had joined the fight. She quickly rolled to dodge another teen lumbering toward her and held her hand out to help her little sister to her feet as she said, "Long time no see, Amanda. Tracked me down, huh?"

"Duh! It's what I do," Amanda replied. She took Crow's hand and sprang to her feet. Crow spun on the ball of her foot and propelled Amanda toward an advancing bully who was quickly pushed back as she kicked him in the stomach. In one fluid motion, they stood back-to-back: Amanda with her gun at the ready and Crow with her sword raised in front.

"Well, let's have some fun then," Crow smirked.

"You betcha!" Amanda agreed.

By this time, the teenage boys recovered from the surprise intrusion and the first kid Crow had kicked recovered enough to get to his feet. Still holding his chest and glaring angrily at the younger girls, he growled, "That's it. You two picked the wrong guy to piss off. Let's send them back to their mommies crying!"

At the mention of the word "mommies" Amanda's expression went cold and she raised the toy gun to aim at his chest. The boys all laughed at her antics, but Crow tightened her grip on her sword and whispered to Amanda, "Stun only, ok sis? These guys are idiots, but they're just kids."

Amanda didn't respond but mentally pictured the gun being set to a stun setting before she started to charge up her shot. As the energy began to flow from her body into the gun, the toy began to glow faintly. Amanda pulled the trigger. There was a strange sound that escaped the plastic barrel as a glowing bolt shot out and hit the boy square in his chest. The blow knocked him off his feet again, and he choked as he crashed to the ground. Amanda stuck out her tongue and turned her attention to one of the others who was trying to catch her off guard. She dropped the gun and spun around to grapple with him while Crow set to work on two that were closest to her. In a matter of minutes, the boys were quickly subdued and lying on the ground in a heap, groaning over their bruises. Crow and Amanda stood over them shaking their heads. Then the two girls walked off, Crow pulling Amanda to where her parents were.

Upon seeing the girl, Crow's parents seemed happy, but there was an undertone of tension that was beyond the girls' notice. However, they took them home and as they prepared dinner, Crow's parents skillfully inquired how Amanda came to be there and find her sister. When it was revealed that she was on her own, the adults immediately knew she was on the run. They made it clear that she was welcome to stay with them whenever she wanted, and Crow was excited to have her sister back.

For a while, Amanda made Crow's house a second home base. She would still go out to hunt, and sometimes her older sister would accompany her. The two became well known among the homeless camps. Whenever the girls got into trouble, there was always at least one person close at hand to assist. All the while, Crow's parents kept a careful watch, though the girls were never aware of it. They were confident they could protect themselves. Where Amanda could use guns that no one else could, Crow could control lightning. They were one heck of a team.

There would be times when it would be days, at most a week, when Amanda would not check in with her sister, but they knew she was more than capable of taking care of herself. That was what she was good at. But there was one night where Amanda got herself into more trouble than she anticipated. It had been a few days since she had last seen Crow when she was near the convention center during a big event. There were people in costumes, and her mental illusions melded them with the inner world only she saw.

She bounced through the crowds of people and snuck into the rooms she should've needed a special card to get into. As she walked the booths, she saw a few selling new guns that she could make use of. Checking her pockets, she realized she didn't have enough cash for the one she really needed. As she stood there staring at it, a boy around fifteen came up and tried to start a conversation with her.

"Well, hey there gorgeous. What are you doing over here? Not many girls hang out around this booth," he asked, trying to sound as suave. Initially, Amanda considered blowing him off, but then she noticed his wallet hanging halfway out of his pocket with money sticking out of it. She figured she could use him to her advantage, so she put on a pout and complained about how she couldn't afford what she wanted. After a few minutes going back and forth, she convinced him to buy two guns for her, and they left the room to hang out in the main area. Amanda could tell that he was interested in her, and she let him buy her something to eat. Eventually she was ready to leave, but he didn't want to let her go. So, she challenged him to a shooting contest.

A few of his friends wanted to see the new girl he was walking around with, and none of them believed that her guns could do the things she said they could. When she proved them wrong, they were angry and scared. They caused so much trouble that two police officers came over, and when Amanda refused to identify herself, they took her into custody. She could feel her stomach turning in knots. She knew the police would call the Department of Child Services, and the hospital would find her again. Her heart raced, and panic started to choke her. Soon, two officers escorted a man in that they said was from DCS to take care of her.

Amanda didn't know what to make of him. He was a well-kept man in his early fifties with dark brown hair just starting to grey at the temples. His accent marked him as British, and his blue eyes almost seemed grey. But what made him stick out clearly in her mind was the scar in the crease of his left cheek near his mouth. She almost mistook it for a dimple, but when he came closer she knew it was a bullet wound. He dismissed the officers soon after entering the room, making it clear that things would be taken care of.

"Hello there Amanda. My name is Charles Ingleson, but you can call me Charlie if you'd like. I'm here to take care of you."

"You got shot," was Amanda's only response. She lifted her hand and poked her finger right into the middle of the scar on his cheek. Taken slightly aback by her complete lack of personal boundaries, he didn't respond right away.

After a few minutes a small smile did creep into the corner of his mouth as he replied, "Yes, I did. In the face that time too."

"Who shot you? Did it hurt? I used to know someone who would shoot people," Amanda fired her questions in quick succession.

He chuckled, "Let's not ask too many personal questions so soon. That can be considered rude, you know."

"Oh, sorry," Amanda responded quietly and looked around the room. It was clear that she wasn't exactly happy with how things were playing out. With what he had been told, Charles didn't quite blame her.

"Now, let's get you taken care of, shall we? Hugo made it clear that he was responsible for you, and I'm here to take care of the paperwork to keep it that way," Charles said, and she visibly relaxed upon the mention of Hugo's name. He escorted her out and directed her to his car while she clutched the two guns she had close to her chest.

"Where are we going?" she asked as she climbed into the backseat.

"First, I am going to get you something to eat, and then I am taking you to Hugo's apartment. He's still on assignment, so he asked me to tell you to wait for him there."

"Am I in trouble?"

"Probably."

Amanda sighed. On the drive, he explained that Hugo had already started to take steps to get custody of her. His way of keeping the hospital from having a chance at her was saying she had been surrendered to DCS pending investigation. That's where Charles came in. He would be the one using the system and paperwork to keep the hospital at bay while aiding in Hugo building a case for full custody to be granted to him. It would be an uphill battle, but one that they would do everything in their power to win. They just needed her to behave long enough for that to happen, or at least not get caught like she did today.

Amanda agreed that she could do that and stayed in Hugo's apartment for a few more days, but she grew restless. She left once again, but she used her resources to stay out of trouble. She would stay with Crow and her family some days, and in the homeless camps other days. Sometimes she would return to Hugo's apartment to leave him notes that she was ok. A few years passed as Hugo waged the legal battle, and Charles kept her a secret from those that would hurt her. In turn, she took it upon herself to help those who couldn't protect themselves.

It wasn't until Amanda was thirteen that things went bad again. During one of her usual rounds in the city, Amanda found herself being drawn toward a specific alley. Her instincts were calling her to it. Amanda knew anything could happen, and she was already charged and ready, but there was no way she could've known what was waiting for her. At the entrance to the alley she could see a pair of shoes jutting out from behind various debris and figured it was either some drunk who was unconscious in the alley, a homeless person trying to find somewhere to sleep, or a victim of a mugging that hadn't recovered just yet. She bounced her way down the alley toward the figure, humming the Battle Hymn of the Republic as she went, and slowed as she got closer. She rolled the unconscious person over and stopped.

"Crow," Amanda whispered, looking at her sixteen-year-old friend. Blood covered Crow's unconscious face. From across her forehead, down her nose and stopping just at her cheekbone, Crow had been slashed open by some unknown weapon. It looked dangerously deep, and there was a strange greenish hue around the edges of the wound that Amanda could not place. All she knew was that if her friend stayed like this much longer, she very well could die.

Amanda administered basic first aid. Ripping off her sleeve, she quickly attempted to staunch the bleeding while trying to clean the green stuff was from the wound. She soon realized her efforts weren't making any difference, so she tossed it aside and struggled to pull Crow from where she was laying. Glancing around, Amanda found that the bag Crow always carried was gone. None of Crow's usual things were with her. The thirteen-year-old dragged her sister through the alley and down to the curb. She leaned her against a light post before trying to wave down any oncoming motorist that would stop to help them. Finding someone willing to help was nearly impossible, but five cars later she had her Good Samaritan, and they were speeding on their way to the hospital not long after.

As soon as they stepped into the hospital's ER receiving room, Crow was whisked off, and her father, who worked as a staff surgeon there, was quickly notified about his daughter's condition. Amanda stayed in the waiting room, unwilling to leave until she saw Crow. For hours, she paced, lost in her own thoughts. She didn't even notice the staff taking note of how she looked or even that they were talking about her. Amanda just thought about Crow, as though just wishing hard enough would make her recover. As soon as she was told that Crow was out of surgery, she rushed to her friend's room to keep watch at her side.

Chapter 5: Crow and Amanda, 2010

Her first thought was that her head hurt. To be more accurate, it was splitting in pure agony. The only other thing she could feel were the bandages wrapped tightly around her head. The fuzziness was starting to go away. Yet, no matter how hard she tried, she couldn't remember anything. Her name? Her family? Where she was? What was going on? There was nothing. All there was to be had was physical, ungodly pain. She could hear shifting close by and someone else's breathing. Someone was holding vigil at her side.

For a time, she lay there, listening to whoever it was that was in the room with her. It was like piecing energy back together after it had been shattered into thousands of pieces. Slowly, she pulled together what little strength she could to open her eyes and found that she could only see out of one. The other had been loosely covered by the bandages. Her vision was blurry, and it took a few minutes for her start making sense of anything in front of her, but once she had, she caught sight of the person in the room.

She was a teenage girl with curly, short, brown hair dressed in dirty clothes with one torn sleeve. There was dirt and grime on the sides of her face, and her brown eyes were wide with panic. She kept glancing from the window to the bed. The girl's dark skin tone was made darker by the amount of dirt and mud caked over her and her clothes, but her hair was mostly held in shape except for a few wild curls that frizzed out of place to bounce in time with each step she took. A quick glance around the room told her that she was in a hospital, but that was about as much as she could understand. The pain dulled her wit and the lack of memory nearly sent her into a panic, but the constant sounds of the other girl's shoes on the floor calmed her enough to keep it at bay.

It didn't take long for this girl to notice that she had woken up and immediately pounce on her with an excessively tight embrace. The girl was gushing, speaking so fast that she could barely keep up with her, but what she gathered was that the girl had been very worried and was relieved that she was ok.

"Who...are you?" she asked in a voice barely above a whisper.

The girl stopped hugging her and slowly pulled back, looking at her with a somewhat astonished expression as she pointed at her and said, "Crow," then drew her hand back to point at herself, "Amanda." The girl, Amanda, pointed back at her, "Crow...what the hell is wrong with you?"

"That's...my name?" she asked her.

Amanda looked at her like she was from a different world, "Yeah...weirdo."

"I...don't remember. What's going on?"

"Well, I was doing my usual rounds, you know like I always do, and I found you in an alley. I don't know why you were there since you should've been home by then, but you were. Your face was all cut up and there was this glowing green stuff that was really gross. So, I brought you here to the hospital so they could fix you. You're safe. I know you're ok and now I have to go. I have to go before they call the people. I don't want to go with the people."

"Wait! Don't leave. What people? Who's going to call them?" Crow's stomach lurched. She woke up with nothing, and now this girl had given her a name. There was more the girl knew and the idea that she was going to leave upset Crow so much that her head seared in pain. Tears blurred her vision, but she blinked them away. She refocused on Amanda and feebly tried to raise her hand to stop her but only made it halfway before her strength failed. Aside from the searing pain in her head, the rest of her body felt numb.

At that moment, the door opened and a tall woman in scrubs walked in looking between Amanda and Crow. Then she focused on Amanda and said, "Ok, little lady. It's time for you to be leaving now so she can get some rest."

"Five more minutes. Please give me five more minutes," Amanda looked at her and Crow could see her panic starting to return.

The nurse looked at her calmly and said, "Well ok, but in five more minutes, I'm coming to get you and we have some people who want to talk to you about where you're staying, ok?"

Amanda nodded and the woman quietly left. Amanda was bouncing nervously on her feet and she was saying, "I have to go. I can't go with them. I have to leave before they get here. I can't go with the people."

"You know who I am...where are you going to go?" Crow asked pleadingly.

"You're going to be ok. You're taken care of. I have to go."

"I'm going to see you again, right?" Crow asked one last time feeling defeated.

"Yes, I will find you, but I have to go. I have to go right now. Work with me ok?"

"Ok."

Amanda leaned over her and quickly started disconnecting all the wires that hooked Crow to the machines. Alarms started going off in the room and Amanda retreated to stand behind the door. It didn't take long for the medical staff to come spilling into the room. Crow closed her eyes and tried to be as still as she could, making her breathing as slow as possible. They were so focused on her, no one noticed Amanda slipping out, much to the confusion and frustration of the hospital staff.

Crow was well taken care of like Amanda had promised, though her memory was gone. Her father had been the one to perform the surgery. He was a brilliant brain surgeon, and even the head trauma doctor at the time conceded that her best chance of survival was for her father to do the operation, and though it was against hospital policy, the Chief of Staff allowed it due to how quickly Crow's condition had been deteriorating. No one else seemed skilled enough to stop it. She made a full recovery, and the only thing that remained was a scar that began on the top left side of her forehead, went down across the bridge of her nose, and ended at the right cheekbone. The thing no one could explain was the greenish hue that tinged the edges of the scar. Some would even say it almost had a strange glow, but Crow kept her black as pitch hair long enough to hide behind when she felt the need. Most of the time she wore the scar proudly, though, and didn't care when people winced at the sight of it.

    Her parents made sure she had everything she needed to recover and were gentle when teaching her how things in her life fit together. They lovingly explained everything that she didn't remember and found a physical therapist just as concerned for her overall well-being as they were. He was a tall British man, in his late fifties with a strong expression, but every time he turned his grey-blue eyes on Crow, there was a kindness that seemed almost out of place. He reassured her that scars weren't anything to be ashamed of. After all, he had a defining scar in the crease of his cheek at the corner of the left side of his mouth. When Crow quietly asked about it, he told her that he had been in the wrong place at the wrong time and that was the souvenir he walked away with. He was friendly, and whenever he saw the brooding teenager for her regular sessions, he always managed to make her laugh – much to her parents' relief. She seemed to be the only patient he had, and on multiple occasions he immediately left the hospital after exchanging a few words with her parents after her session. Crow kept this observation to herself, however, and focused on rebuilding the relationship with her doting parents.

When she was finally well enough, she went home with her mother and father. Though her memory never came back, and despite the unconditional love of her parents, it was difficult for her to handle in good humor. It set her on a path of wanting to help others, and if helping others led her to a chance to help herself, so be it. Three years later, when she turned nineteen, Crow found herself working in the very hospital she had woken up in that night.

Chapter 6: Crow, Amanda, and Hugo, 2012

One night, after working well past her expected time, Crow snagged the CAT Scan results she had done on herself and was looking over them as she bid the front desk nightshift good night. Though the day had been busy, the night had, thankfully, calmed down. She slowly walked out, looking over the results, hoping that maybe she would see something she hadn't before, something that could lead to her recovering even some of her memories, but alas it was the same. Crow was no closer than she had been two years ago. She paused just outside—flipping through the results before gently putting them in the messenger bag she always carried—and looked up when she heard a car idling in front of her.

The rest of the street was completely empty, but oddly enough, there was a limo pulled up to the curb directly in front. She paused in the middle of the walkway and quickly scanned the streets. To her knowledge, there was no high-class person in the hospital needing treatment, and there was no reason that it should be there, but what unnerved Crow more was the man who got out of the limo. All she could see of him was from the light that was cast down from the streetlamp, and she caught the glimpse of his expensive-looking suit and tie. He started to move toward her. She scanned the area and noticed an alley nearby that she could get to before he had a chance to get back into the car. Without hesitation, she ran as fast as her legs could take her.

She was halfway through the alley, thinking she had given them the slip, when she heard it: the sounds of tires skittering across the pavement and the flash of headlights as the limo pulled up to block the alley in front of her. Her heart nearly leapt out of her chest, and her mind was quickly sorting through all the possible ways she could defend herself. As it was, she always had her backup, and if things came down to it, and she would look forward to hearing on the news how they would explain the random bolt of lightning that would fall from the sky on a perfectly clear night. Crow watched as the figure got out of the car once again and looked at her as he adjusted his tie, "Ms. Crow. I've been looking for you for some time now."

"Uh-huh, I'm sure you have. And why exactly have you been looking for me?" Crow inquired, staring him down. She wasn't inclined to trust a man in a suit who had been waiting for her outside the hospital in the middle of the night.

"We just need to talk to you Ms. Crow. That's all," he answered simply.

"In a dark alley? That's one hell of place for a conversation," Crow sneered.

"You're the one who ran here. I was parked under the light, in the middle of the street, where the car was easily seen," the man answered coolly.

Crow bit the inside of her cheek in aggravation. "Well, being a female alone in the night, you don't exactly walk to the lone car when no one else is around and you don't know the people inside of it."

"Still, this was your choice, not mine," he said, gesturing widely. The more he talked, the less she liked him.

"How do I know this is legit?" she hissed.

Sighing somewhat, he reached into his coat. Crow tensed, waiting for him to make an aggressive move. Instead, he pulled out a small, square object and tossed it to her. Crow caught it easily and flipped open the leather wallet to see a federal agent ID for one Hugo Aberline. The picture matched the man that stood before her from his long, black hair tied in a neat ponytail at the base of his neck down to the same folds in the collar of his button-up dress shirt. From what she could see, it was real.

"Will that suffice?"

Crow tossed it back to him and crossed her arms tightly over her chest. Her eyes narrowed and she shrugged, none too happy about the situation she had fallen into.

"Well, where would you prefer to talk?" he asked.

Crow was quiet for a minute. Somewhere she could get out if things went south, and somewhere he didn't have the advantage. An idea popped into her head. "There's a coffee shop not too far from here that I always go to after my shift. It's the only place that stays open this late. We'll meet there."

"Very well, we'll meet there in two hours. Until then, Ms. Crow." He got back into the limo and it drove off.

Crow watched in shock. Whoever was driving that car was one hell of a driver. She sighed heavily in relief and collected herself as she leaned against the nearby wall. Her long, raven hair fell around her face like a curtain, and she buried her face in her hands. The thought of not going, of hiding out, crossed her mind, but she was curious as to who the hell this guy was and what he had to say. If he really was a federal agent, he would have been watching her for some time before finally approaching her. He knew where she lived and which coffee shop was her usual spot. He probably knew quite a bit more than that, but she wasn't going to think about it all just yet. After mulling it over, she decided she would go, but she prepared herself for a trap.

Ready for a fight, she arrived half an hour early and saw the limo waiting outside. It was idling, but the tint on the windows was too dark for her to see the driver sitting inside. In fact, she couldn't see anything through any of the windows. Looking into the restaurant, she could see where the agent was sitting, and it looked like there may be someone with him, but she didn't have a clear view from where she was. Crow quietly went around to the second entrance and snuck in, keeping as close to the wall as she could to remain unseen. She looked over the patrons in the shop and saw that they were too engrossed to notice her strange behavior, so she turned her attention to the table where the man was sitting.

She had been right, there was someone sitting with him, but all she could see was the back of another girl's head. From what she guessed, the girl was relatively close to her in age and focused on eating while the man in the suit read the paper. Something about the female nagged at Crow's memory, so she stopped one of the waiters who knew her well. "Hey, do me a favor, and there'll be twenty bucks in it for you."

"Uh...what exactly are you expecting me to do, Crow?"

"You see that girl sitting over there with the overdressed guy? All I need you to do is accidentally bump her so I can see her face. That's it." She held out the twenty-dollar bill to the waiter. He looked over at the table and smirked before turning to take it. If Crow had been paying attention, she would have noticed him acting a little skittish, but the nineteen-year-old was far too focused on the duo.

Crow hid off to the side and waited. Just like he promised, the waiter walked over and acted as though he tripped, managing to jostle the girl around enough that Crow could see her face. It was the girl who had been in her hospital room three years ago when she had lost her memory. She had cleaned up, and the dirt and grime no longer marred her rich bronze skin. Her hairstyle was reminiscent of the thirties where the roots started smooth and her slightly frizzy curls flared out at the ends. Crow was caught off guard, but now she was more curious than ever. Amanda was giving the waiter a hard time for brushing her, and the agent never once looked up from his paper.

Crow walked quietly over to the table, standing behind Amanda, not sure how exactly she should proceed. The dull buzz if the café was slowly turning into a deafening roar in her ears. The longer she stood there, the more anxious she felt. Amanda passively glanced around the room and saw her standing there unable to move. Without a moment's hesitation, she jumped to her feet and seized Crow in a tight hug. Crow hugged her back awkwardly and looked over the man before saying, "Who the hell is he?"

"That's Hugo, He's my brother! Hugo kept me away from the people and even got my scrapbook back with my memories. He's the one who helped me find you."

Hugo still held the newspaper with one hand, but with the free one, he slid a strange folder across the table. Crow eyed it carefully and looked back to Hugo, who was far too interested in his paper to even look up at her.

"Uh-huh…" she said as she sat down and touched the top of the folder thoughtfully. Reading the name "Ren Yoshida" across the top of it, she felt her curiosity flare up, but both Amanda and Hugo didn't seem up to divulging just what all was going on. Crow wrinkled her nose. "Not that I'm not happy to see you, Amanda, but how long have you been looking for me?" Crow asked curiously.

"Since I got away from the hospital."

"I haven't gone very far. You got out of there ok, right?" Crow asked.

"Yeah, but people were watching you to find me, and I had to put some distance between us, and when I came back you moved, and it was a major pain to find out where. Oh yeah. Good job, by the way, with the playing dead thing. They were so worried about you, no one paid any attention to me," Amanda answered. It was then that Crow noticed just how many empty dishes were on the table in front of them. At first, she assumed that Hugo and Amanda had shared a meal before her arrival, but upon further inspection of Amanda's eating habits and the fact that it didn't even seem like Hugo had even been given eating utensils, Crow was quick to deduce that Amanda had eaten all of it on her own. Crow couldn't help but wonder, just where was all the food going? Did she have a second stomach or a hollow leg? For someone her size, Crow figured that her metabolism would have to be off the charts in order to burn that much energy and still have room for more.

"No problem. It was the least I could do for someone who remembered who I was when I didn't. What have you been doing for the past three years?" Crow inquired looking sideways at her friend.

"Hiding," she answered after a few seconds of trying to decide just exactly what she wanted to say. There was a moment of silence, and Crow realized that her friend wasn't going to elaborate, but before she could ask, Hugo beat her to it.

"Don't forget getting in trouble, getting arrested, getting me called off jobs to come save you. You've been up to quite a bit more than just hiding, Amanda," Hugo said in a cool monotone as he finally put down the paper and looked at her pointedly.

"I didn't ask you to come save me," Amanda said in a defensively child-like tone. "But I appreciate it all the same."

"You don't call me, but everyone else does," Hugo responded. As Crow looked between them, she could see how relaxed they were with each other. Though Hugo retained his professional demeanor, he was in fact very at ease with their surroundings. This brought Crow off her guard, though she would not admit it. While they were occupied with their sibling spat, Crow went to looking over the folder that had been slid in front of her.

The name was calling out to her, but no matter how hard she tried, it didn't ring any bells. She reached out and hesitated only a few seconds before flipping it open. Crow didn't know what she had been expecting, but she was not prepared for what she saw. There was basic medical information inside; date of birth, blood type, weight, height and health condition. There were pictures of a small Japanese girl playing alongside of who she imagined was a younger Amanda. There were even pictures of her parents carrying a very happy, smiling young Crow in their arms. Then she saw them: adoption papers. Crow felt like she had been kicked in the chest. It was a closed adoption, and all dates or anything relevant to when had a black bar over it. In fact, the dates and other information had been blacked out on most of the papers. This left more questions than answers, but some of them she could fill in herself.

The first was, who was this Ren Yoshida? That was simple enough for her to gather. This is part of what she had been missing: her real name. The pictures she was looking at were before she lost her memory. This is who she had been before, but even then, there was more than what her parents had told her. She was adopted. All this time, the little family she had been clinging to was not her biological family. This didn't change the love they had shown her, nor did it change the love she had for them, but still, nagging ideas broke through the torrent of thought. Who were her real parents? Why had she been adopted? Why was so much of the file blackened out? How had this man, Hugo, found out so much? How long had she known Amanda? Why hadn't her parents told her anything?

A slight pang of a headache twinged in the corner of Crow's forehead. She put the file down flat on the table and pinched the bridge of her nose. Amanda and Hugo stopped their bickering to look at her. Amanda leaned over and said gently, "Are you ok?"

"What? Oh...yeah I'm fine...I'm...I think I just need to go home," Crow said as she placed her hand on the folder and looked at Hugo. He gave her a small nod, and she quickly slipped it into her bag. But just as she made mention of going home, Amanda jumped in excitement.

"I'll go with you!"

"What?" Crow blinked in surprise. Hugo was rolling up the newspaper and tucking it safely away in his coat. Sensing that the decision had already been made, Crow sighed and ran her hand through her hair.

"Are we good here?" Hugo asked looking at each of the girls. Amanda nodded her head in excitement, and Crow nodded as well. "Good. We will meet you at your apartment in an hour." Hugo reached into his coat and pulled out a rather large bundle of money. Crow looked at it with wide eyes as he started putting bills on the table. Her shock only deepened as she counted just how much he was putting down. Hugo paused just as it reached two hundred and muttered under his breath thoughtfully, "That should cover our meals and coffee for twenty-three other agents…" There he paused and glanced around the shop for a few seconds before placing a few more bills on the table, muttering, "Maybe another hundred for the coffee." Then he sat back and spoke into a small mic that was hidden in the collar of his shirt, "We're done here. All units can release their positions. You're all relieved for the night. See you tomorrow."

In one fluid movement, every single customer in the shop got to their feet, and after gathering their various items—purses, bags, etc.—walked out, chattering like mildly invested coworkers. Crow opened and closed her mouth wordlessly for a few moments until finally, even Amanda and Hugo left as well. She was alone with the waiter she bribed. Crow plopped back down into her chair flabbergasted as he walked over. He looked over her and inquired, "You are OK, right?"

"You knew about all of that? You knew they were all federal agents? You knew that I walked right into all of it?" Crow asked in a weary voice that sounded like she was on the brink of shattering.

"Hey, they told me that if I kept quiet there would be a really good tip in it for me. Besides, that guy you were talking to said if I were to interfere with a federal investigation that it could end really badly for me, and no offense sweetheart, but I'm not going to federal prison for you," he said as he held out the drink in his hand to her, "Here's your usual on the house."

"More like it was paid for by their money," Crow responded, taking the drink out of his hand as she stood and giving him a quick swat to the back of his head. He responded with a laugh and, shaking his head, walked back to the kitchen. She turned and quietly left the shop, feeling just as worn out as she had when she had first been released from the hospital. An hour later, Crow was in her apartment sitting on the couch watching television, waiting for the inevitable knock she knew was going to sound at the door. Just a little after that hour, there it was, and when Crow answered the door, in bounced Amanda with a bag slung over her shoulder. Glancing down the hall, Crow didn't see Hugo, but she was sure that he was close by, watching over his little sister to make sure nothing would happen to her. Crow closed the door and turned back to see Amanda looking over the apartment.

"Nice place you got here," she said, plopping the bag down and sitting on the couch.

"Thanks, it's nothing big, just something my parents got me when I was thinking of going to school and work." Crow trailed off, thinking back on her earlier discovery, but quickly shook it off to look back at Amanda's bag. "What all do you have in there?"

"Just the things I don't go anywhere without: my guns, my scrapbook, things like that. The things Hugo saved for me," Amanda chittered away as she started pulling some of the things out to show her friend. Hearing the word "guns" had intrigued Crow, but as she came to get a closer look, she realized they were mainly toys. Some were paintball guns, and some looked like toys that could only shoot foam darts or something similar. Crow arched an eyebrow and took a sideways glance at her friend. Amanda was still chattering away, quite involved in what she was showing her, and Crow was inclined to believe that she thought these guns would really fire.

"You can really shoot these?" Crow asked in disbelief.

"Duh! You have the lightning, and I shoot the guns. That's how this works. You really don't remember anything, do you?" Amanda looked at her as she picked up one of her guns and showed it off to Crow excitedly, "Don't worry, I'll be here to remind you."

"Thanks, Amanda. Why don't you show me how you shoot those guns of yours?" Crow asked as she got to her feet, and Amanda practically jumped in excitement.

"Ok!" She went to Crow's patio door. The two went outside, and Crow took in the night air. Then she looked at Amanda, who seemed to have been scanning the night for a suitable target. As they were looking out, Amanda smiled and pointed out at the golf course across from her apartment, "Ok, ok. You see that sign all the way there under that light?"

Crow nodded. Amanda grinned and leaned against the railing, looking down the scope of her gun. Crow watched with guarded interest, doubting that anything of real significance was going to happen, and couldn't stop her jaw from dropping when Amanda fired an energy bullet from the toy gun. Her aim was true, and she shot the exact middle of the sign. She looked up to see Crow's expression and laughed. Crow shook her head. "That was a good shot."

"Duh! That's what I do," Amanda said with a smirk. Crow was starting to think that it wouldn't be so bad having Amanda around when there was the sound of gunshot. Crow looked to see what Amanda was aiming at and instead saw her staring back just as shocked as she was. The light on the street below the apartment went out, and the area went dark. Two more shots rang, and Crow could see the sign Amanda had shot now had two more bullet holes in the corners of it.

A groan of terror rose in back of Amanda's throat, and Crow heard whistling when she reached out to her friend. After listening to it for a few seconds, she recognized the tune. It was the same song she had heard Amanda humming: The Battle Hymn of the Republic. However, hearing it whistled seemed to have an adverse effect on Amanda, and she visibly panicked. The things coming out of her mouth weren't comprehensible, and the younger teenager ran back into the apartment. Just as she did, Crow heard two more shots, and turned to see the sign now had bullet holes in all four corners around Amanda's shot. Crow ran back into the apartment to see her friend throwing her things back into the bag she had brought with her.

"Amanda…what's going on? Do you know who is shooting?" Crow tried to ask her friend. When she looked at her, Amanda's panic was as clear as day.

"I have to go. I can't be here. I have to get out of here," Amanda clamored. No matter how hard Crow tried to get anything else from her, that's all she would say. Amanda's bag was packed, and she was out the front door before Crow could stop her. Crow stood in shock until she looked down and saw one of Amanda's guns on the ground. She couldn't explain what possessed her to do so, but Crow snatched her own messenger bag off the ground, along with the gun, before running out in an attempt to catch her friend.

Crow reached the street in front of the building in time to watch Amanda jump into the back of the same limo that she and Hugo had been in earlier. The door slammed shut before Crow could call out to her, and in a blink, they were driving at high speed as they rushed out of sight. This left the nineteen-year-old standing alone, absolutely lost and confused about what had just happened. Despite the whirlwind of questions, there was one coherent thought that ran through her mind. From the trajectory of those bullets, the shooter was on the rooftop of her apartment building.

Summoning the power that she had stored within her, she pointed her hand at the building, and after a little focus, called down a raining storm of lightning all over the roof. Whoever had been firing those shots wouldn't have been expecting that. A small smirk of satisfaction crept across her lips. No one could've gotten away from the lightning storm.

Without warning, an explosion so fierce knocked Crow straight to the ground, and when she came out of her daze, she looked up to see the apartment building smoking and flames licking the exterior walls. Slowly, the teenager got to her feet, and her heart froze in her chest when she saw that the source of the explosion was her apartment. Clutching the bag tightly in her hands, she stared in horror at what had once been her home. While terrified residents spilled out of the building, screaming in fright, Crow stood in the middle of the street trying to piece together everything that happened.

But no matter how hard she tried, none of the pieces fit, and all she could do was stand in the street looking at the burning remains of her apartment until the fire department and police arrived on scene to investigate. When the authorities discovered that her apartment had been the one that went up in flames, she was taken into custody for the night for her own protection, as they said. Much to her irritation, they questioned her and decided they would not let her go until she had somewhere safe to stay, so she called her parents. This satisfied the police, and she was released into their care.

While her parents were fussing over her in concern, she noticed something in her mother's demeanor that was highly unusual. As they were escorting her to the car, her mother was abnormally alert and scanned the world around them. As much as Crow could remember, her mother would get upset, but she was never tense. Her father slipped into the driver's seat, and Crow sat in the backseat with her mother. Through the entire ride, her mother didn't take her arm from around Crow's shoulders, and she kept staring out the windows like someone was going to attack at any moment. This continued until they arrived home.

Crow did not comment on the strange behavior of her parents, and her mother ushered her into the house before her father even had a chance to turn off the car. After a bit of shuffling around, her old room was prepared, and when her mother finally calmed down, her parents kissed her goodnight and went to bed.

Crow sat down on the bed and cleared her mind. There was more going on than she was being told, and she decided it was time she did some investigating of her own.

Chapter 7: Crow, 2012

Sometime after the explosion, Crow went back to her apartment alone, much to the aggravation of her mother and father. She walked through the charred remains of her room and picked through it, looking to find anything that could be salvaged. But nothing survived the blast. She was relieved she had kept her most valuable documents and pictures in the bag with her. When she saw that there was nothing left, she went to the roof which had been left untouched. As she slowly walked the rooftop, she could see the scorch marks left from the lightning. There was no way someone could have evaded it. Every inch of the roof was covered in burns. So why hadn't anyone been found?

She slowly approached the corner that was just above where her old apartment had been. It was then that Crow felt a knot of dread form in the pit of her stomach. She came to a stop and saw a perfect square left completely untouched. Someone had anticipated her attacking. She thought no one outside a select few knew of her powers. The whole thing left a bad taste in her mouth. While it was true that once in a great while her emotions overwhelmed her and a nearby bulb would burst, she had never given any indication of abnormal abilities to anyone. Someone knew far more about her than she had anticipated, and they had prepared specifically for her. She stood, feet in the center of that perfect square, and looked over it carefully. As she intently scanned the roof, she noticed something at the edge of the rooftop glinting in the light. Curiously tilting her head to the side, she walked over, and there – sitting perfectly on the edge of the building – was a bullet pointing straight into the air. She looked over it for a moment and picked it up. Looking it over, it appeared to be a standard rifle shell, possibly military, but what caught her eye was the "W" scratched on the side. She had no idea what it meant, but she was positive it was a message from the shooter. So she placed it in her pocket and turned, deciding it was time to go back to her parents' home.

     For a few weeks, she kept her silence. She didn't say a word to her parents without thinking over her wording carefully. Crow knew them well from the experiences she had of the past few years, but there was no guarantee on how they would respond. Besides, the internal strife she felt about possibly hurting the two people who loved her unconditionally was beginning to make her physically sick. No matter how she tried to hide it, her mother was still there, doting on her, lovingly trying to make her precious daughter feel better. Crow kept the file Hugo had given her close by, carefully ensuring her parents would never find it, but the truth was beginning to burn in her breast. The desire to know why they never said a damn thing about her adoption, or even use her real name, was overwhelming. She understood the hell it had been after she lost her memory. Her mother and father had worked hard to bring her out of her isolation, her depression. They gave her as much love as was possible, and they rebuilt her. A small part of her wondered how different she was compared to who she had been. That nagging thought was enough to push her to bring it up, but she wasn't sure when the best time to say something would be. She had been told that an incident had given her mother a delicate condition. That could be used to her advantage. As much as she didn't want to exploit her mother's illness and felt terrible for even thinking about doing so, she understood how stubborn her father could be if he didn't want to divulge anything, and the only weaknesses he had were his wife and daughter. So, if she had to take advantage of her mother to get her answers, she would do what she must.

So, Crow left to go to a nearby cafe. Though it was different from the one she had met Hugo and Amanda in, she found herself expecting to see someone who didn't belong. But if there was, they hid themselves too well for her to notice. She sat down with her usual drink and plopped the file down on the table in front of her. Staring at it intently, she began thinking over the electric currents in her childhood home. Crow knew the workings of wires and electric currents well throughout the entire dwelling, and she knew her parents' routines. She knew the general areas in which they would spend most of their time, and she knew which electronics they used the most. Methodically, she reached out and flipped open the file to look things over. She stared hard at every picture in the file and every word on the papers that struck an emotional chord with her. Her power started to spring alive inside her as her emotions intensified, and once she had it almost crackling through the ends of her long black hair, she closed her eyes to picture the house she was living in with her parents. She focused on specific electric currents surging through the house and started causing them to overload. She imagined the lights flickering and the electronics reacting to the sporadic surges of power reaching them. She could almost hear some of the bulbs burst as they were overloaded with electricity, and she could feel the currents flaring through the house.

She kept this up for an hour or so. Whenever her conviction would falter, she would look back at the pictures of when she was a kid. When she felt cruel, she looked at the adoption papers. When she was about to cry, she thought about the things her parents should have told her. It was true, they had given her as much as they could, but surely keeping this from her wasn't necessary. Why hadn't they told her what her real name was? Why had there been so many strange secrets since she lost her memory? Who was she? Did they know about her powers? She had tried to keep them hidden the instant she recognized them. She was terrified to show them, but now she knew they had to know. So why hadn't they told her about them?! Why had they let her think she was completely alone?!

When she was sure her parents had suffered enough, she calmed her raging emotions and reached into her bag to pull out her cell phone. Taking a deep breath to further settle herself, Crow dialed her father's number and waited for him to answer. He must've been close to the phone, for it didn't take long for Crow to hear his calm voice on the other end, "Hello Crow. Are you alright?"

"Why wouldn't I be?" Crow asked somewhat defensively. She bit down on the corner of her mouth and dug her nails into the table she was sitting at. It was more difficult than she thought it would be to keep herself under control. She was frustrated with her own raging emotions.

"Well, after the incident with your apartment, can I be blamed for worrying about my little girl?" her father responded calmly as tears burned the corners of her eyes.

"Yeah, sure..." Crow answered, trying to pull together the dialogue she had planned, but no matter how hard she tried she couldn't focus enough to retrieve it.

"What's wrong, Crow? I know something is bothering you. I can hear it in your voice," he asked.

She wasn't ready to get into things just yet, so she beat around the bush just a little longer. "Just been thinking lately dad...How's things at home?"

"Things are just fine here, Crow." His answer was a lie, and Crow knew it. There was no way things were fine after all of the hell she had been causing at the house with her electricity. Surely her mother was panicking, and he would've been trying to comfort her. The lie only angered her further.

"Oh really? Nothing out of the ordinary?" she growled quietly. She allowed her power to surge through the lights in the hallway near his study, where she guessed he was sitting. Through the phone, she heard crackling and then shattering. Crow quickly calmed it and asked almost innocently, "What was that dad?"

"Oh, just the lights in the hallway. We probably need to call an electrician. We might have a wiring issue. It was distressing your mother, so I had her go into the bedroom and relax. I made sure to unplug the electronics and take out the bulbs in the lights so nothing will bother her while she rests," he said dismissively. Crow's brow twitched in annoyance. Her father was a clever man.

"I'm sorry to hear that, Dad. It's a shame electricity can be such an unpredictable thing," Crow replied as she flickered the lights in his study. She could hear it through the phone, and she heard her father sigh heavily.

"It's nothing we can't handle, Crow. We have dealt with worse than this. Is there something else bothering you, sweetheart?"

"Dad, you remember the night my apartment went up in flames, right?"

"How could I possibly forget that, Crow? We almost lost you again."

"Well, there was more that happened that night. I was visited by a FBI agent when I was leaving work," Crow explained as she ran her hand through her hair.

"Oh?" her father inquired.

"Yeah. He had someone else from my past. Someone I think you know. He had a girl named Amanda with him. Dad, who is Ren Yoshida?" Crow asked. There was a pause, and Crow was almost sure she had him.

"I don't know what you're talking about, Crow," he answered in a calm, calculated sort of way. Crow let out power surge in anger. She heard a bulb near the phone burst into pieces in the lamp that held it.

"Oh really? You don't?" Crow asked pointedly.

He sighed, "Crow, is that really necessary?"

"Is what necessary, Dad?" Crow hissed as she sent another surge through his study.

"You know what I'm talking about."

"I actually don't know what you're talking about," she mimicked him.

"Children," he grumbled in exasperation. Crow bit down on the inside of her cheek and let one more surge flare through the house. This one was a little more powerful than those previous, and she heard her father slam his hand on the desk. She had crossed the line. "That's enough, Ren!"

At first, Crow couldn't speak. It must've been pure reflex on her father's part, and she wished that it had triggered something for her. Yet, nothing came. No memory. Nothing. It hurt just as much as finding out she had been adopted. Crow pulled herself together long enough to ask, "What did you just call me?"

Her father fell silent. Crow shifted, uncomfortable in her chair. The seconds wore on. After a minute or so, her father sighed, "I said that's enough, Crow."

"No...you said Ren," Crow choked.

"It was nothing, Crow. Just a slip of the tongue." There was a tone in her father's voice Crow had never heard before that disturbed her. She leaned over the table and could feel her stomach churning in anticipation. However, her father recovered and cleared his throat to say, "Your mother is awake, and I need to check on her. When will you be home for dinner?"

She was angry. She finally caught her father in the lie she expected, but it was such a shock that she couldn't immediately pursue it. She was shaking with all these new revelations, but she couldn't continue interrogating him. The child within her was screaming and the teenager trying to be an adult was doing everything she could to smother it. So, she grit her teeth tightly as she closed her eyes while bowing her head to say, "My usual time."

"See you then." Then the line disconnected.

Crow sat in her chair for twenty minutes, unable to move, numb. When she finally could think, she wanted to forget she was adopted. She wanted to forget everything she learned the night

Amanda and Hugo found her. More than anything, Crow wanted to go back to the boring routine when things were normal or at least somewhat normal for her. The pieces of the puzzle that was her life were coming together, but there were many more pieces missing than she had initially realized. There was instinctive anger, but she had no idea where to direct it. True, her parents were hiding things from her, but there had to be some reason for it. Just what was that reason, and why did it seem like there was something lurking around the corner waiting to strike? These were things Crow couldn't answer, and they made her feel worse. A few hours passed in this way, and when it came time to leave, she rose and mechanically gathered her things. All she wanted to do was scream, but she maintained her composure. She slowly walked out of the shop and stood on the sidewalk, staring up at the sun as it was beginning to sink. After a minute, she trudged back home.

 By the time she reached home, Crow was her usual calm and happy self. Her mother was in bright spirits, and aside from the earlier stress from the electric surges, she was relaxed. Crow's father was his usual temperament, and it was almost like their prior conversation never happened. So, they sat down to a wonderful dinner that turned out to be Crow's favorite meal. Her mother happily chittered away about the electrician that had fixed the wiring while she was sleeping, and about how today was a good day. Crow wasn't sure exactly what happened to her mother because the incident had been before she lost her memory, but from what she had been told there had been an accident that had left her mother with severe brain damage. Due to her father's care, she recovered wonderfully and made more progress than any other doctor had expected her to. But there were still days where her mother would sit in a chair and stare at the wall with a furrowed brow, trying to figure out something in her head that wasn't connecting the way it should. During these moments, she wouldn't speak, and even Crow's father said it was better to just leave her be. But there would be other occasions, like during dinner, that she was fully coherent and laughing like nothing was wrong. She was so clever and quick-witted that it made Crow proud to call her Mom.

Crow tried her damnedest to make sure her mother didn't catch on to her inner turmoil. She tried with everything she had to keep a smile on her face and behave with her parents like she always had. Her father did the same, and at the end of the night she hugged her mother as her father escorted her to bed. In fact, she hugged her tighter than she had in a long time, feeling guilty for her earlier actions. However, before her father excused himself, he quietly told Crow to go into his study and wait for him there. There was something they needed to discuss. She did as she was told and she waited. It was all part of the routine. Her father would escort her mother to bed, talk with her a little and then stay with her until she fell asleep. It was a routine with so much love in it. It was more proof that the people she had known as her parents were truly good people.

After a while, Crow's father appeared in the doorway. Before Crow could open her mouth, he held a silencing finger to his lips. He went over to his bookshelf and messed with a few things, and Crow could hear a faint clicking sound. He quietly went to a few other places in the study and did the same thing. Crow watched him intently, but kept her peace while he sat down in front of her reached out for the phone. He turned it over in his hand and flipped a strange switch in a hidden compartment on the bottom. Crow heard a faint buzzing as he sat it back on the table before saying, "Alright, now we can talk."

"What was all that?" Crow asked indicating around the room.

"Can't a father want to speak to his daughter without anyone possibly listening in?" was his calm reply.

"Who would want to listen in?" she asked curiously.

"You'll find out in time. Now, I spoke with your mother and both of us decided that it was time to have this talk. Ask anything you want to, and when you're done, I'll explain the things you need to know," he said as he looked over her carefully. For a few minutes, Crow didn't have the courage to speak.

"I'm adopted?" Crow asked finally.

"Yes."

"Why didn't you tell me?"

"We did before your accident."

"Why didn't you tell me after?" Crow hissed in frustration.

"Because it didn't matter. You're our daughter. You must understand something, Crow. You knew everything before you lost your memory. You knew you were adopted. You knew about the ability you have and you knew far more at your age than most have to know in a lifetime. You almost died when you got hurt. Your life hung in the balance, and even when you were healing, you were fragile. Why would I risk adding to that stress? Why would I risk your health and mental wellbeing by saying something that doesn't even matter? You're our daughter, and we love you more than you will ever know," he responded with such fatherly command that Crow immediately fell silent. She hung her head, realizing how childish she had been.

"Who were my biological parents? Why was I adopted?"

"Well, you were given to us to raise until the time when your parents would come back for you. At first, that was the plan and we stuck to it. You had a preordained future ahead of you, and though I never knew exactly what it was, your mother did. But, your mother and I realized that we had fallen in love with you and we couldn't give you back. You were our little Ren, and through everything, there's no one who could've loved you more than us.

"One night, your mother took me aside and told me we had to run. We had to take you and disappear for the sake of your future. I never questioned it. I knew the kind of family she came from, and when she told me we had to run for your sake, I wrapped you up and we ran. We've been running ever since. Everything we've done has been to protect you. Everything we have done was to keep you safe and keep those who have been sent after you off your trail. We're not perfect by any means and I'm sure there are things we've done wrong, but everything was because we love you," he explained as he reached out and took her arm and made her look up at him. Crow saw clearer than ever before just how much her parents loved her, and there was no doubt in her mind that they would go to hell and back to keep her safe.

"So, we've been running all this time?"

"Yes, and we've had a few close calls. Your mother's head injury being one of them. Yours being another. You're not the only one with power, Crow. Your mother and I have our own, and the people who've been chasing us have theirs as well. When you didn't remember that, we thought you'd be safer not remembering. So, we made the decision we thought was best at the time and didn't tell you, but you found them all on your own. Maybe it would've been better to tell you everything, but we couldn't risk you. We've fought tooth and nail to keep you safe and now, you're going to have to fight too. You didn't ask for this, but you'll have many people chasing you. You're going to have people out to kill you and others out to make you part of them. It's going to be up to you who you choose to be and who you choose to associate yourself with." Crow's father slowly got to his feet and moved over to his desk. He opened the top drawer on his left and began sorting through the contents, causing a sense of dread to swell in Crow's chest.

"Dad…what are you talking about?" Crow's voice cracked as she felt her stomach turn into a knot. She got to her feet and realized she was shaking. The things her father had told her scared her, but the way he was acting was even more terrifying, "Dad, What's going on?"

"Your mother and I are staying here. You have to run, Crow. You have to get somewhere safe, and don't stop until then. Don't look back, and remember one thing—as you go, you're going to learn a lot of things, and you're going to learn the truth about everything that has happened to you. I'm not going to lie, Crow, some of it will have you deeply conflicted. There's only one thing I want you to understand. No matter what you're told. No matter what you find out. No matter what happens to you. Everything your mother and I have done is out of love and we never once regretted who we became after taking you into our lives. You are everything to us. Never doubt that." Her father straightened up and held a set of keys in his hand. Crow's eyes widened as she realized the keys in his hands were to the cherry red convertible corvette that he prized and babied almost as much as he did her. He walked away from the desk and gently took his daughter's hand to place the keys in them. As he wrapped her fingers around the keys, he looked at her and said, "Now, I need you to run, Crow. I need you to run and not look back."

"Dad... No... I'm not going anywhere without you and mom," Crow started to plead as she held on to her father; clinging in terror. The very idea of facing the world without either of them was almost more than she could handle. She felt shell shocked as he placed her bag over her shoulder and secured it so it wouldn't fall. Then her father held her by the arm and gently but firmly led her down the hall to the front door. She realized what was coming and tried again, "Dad. Please. Don't send me away. Dad, I can't do this."

"Yes, you can, Crow. We raised you to be strong. Now it's time to make us even more proud of you," he answered with a small choke in his own voice.

"No...Daddy please," Crow tried to pull away from him and stand her ground, but her father's pace never changed. She could feel his hand shaking slightly as he stopped at the front door and pulled it open. He leaned forward and placed a small kiss on her forehead.

"Damn it, Crow! I told you to run!"

Before she knew what happened, Crow's father had thrown her from the house and slammed the door shut as she sprawled across the ground. When she finally got her senses back, she was on her feet and trying to open the door but found that it had been locked tight. She slammed her fists on the door and yelled for her father to let her in. Tears were burning the corners of her eyes, but no matter what she did, the door wouldn't budge. However, she heard that her mother had gotten up. Within earshot of the door, her mother and father were speaking quickly back and forth in Japanese.

Crow couldn't catch what exactly was being said because of how quiet they were, but whatever was said was urgent. After a short conversation, both her mother and father commanded in perfect unison, "Run, Crow!"

Crow slowly stepped away from the door. The tone of their voices was the same as when she had done something to scare them. It was the tone of voice they used when they were telling her not to do something that could end up getting her hurt. It was enough that she turned on her heels and rushed to her father's car clutching her bag. She practically flung herself into the driver's seat when she opened the door and threw her bag into the seat beside her. After fumbling a few tries, she was able to get the keys into the ignition and was off like a shot. Crow flew down the drive, holding the steering wheel so tight that all her knuckles turned white, and stopped three blocks away. Something was nagging at the back of her head. She slowly got out of the running car to look back at her house. She could make out the silhouette of her mother and father holding each other through the living room window. Just as she locked eyes on their image it was as if she could hear her mother's voice in her head telling her to run, but before she could ponder this, there was a loud explosion that knocked her into the side of the car. When she pushed herself up using the car as a brace and looked back, the sight that met her eyes was enough to knock the wind right out of her chest.

Flames burst from the house and black smoke flew into the air. A ball of fire flew up from the house and Crow distinctly saw the shape of a dragon rise from the ground. Crow stood frozen in absolute horror. The fire was so intense that the structure of the house was already falling in on itself. All Crow knew was that there was no possible way her parents could have gotten out. There would be nothing left. They were dead. No amount of hope or love could ever change that. Holding onto the side of the car, Crow screamed in emotional agony as that realization hit her. As she screamed, the lights on the side of the street flickered and flared before bursting from the surge; showering glass on the ground. Lights for a mile out in all directions went completely dark. The sound of shattering glass and roaring flames sang through the otherwise quiet night. The only light was cast from the moon, the stars, and the fire.

Chapter 8: Crow's Return, 2012 to 2016

Crow was alone, and she knew she needed to get as far out of dodge as she possibly could. She was out of Indiana before she thought anyone could think to look for her, and she didn't even consider going back. She didn't need to. The first time she stopped, she looked in her bag and saw a card with a note taped to it. Inside was her father's account number, routing number, and PIN. She also found official IDs with her real name, Ren Yoshida. She didn't know how to feel about those but kept them close nonetheless. She withdrew the daily maximum and did everything she could to disappear off the map. Crow never stayed in one place too long. She was far too paranoid, and the fact that she didn't have her parents there to look out for her frightened her.

She stayed out on the road going state to state, keeping as low a profile as she possibly could. Things were quiet, and Crow kept on the move. She didn't socialize with anyone, and she didn't make herself a regular anywhere. She changed her appearance: Where she once had long hair black as pitch, it was now cropped short around her face and highlighted with red streaks. She was never ashamed of her scar, but now she kept it covered with makeup, constantly concealed. She dressed mostly in black, and her usual attire consisted of black knee high combat boots with red belts crossing over them, black canvas pants, a red tank top, and a black coat with a red crow across the back. When most people saw her coming, they avoided looking at her or acted as if she didn't exist. This was more than fine. She spent two years this way until she was going for breakfast to a cafe she had only been in once before when she caught sight of the newspaper on the front stand. There were three people ahead of her waiting to be seated, so Crow picked up the paper, intending to quietly wait her turn. The headline wasn't anything of real concern to her, but there was a small side article that immediately caught her attention. Completely forgetting her hunger, Crow quickly sat on the waiting bench and flipped the pages to the article in question.

There was an estate auction being held in her hometown of Indianapolis. There was a grand show and hullabaloo over it due to the family name, and that specifically was what caught Crow's interest. Apparently, everything that was being auctioned off was from a well-off Japanese family whose last living member in the USA had just passed away leaving no one to lay claims to the items left behind. The surname was Yoshida. There was a call out, asking for any remaining relatives to come claim the items before the auction so that they could be returned to their rightful owners. Crow stared through the newspaper in her hand. The auction was in little over a week, and it would take her two days to get back. The auction was being held in the convention center, and there was a hotel attached to it that, more likely than not, would be booked to near capacity. She didn't have a lot of time to plan, and she hadn't planned on returning to Indiana so soon. It wasn't until the young hostess of the cafe stood in front of her and cleared her throat, annoyed Crow hadn't been paying attention, that she snapped out of her daze. Crow practically jumped out of her skin when the hostess spoke to her, and she jumped to her feet, holding tightly onto the newspaper she had been reading.

"Steady there girlie. I didn't mean to startle you. Is it just you today or are you waiting for someone?" the young woman asked, tilting her head to the side.

"I...ah...Actually, I just realized I have somewhere I have to be. How much do I owe you for the paper?" Crow asked as she dug into her pockets looking for change.

"Don't worry about it. We throw them out at the end of the day anyway. Besides, it's not like missing one paper is gonna throw off our whole day."

Crow bowed slightly, "Thank you."

She was out of the cafe like a bullet shot from a gun and was running back to where she had been living. It was a small apartment, furnished simply with a table, a single chair, and a small television set on the floor in the corner of the living room. She had only been there for a few weeks. She sighed. It was a shame to waste the money she had spent for the entire month, but there were more important things she needed to worry about. She didn't have time to waste. Gathering up what little effects she had, she was packed in a matter of minutes and on her way to the garage she had paid to store her father's car. She didn't like the idea of it getting dented or damaged by some unaware moron who wasn't paying attention to where they were going. And it would've been too conspicuous leaving a dead body behind for damaging her late father's car.

It wasn't a long trip, and soon she pulled up to the storage door to look over her father's car, her car. A small tear slipped down the side of her face, and she paused for a few minutes to gather herself before putting her bag in the trunk and slowly easing into the driver's seat. Memories of car rides with her father and road trips with her parents came to mind, things that would constantly keep coming back to her once she got back home. Crow didn't immediately see it, but as she looked at her hands gripped on the steering wheel, she noticed that not only were her knuckles white, but her arms were shaking so severely that she had to hug them tightly to her for nearly fifteen minutes before she could finally put the key in the ignition and drive off. She was a few streets down when she had to take a sharp turn to avoid another driver who pulled into the intersection without looking to see if there was anyone coming his way. Just as Crow managed to avoid him, she heard something come loose and started thumping around in the trunk that she was sure hadn't been there before, and it sure as hell wasn't the bag she just put in there. She swiftly pulled off into a somewhat empty parking lot and got out of the car. She hesitated with her hand on the lid of the trunk for a minute, trying to gather the courage to open it and see just what exactly was banging around.

Finally, when her hands were stable enough, she opened the trunk and looked around. At first, she didn't see anything. Out of respect for her father, she had kept the car in pristine condition and made sure her bag of stuff hadn't caused any sort of damage to the inside. There was nothing that would've made a thumping sound from making a sharp turn. Crow placed her bag on the ground beside her feet and slowly ran her hands over the trunk. It was then that she found the handle of the storage compartment for the spare tire. Crow had never thought to look inside of it. She only hesitated for a few more seconds before she pulled open the compartment. Sitting where the spare tire should've been was one of her father's medical briefcases. She blinked and looked to see old tape had worn away from where it had been secured to the bottom of the tire compartment. It seemed to have given way over time. It had been so long since Crow had seen one of her father's medical briefcases that she slowly picked up and held it to her breast, lost in the feel and smell of the worn leather. She replaced her bag in the trunk, closed it and returned to sit in the front seat. Gingerly, she placed the briefcase on the seat and ran her hands over it, remembering her father. Then she flicked it open and carefully began inspecting the contents inside.

It was her medical file following the injury to her head. As she read through the notes, she learned something that almost stopped her heart in her chest. While the initial injury had, in fact, been severe, it had been semi-stabilized before she was taken to her father, and her memory loss had not been caused by the initial injury. No, the memory loss had, instead, been caused by her father. She read his handwritten notes intently and saw that he had, with unnatural surgical precision, cut out a specific part of her brain and fully removed it. He had removed a part of her brain that wouldn't cause any visible or physical damage, but would permanently erase all her memories. Any normal surgeon wouldn't have been able to do such a thing, but her father was talented. After all, he told her that he had powers, just like she did, except that his involved his surgical skills. That was why he was the best at his job. There was something at the end of his notes that struck Crow. He wrote that it was a success, and now that he had taken away her memories, his beloved daughter would now have a better chance of being safe. Crow put the file back in the briefcase and closed it as tears silently swept her cheeks. It was her father that had taken her memories from her. He did it out of fear for her safety. A fear that she didn't quite understand, but she knew enough about her parents to know that they only did the things they did out of love.

    When she was able, Crow replaced the briefcase in the trunk of the car and drove back to Indiana. The only times she stopped were to get gas.

    The city was just as she had left it. Though she didn't honestly expect much to change in just two years, she had built up so much in her mind about that Crow wasn't sure how to feel about it. She spent a few hours driving around downtown, looking at everything before she stopped in front of the Westin connected to the convention center. Something in her gut told her that stepping through those doors alone was a very bad idea. It proved to be a problem, considering she didn't have anyone else to go with her, but she figured if she managed some decent reconnaissance, that would make up for it. However, she needed somewhere safe, and she glanced along the street to find neutral ground, landing on the Marriot hotel.

    "Besides," she muttered thoughtfully to herself, "There's three days left before the auction. I should be able to cover my ass in that time, I hope."

She drove over to the second hotel and parked her car in an empty section of the garage. She glanced around and smirked before charging the air within a short distance of the car and using the lights above her as boundary lines to keep a closed circuit. Now all the lights in the area would flicker whenever someone entered the space. She hoped that everyone else would shy away. Midwest superstition worked to her advantage. Crow, on the other hand, knew she could handle anything some street thugs might throw at her. Satisfied that her father's car would be safe, she walked into the hotel and slowly approached the front desk. After a little chat with the manager, she had a room and was on her way up in the elevator.

Crow was lost in her own world, trying to plan just how she was going to go about scoping out the Westin. It would be difficult to get into the areas dealing with the auction, and she wasn't exactly easy to miss. A five-foot-five Japanese woman would easily stick out in the middle of the convention center without a convention going on. Then again, the auction was of a Japanese family, so they would probably think she was merely an intrigued tourist. The worst she thought would happen would be that they would ask if she were related, and a few well spun lies could keep that under wraps. Hopefully, no one would want to see any identification from her.

The elevator stopped, and she gathered up her things to step out. She walked quietly, thinking to herself, and arrived at the door. She pulled the keycard from her pocket and opened the door. Lost in thought, she slipped into the room and kicked it shut behind her. There were dozens of thoughts bouncing around in her mind, but those all went away quick enough when she felt the barrel of a gun press against the back of her head. She dropped the bags she was carrying and froze on the spot staring at the window in shock. How had she not noticed there was someone else in the room with her? Crow silently cursed her oblivious nature and channeled lightning through her hands, ready to strike down the foe.

"Pew! Pew! You're dead!"

"Fucking Amanda," Crow half groaned, half hissed. She turned around and looked at her friend, who grabbed her in a tight embrace. Crow wrapped one arm around Amanda and kept the other at her side. After giving her a moment to hug her, Crow growled, "What the hell is wrong with you, Amanda? Normal people don't put guns to the back of their friends' heads!"

"I dunno. Hey, what's wrong with me?! What's wrong with you! You're the one who doesn't send any post cards. You don't call. You just up and disappear for two years. That's rude, Crow! Rude!" Amanda responded defensively as she stepped back and allowed her friend to walk into the room. Crow snatched her bags from where she had dropped them and plopped them on the bed closest to the window. She glanced over the room and noticed that it was a standard room with two beds, a television, two lights, and a phone. An idea popped into her head. Hugo must have been anticipating her actions and not only had the room prepared for the two of them beforehand, but also made sure the person at the front desk would give her the key to the room he had Amanda waiting in. She wrinkled her nose and barely kept herself from muttering something about how aggravating it was to be meddled with by the government.

"Gee, Amanda, I'm sorry I was a little preoccupied with my parents' house bursting into flames and running for my life that I forgot to send you a postcard of all the rundown apartments and hotels I was staying at," Crow grumbled quietly as she sat down on the bed.

"You know that's not really an excuse. I run from people all the damn time. I mean look at me right now, still on the run from people. It's not my fault they don't know how to use my weapons. Maybe if they did the right training they wouldn't look stupid," Amanda said as she plopped down on the second bed. Crow took a moment to look over her friend and noticed that for the most part Amanda had cleaned up. She wasn't covered in dirt and grime like she had been the last time, and she was dressed in what Crow thought was a cute retro 1930's dress. The only thing that brought her look down was the dirty trench coat she wore over it.

"I'm not even going to pretend I understood half of what you just said," Crow muttered. "You're going to watch my back while I scope out the hotel before the auction, right?"

"That would be why I'm here," Amanda replied, looking at her like she was stupid.

"Then let's get to work, shall we?" Crow said as she got to her feet and reached into her bag. She pulled out a few throwing knives and hid them up her sleeves. Amanda bounced off the bed and moved to her friend's side, reaching into one of the many pockets of her own trench coat.

"Oh yeah. Before we do, I have something for you," Amanda said. After rummaging in her pockets for a moment, she produced a small box with a thin red ribbon wrapped around it. It fit perfectly in the middle of her hand. Two rubber bands were wrapped tightly around a white piece of paper on the side. "Wait, one second." Amanda said, quickly turning away with the box. After fighting with it for a minute, Amanda turned and held it back out to her with a smile on her face, the paper and rubber bands gone.

"What's this?" Crow asked titling her head to the side as she reached out and gently took it from her friend. She looked over it and couldn't help but smile. It had been two years since she had last smiled, and Amanda knew it.

"It's for your birthday, duh," Amanda answered, rolling her eyes at her blatantly oblivious friend.

"My birthday isn't for another two months," Crow laughed as she gingerly sat beside her bag on the bed and began to pull off the ribbon on the box carefully.

"You have this habit of disappearing. I've gotta give you things when I can."

"I'm not the only one who disappears."

"I explained that."

"Touché," Crow laughed and opened the box. She was shocked upon laying eyes on a beautiful jade comb with a crow on it. She turned it over in her hands and lifted it up to look at the intricate designs etched into the jade. It was gorgeous. The shade of green was the exact same as the green hue that tinged the edges of her scar. There was no doubt in her mind that Amanda had made a similar connection. Crow smiled at Amanda, "Thank you."

"You're welcome. It made me think of you."

"I can imagine. While we're exchanging things, I have something of yours as well," Crow said as she gently replaced the comb in the box. Then she sifted through her things and finally found what she was looking for. She pulled out the gun that Amanda had left behind two years ago just before Crows apartment had been blown up. "I thought you might what this back."

Amanda laughed and took the gun. It was quickly put away in one of the trench coat's many pockets, and the two started to plan their three-day recon mission before the auction.

Chapter 9: James' Departure, 2016

At eighteen, James was still quite the recluse. However, in an attempt to move on in life, he made the decision to move out of his fathers' house. If he was going to become a man of his own, he needed to make his own way. This was only agreed upon by his fathers on three conditions: He would at least write and give them updates if not call to check in once in a while. James had no problem with this. While he was moving out, he wasn't trying to cut ties with them. The second was that he had to finish his court mandated visits with his therapist, Jim Gallamore. Another point he could not argue. After all, he knew that the only way he could move on was by getting past what happened to him and what he had tried to do. The third was that he always kept his scrapbook close by with assorted things he could use to keep himself safe. James readily agreed to these conditions, and the day finally came when he finished his last session assigned by the court.

James kept mostly to himself, and many didn't bother him. His appearance was that of someone who made it a point not to draw attention, and at 5"5, one hundred and thirty pounds, he didn't make much of an impression when he entered a room. His short brown hair was often well kept and his hazel eyes were mostly cast off in the distance when he was in a social setting if they weren't focused on the floor or wall. He wasn't one for airing his thoughts to the world, and the particular therapist he had been working with had done well to make him feel like progress was quietly being made despite his habit of keeping almost everything to himself. In fact, he had given James a newfound confidence he had been lacking before.

Jim Gallamore was in his early sixties with a British accent, but as to the specific area of Britain he came from, James wasn't well versed enough to know. He was a calm looking man who seemed like he had quite a bit of experience under his belt, but at the same time James couldn't help but notice that he seemed in rather good shape for a man his age. His eyes were blue, but when James had first seen them he almost mistook them for grey. The most defining piece of his appearance, however, was a strange scar in the crease of his left cheek that from afar could almost have been mistaken for a dimple, but upon closer inspection it was clear it was a bullet wound.

James wondered what happened to walk away with a scar like that. However, he dismissed these odd things and focused on the goal of getting through his mandated sessions. From the moment he walked in on the last day, James was watching the clock, and even the elder man seemed somewhat distracted. When the final minutes ticked by, his therapist sighed and pulled out the paperwork that he would need to fill out for the court. It was at that moment that James noticed a manila folder sitting next to the paperwork that had not been there a minute before. He didn't remember seeing Mr. Gallamore put it there, but he didn't have much time to think it over as his therapist rose to his feet.

"Well, James, you have made quite a bit of progress in the time we've had. Though there's still a few things that you will have to face, and you will have to do so on your own. By the court's ruling, you have finished your time with me, and I wish you the best of luck in the future. However, I suspect that though this particular chapter in your life is closed, the next will be starting all too soon and you won't have much time to catch your breath," he said and absentmindedly placed his hand on the manila folder sitting beside his paperwork. He looked at James carefully down the bridge of his nose and seemed to hesitate. It was clear that there was something bouncing around in his head dying to be said, but he was unsure of the best way to go about it. James signed the paperwork that he needed to and it was sealed with the elder gentleman doing the same. It was then that James felt his therapist firmly grab his upper arm and lean in as he whispered, "I know things have been difficult James, and I know that you are better suited to handle them now than you once were, but I cannot stress enough that to handle what the future holds in store for you that you have to become stronger. It would be a shame to see the man you have become disappear and break."

"What are you talking about?" James asked in confusion. Up to that moment, he had thought Mr. Gallamore to be a calm, mild mannered man, but looking into his eyes at that moment there was something hiding that James didn't understand. There was something lurking in the depths of the British man's eyes that sent chills down his spine and he wasn't quite sure he wanted to hear what would be said next.

"I got this in the mail the other day," Mr. Gallamore said indicating the folder he was now holding in his hand. After releasing James, he stepped back and turned the folder over in his hands a few times before holding it out as he said, "I'm still unsure what possessed me to do so, but I opened it the moment I saw it was addressed to you. I don't quite know what to make of the contents. I'm sorry, James. I'm truly sorry in more ways than one that I have to deliver this to you."

The solemn look in the man's eyes further chilled James to his very core, and he slowly took the folder from him. James couldn't explain it, but he knew beyond the shadow of a doubt that there was something in the envelope that his therapist was concerned would cause him to go down the same path that had nearly taken his life once already, and a small part of James didn't know if he was strong enough to choose otherwise. He screwed his courage to the sticking place and opened the folder. There were two pieces of paper inside.

One was a paper that had an address written on it. The other seemed to be a picture, and James had to slip it out of the folder to get a proper look at it. But once he had, he froze.

It was a dark picture likely taken in a basement or other shut away place that the sun couldn't reach. There was a chain link fence against a wall, and lying on the ground in front of it were a few different strange tools that James wasn't quite sure their purpose. However, the sickly stains on the ends of them reminded him of dried blood. In the middle of the picture, two figures were chained to the fence and it looked as though they had nearly been beaten to death. His fathers' battered bodies were leaning against the fence clearly unconscious, and James could only imagine the tortures to produce the horrific wounds he was now looking at. Blood was oozing from various gashes across their faces and necks.

Horror swept over him. All the pain he had suffered was nothing now compared to the pain he could see his parents had been submitted to. A deep bubbling rage began to rise to the surface. The meek man he had become from the horrific scars that had been left on his psyche seemed to melt away, and in its stead was a determined man ready to draw blood from any who dared treat his fathers this way. He flourished in defense of his loved ones, and with that rationalization he was quick to focus his thoughts. He would find his parents, rescue them, and then he would find the soul or souls responsible. When he did, he would make them pay more dearly than they could ever imagine.

"What the hell is this?" James asked sharply looking at Mr. Gallamore. He shook his head.

"I honestly don't know, James. There was no return address, and when I went to the post office, there was no record of it being dropped off at my residence. My curiosity got the better of me, and I opened it. Although frankly I wish I hadn't. At first, I was torn about if I should even show this to you and go straight to the proper authorities. Most would agree that I shouldn't have risked your mental well-being by showing you such a disturbing image, but from what I have learned in my time with you, I had no other choice. They're your fathers and I had no right, even in my profession, to keep this from you. So, I called in a favor from a friend and had the image blown up to make out the address on the second piece of paper there,"

Mr. Gallamore replied as he looked over James carefully. His eyes were still unnerving to James, but from what he could see the old man was telling the truth. Although, there was something that James could not altogether place, and it was enough to set him even more on edge than he already was. James replaced the disturbing images of his fathers in the folder and pulled out the address.

"Indianapolis, huh? Seems like I'm going to be taking a trip," James muttered to himself. As he thought over it, James noted that if he were to take a train straight into downtown, it would only take him three days' time to get there, and from there he would just need to find the address. Then again, all the time he was on the train would be spent finding a route to the location and planning the rescue of his fathers.

"Listen James, I have no idea what possibly could have happened to put your fathers in a situation so horrific, and I know telling you to let the police handle it will only serve to anger you further. However, I urge you to be vigilant and watch yourself. There are people in this world who would sooner kill you than look at you. You have been pulled from death's grip once. I wish there was more I could do to help you."

"You have helped me quite a bit already Mr. Gallamore. Now if you excuse me, I have a train to catch." Before the elderly therapist could say another word, James was gone. His course was planned. First, he would return home to pack what he would need. Then he would leave for the train station and in three days, he would be in the thick of whatever hell awaited him. The rage boiling in his chest made the fear of what was in store almost meaningless. He would find his fathers.

James Vinci had been reborn.

Chapter 10: Sek's Awakening, 2016

Sek dove into his work. It challenged him and it kept him well occupied. As a young, determined twenty-two-year-old, he had plenty of energy to devote to it, and his mind was sharp. His parents and sister even came back to live in the states for a while. But aside from the first week of welcoming them back, Sek didn't see them much. He was far too busy and had too much to offer to the field to slack off. At least, that was how he saw it.

It was in this field of study that he would unwittingly develop his powers. Working with a machine called a G.R.E.E.B.L.E., Sek was studying the effects of Molybdenum Sulfate and Platinum Rhodium on a ceramic. When placed under extreme temperatures and electric conditions, it generated a massive physical strain and magnetic field. However, the sample was unstable, and during such an experiment the sample exploded, severely injuring Sek. The blast was so violent and the injuries so severe that it put him into a deep coma. He was the only survivor as the blast took out those he was working with and caused the building to partially collapse, taking even more lives.

For a time, the doctors weren't sure if he would survive the event, but his parents reassured the hospital staff that he would pull through, and they were to do everything necessary to get him on his feet as quickly as possible. Strangely enough, though they had made it clear that he was to be well taken care of, not once did his parents visit him while he was unconscious. Sek's sister, however, visited him every day and would talk to him. She made it her job to tell him the things that were going on and that she would be waiting for him to wake up.

Six weeks passed.

Sek was getting stronger. His vitals were steadily returning to normal and in some cases almost seemed better than they were before the accident. In fact, he was progressing far better than anyone could have anticipated. Two weeks after the incident, when he started taking a turn for the better, strange things began to happen in his room. The machines would start to surge at random times. When they were checked by hospital IT, it was as though a heavy-duty magnet had wiped the hard drives clean. Many of the machines had to be replaced only for them to suffer the same fate a few days later. Yet, no matter how hard they tried, no one could find the source of the phenomena. When the doctors had to explain the constant shifting of machines to the family, they were surprised to be greeted by small smiles from his parents.

One day, a nurse was trying to get one of the numerous machines hooked up to the young man to read correctly, and she set her clipboard on the bed, accidentally nudging his hand. The small, sudden movement was enough to rouse Sek from his coma. It took a moment for him to acclimate to his surroundings and realize what had happened, but then he became aware of the second person in the room. She was far too concerned with the machine and its off-the-chart readings. After a few minutes of Sek trying to calmly get her attention, he said, "Ya know, pushing the same button over and over again isn't gonna give you a different answer. Even lab rats can learn that and try something else."

The nurse practically jumped ten feet in the air and back to the door; her wide eyes fixed on the comatose man who just spoke. Sek could barely conceal his amusement and waited for the poor woman to swallow her heart. When the color finally returned to her face and she could form a coherent sentence, she checked his basic vitals before advising him on the situation. Though slightly surprised to hear he had been in a coma for six weeks, he was intrigued by the fact that as he was looking at the very machine she had been tinkering with, he could see a strange magnetic field around it. Considering his field of study, he wasn't surprised by the magnetic field itself. What surprised him was the fact that he could so vividly see something invisible to the human eye. He faintly heard her saying something about alerting the other doctors that he had regained consciousness, and then she scurried out the door and left Sek alone to his thoughts.

He knew that without the proper equipment, he shouldn't be able to see the magnetic fields as clearly as he was at that moment. He inspected them and could even see how the other machines were affected by the abnormal fields coming off it. Sek carefully looked it over and knew exactly how to get it working again. As soon as he worked it out in his head though, it seemed to fix itself. But before he could examine it any further, multiple doctors flooded the room. None of them could understand how he had recovered so quickly and went about running as many tests as they could. Sek was rather impatient about wanting to be released from the hospital, but when his sister arrived, he found that he couldn't argue with her demand to stay until he was given a clean bill of health.

When he was alone, he would look at the paperclips and other likewise metallic baubles left behind by the nurses and manipulate them. It took a few tries for him to figure out the mechanics of it at first, but soon he was having them bend and flex without physically touching them. He could even manipulate the readings on the machines in the room. He was interested in seeing just how far he could push these newfound talents. Unfortunately, he was limited in the things he could do in the hospital since he wasn't just yet ready to let others in on it.

The day finally came that there was no medical reason as to why he couldn't be released from the hospital. Sek was relieved that they could no longer keep him, and his sister had started to get anxious about his release. But due to some family matters, she was unable to be there. It was all the same to him. All he had to do was wait for the doctor to come in and bring the final papers to sign that he was clear to leave. Sek's sister had brought him clothes from his apartment, and he was dressed long before the doctor walked into the room. While he waited, he amused himself with a paperclip. He would bend and twist it in ways that would be difficult to do with just his hands when he heard the door clicked out of place. Sek hid the paperclip in his pocket and looked up to see a doctor stepping into the room that he hadn't seen before, which was a feat considering his medical miracle had made him quite popular with many of the staff.

This doctor was in his early sixties. His hair was greying along the sides though for the most part was still fairly dark. He looked in relatively good shape for someone his age, and Sek felt there was something slightly off about this man that he couldn't immediately place. As he approached, Sek looked into his face and quickly noticed two things. First, there was a bullet wound scar in the corner of his cheek on the left side. Second, when he looked into this man's grey-blue eyes, he couldn't easily read them and knew that this man was no mere doctor. He may have been dressed in the uniform and he was carrying a clipboard with all of Sek's medical charts, but he was sure there was something else this man was hiding. However, he kept quiet until the doctor spoke first.

"Hello there, Sek. I'm Mark Staskim. I was the surgeon that took care of your case following your unfortunate accident. I do apologize that I haven't been able to check in on you before now, but it would seem that you have recovered quite well. I just have to document the last readings before I can finish your discharge papers," he stated as he brought up the clipboard and started to scribble something down from the machine.

Sek didn't say anything and just looked over this man carefully while he was focused elsewhere. So much about his appearance seemed familiar to him even though he had never met the man before, and it was nagging at him. While Sek was trying to work through where he could have known the man, his powers began interfering with the machine. The harder he concentrated on what it could be that wasn't making sense, the more distortions in the data appeared on the screen.

The doctor glanced over the clipboard at him, "You know you're never going to get out of here if you don't let me get these readings."

Sek was taken aback. Almost immediately, his power subsided and Dr. Staskim quickly finished documenting everything he needed. He stepped back and finished filling out the last bit of it before signing his name across the last sheet. He handed the clipboard over to Sek, who quickly signed what was needed of him. When all of that was finished, Sek was on his feet and holding the paperwork out, saying, "Right, so that's it then. I can get outta here?"

"Legally, you have been released with a clean bill of health. There's no reason for you to be kept in this hospital. I do have something for you though, Sek," Dr. Staskim said as he reached into his pocket and produced a small, white business card. He held it out to Sek and continued, "This is my card. Before you leave, I have something I would like for you to think about."

Sek took the business card and looked over him warily before saying, "Ok…"

"You, my young friend, are about to find yourself thrust into a world you never knew existed. Things are fast changing from the routine you've acquainted yourself with, and I'm sorry to tell you this, but I doubt you'll be able to return to your research. There are many factions in this world that you'll be made aware of in time, but there are two coming to the forefront of this fast approaching conflict. You know as well as I do that you are no longer what you once were. You have kept your secret well, but I am no mere man. You are one of us. You are special.

"The normals will hunt you down and try to exterminate you out of fear of what you can do. There are many groups that will recruit you to use for their own purposes, and as I have already said, there are two that have found you. I represent one of them. Our main focus is to teach the younger generation of our kind and provide sanctuary. We have a stable base of operations to help not only our kind find safety, but also attempt to work with the normals in hopes that one day, we may live freely. The other will make itself known soon enough, and I warn you. They will use you until you have nothing more to offer, and when you have served your usefulness they will dispose of you. If you wish to join us, just call that number. Unlike many of the other groups, we do not force ourselves on those we extend our offer to," the doctor said, fixing Sek with a serious, intent stare.

The implications of everything he said were bouncing back and forth in Sek's mind and there were quite a few things that he could have said. Yet at that moment, all Sek cared about was getting the hell out of that hospital.

"That's great and all, and don't get me wrong I appreciate your warning…but I've got somewhere I'd rather be than here," Sek said as he took the business card and slipped it into his pocket. Before anything else could be said, he darted around the doctor and made his way out of the hospital. It wasn't soon enough for him when the doors opened and he was able to step out into the fresh air and feel the wind on his face. He glanced around and could already feel the tension that the strange doctor had caused him. Whatever he had been talking about, it wasn't his problem at that moment, and he would handle it if the issue ever presented itself. Until then, what was the point of stressing himself out over it? Not to mention he sounded like one of those crazy conspiracy theorists that weren't exactly all there in the head. Already feeling more at ease, he decided he would walk back to the college campus and look over the labs to see what had been done in the six weeks he was out of commission.

Sek made his way down the steps toward the parking lot and was lost in his own world when a body slammed into him out of nowhere. Sek was startled and stumbled back a few steps while a doctor in his late forties quickly scrambled to snatch the papers that flew out of the bag he had dropped. When Sek had recovered enough to help grab a few of the papers that had gotten away from the doctor, he looked to see that the man was shaking his head. He thanked Sek for his help and said, "Just coming back from vacation and my head is just not in it. I'm sorry to have bumped into you like that. Thank you again."

Just as Sek was going to respond to the man, his eyes caught sight of the name on his badge that was hanging from his coat pocket. Normally, he would've had something clever to reply with, but seeing the doctor's name as Mark Staskim threw him off his game. The doctor quickly excused himself, explaining that he was late and needed to get himself caught up on his cases. After a few minutes of just standing there, Sek shook his head and looked around, wondering just how much stranger his day could get.

That was when he spotted a man about ten yards away walking a dog, staring at him intently. Even when Sek looked back at him, he didn't break eye contact. Even the dog seemed to be staring at him and didn't move an inch. Deciding that everything had just exceeded creepy limit for the day, Sek made his way down the rest of the stairs and set off walking back to campus. It was a nice day, and he was grateful for the walk after so much time inside. But after turning several corners and walking on all different streets, he continued to see the same man walking a dog every few minutes. He was almost positive it was the same man because he never once changed clothing, but every few turns Sek was certain that he was walking a different dog.

It was an hour before he arrived on campus, and the constant visual encounters with the dog walker had him slightly on edge. It was strangely quiet, and he wondered where the students and faculty were. Though he instinctively wanted to head back to his apartment, he couldn't help but be curious as to what the lab looked like after the explosion. Glancing around to see if anyone would acknowledge that he was there, Sek was almost relieved to find it deserted. Perhaps there was a break or something that he had not known about, and that was why there was no one on the campus. So, he made his way to the lab he had been working in. It was still roped off and thoroughly decimated after the explosion. There were notices that it was declared unsafe and under construction, but it seemed to him as though they hadn't even managed to start picking it up. He slid through the barriers with relative ease and walked over to where he had been when the whole thing went down. The memories of the incident were coming back to him. Was there something that could've hinted at what was going to happen? What caused the explosion in the first place? How many others were injured? Was there anything he could have done differently to stop the experiment from detonating as it had? As these questions were coming to his mind, he noticed something glinting on the ground nearby.

He carefully moved through the debris to where the items were. They were buried beneath some charred remains of chairs and a desk. He glanced around, hoping to find something he could use move the remains without getting his hands covered in the dirt and grime. Finally, he decided to shift it with the toe of his shoes and was pleasantly surprised to see two piezoelectric ceramic cubes that he had been working with laying there. A small grin crept across his face, and he glanced around to make sure he was still alone. It was eerily quiet, and once he was thoroughly satisfied there wasn't anyone nearby, he raised his hands over the ceramic cubes. After focusing on his new abilities, the cubes shot into the air and smacked into the palms of his hands. When he turned them over, applying the theories he had been testing before the accident, he started to cause them to shift and change into various shapes. Sek smirked, content with his findings, and returned the ceramics back to cube form. Hiding them away in his pocket, he took a glance around to see if there was anything else that he could scavenge before returning to his apartment. When he found nothing, he swiftly maneuvered his way out of the destroyed lab.

Things were still relatively quiet, and after the bizarre events he had been a part of, the main thought in Sek's mind was to get to his apartment and sleep some of this off after he had relaxed with a good smoke or two. Sek had a good stash of pot waiting for him, and it had been a while since he had a relaxing joint to take the edge off. The walk to his on-campus apartment was quiet and calming. As he neared it, he even began to forget about the strange things that had happened that day until he saw that same old man with yet another dog standing in front of his building. He stopped in his tracks and stared at him. What interest did he have in him? Sek was positive this was far more than coincidence, and he was going to confront him.

Sek approached him. This time he seemed far too interested in his dog, and when he was close, Sek had to speak in order to get his attention, "Hey, you! You with the dog. What are you playing at? Why have you been following me around?"

The man looked up at Sek slowly, like he was surprised at being addressed, and motioned for the dog to sit at his feet. He looked over Sek with a strange smirk curling at his lips and waited a few moments before replying, "I have no idea what you're talking about, but it sounds like you have people watching you doesn't it? Maybe you should be careful." He motioned for his dog to follow him and went on his way like nothing happened.

Sek watched him until he was out of sight and shook his head. No matter what the guy said, Sek was not impressed with the display. He felt assured that he would be seeing the creepy dog walker again. Putting it to the back of his mind, he went into the building and searched around in his pockets for the key to his apartment. As he did, his hand brushed the card that the British impostor had handed him. He paused for a moment, thinking over the warning he had been given. He found his key and opened his apartment door.

Chapter 11: Sek's Misadventure, 2016

For the most part, Sek was relatively relaxed, but there was a certain quirk to his personality most didn't know about. Sek had a mild case of OCD and a worse aversion to germs. In fact, he carried so much hand sanitizer with him that it had inspired quite a few jokes from his sister. So, the state in which he found his apartment after the door swung open was highly distressing for him. After freezing for a few moments in shock, he slowly stepped into the apartment and closed the door behind him, scanning everything carefully.

It looked as though a hurricane had passed through his home. His furniture was scattered around the room. Things that had been neatly put away in drawers and cabinets were strewn about on the floor, and there was broken glass glistening in the carpet. Not a single possession was remotely where it had been before he was taken to the hospital, and the fact he didn't know what grubby hands had defiled his pristine living quarters fueled his steadily boiling temper. Just as he was coming to grips with the scene before him, Sek heard something strange coming from his bedroom. As he listened further, he was able to determine that someone was still in the apartment.

Acting on instinct, he turned the two ceramic cubes he had plucked from the ruins of his lab into knives and quietly crept toward the bedroom. Sek moved soundlessly in a way that no one could have gone past him without his knowing. He swung around to stand in the doorway with his knives at the ready. Yet when Sek stared into the room, there was no one there. He blinked in surprise and stepped inside, trying to find whatever clues he could. It was at that moment that he heard someone ransacking the living room as if it wasn't destroyed enough as it was.

    He was out of the room and down the hall like a shot, but once again when he made it into the room, there was no one there. Irritation began to swell in his chest, and Sek's mind went to the card in his pocket. If anyone were going to have answers about what was going on, it would be him. Scanning the room carefully, he walked over to the phone and took out the card to look over the number. After a few rings, it was the impostor doctor who answered, "So, I assume you have made your decision then, my friend?"

    "Well, it seems like I don't have much of a choice. There's enough freaky shit going on, and as it is, I can't stay here anymore," Sek answered in annoyance as he looked over his destroyed apartment. There was a small voice in the back of his head trying to remember exactly where he had put his stash and wondered if it would still be there.

    "Unfortunately, that is the way the world works. I will have a plane waiting for you in the morning. Ten o'clock sharp. It will be completely taken care of and paid for under your name. All you will need is identification to prove it's you at the airport and you will be safely on your way." Sek could hear a hint of relief in his voice on the other line.

    "How do I know I can trust you? I don't even know your real name, mate. I saw the doctor you were masquerading as walking in when I was leaving the hospital."

    "You can't afford not to trust me. After all, I got you out of the hospital in once piece, didn't I? It doesn't matter that I had to use someone else's name tag to do it. Now, just wait until tomorrow for your plane and do your best not to draw attention to yourself alright?"

"Yeah. Yeah. I'll see what I can do." He hung up the phone and glanced around, wondering where in the hell his stash was. After everything that happened and his entire apartment being a total mess, he seriously needed a good hit to calm the hell down. It was then that he noticed a human form had appeared under the curtain that hung across the sliding glass patio door.

"I would not leave town if I were you." The voice sounded as though it was being heavily processed through some type of voice modulator. "You belong to us. You'll be contacted with your instructions tomorrow. Until then, don't do anything stupid... and stay fucking put."

Something in the voice rubbed Sek the wrong way, and considering he wasn't one for taking orders in the first place, he promptly launched one of the knives he had made from the ceramic cubes at what he imagined would've been the form's chest. But before making contact, the shape in the curtain went flat, and the knife impaled the wall just beside the glass.

"I'm a fucking shadow. You can't hurt me, track me, or catch me, but I can do all that and more to you. Believe me, if the boss tells me to, I will ice you in a heartbeat."

Sek warily approached the curtain as the voice faded away, expecting something to jump out at him, but nothing happened. Nothing was there. Just his knife stuck in the wall. After looking around, satisfied that he was the only one left in the apartment, he ripped the knife out and reshaped it into a cube before stuffing it in his pocket, faintly awed by what he could do with his new powers. Still through all of this, his first concern was finding just where in the hell his pot was. Eventually he found it under some various items that had been ripped out of his desk and strewn about the hallway. His own irritation was beginning to boil over, and to distract himself he flexed his powers, causing various metallic things in his apartment to bend and move at his will, officially making it so no one would be able to use them again unless they carefully bent them all back into place. All he could do was bide time until tomorrow. That was when everything would go down and he would have to make a choice. A choice he somehow knew would decide the path for the rest of his life. Eventually, he slipped into a relatively calm sleep relaxing after he made good use of his stash.

    The next morning came with no event. Sek awoke with no one waiting for him. No ringing from the phone. Absolutely nothing was out of the ordinary, aside from the destruction of his apartment that he didn't bother to clean up. It was as if he had been completely forgotten, but Sek knew better than that. He looked over at the clock and saw that there was just enough time for him to pack the essentials and get to the airport to make the flight. Sek wasn't sure exactly what would be waiting for him, but as he rode in the taxi to the airport, he continued to see the same man he had the day before. He was still wearing the same shirt and appearing on occasional street corners with different dogs in tow. At each meeting, he was sure to make eye contact with Sek and stare him down with a fierce gaze. There was no doubt in his mind that this was a display that was meant to be intimidating, but Sek was unimpressed. In fact, he went so far as to keep count and by the time he reached the airport, he had seen him on ten different streets with ten different dogs. Thoroughly aggravated and tired of feeling like he was being followed, Sek took a quick walk around to see if he could find the man instead of immediately going to the main terminal of the airport. He had time to kill without missing his flight. Just as he was walking back from his search, beginning to think that he in fact hadn't been followed there, Sek finally spotted him. He was standing at the entrance of the parking garage with his damn dog, talking to one of the many security guards that did rounds to help people who were lost.

    Sek stopped a few yards away from him and for the first time took a moment to look over the man and his appearance. The man was tall and thin, somewhere in his mid-sixties and dressed like he came out of a children's television show. Dressed in a striped sweater that looked like it came out in a decade long since passed, worn khaki pants with brown sandals and black socks, he looked a little out of touch with the world around him. What made it worse, in Sek's opinion, was that the damn poodle he was walking was wearing a matching sweater! Sek couldn't explain it, but as he looked over the dog walker he could feel something sinister lying underneath the facade of an old man so far out of date. It was highly disturbing. He finished the conversation he was having with the security guard and turned around to look at Sek as if he knew he was waiting for him to turn around. Sek waved him over and waited for him to approach. When he was within speaking range, he looked at Sek and said, "Well, well, well. I was wondering if you would come or not. Cutting it rather close, aren't you?"

"I do that. Anyway, mind telling me exactly what the hell is going on here, mate? I get the need for theatrics and all that, but I'm not particularly impressed," Sek asked, looking over him carefully. The feeling that something was horribly wrong with the man standing before him made Sek feel on edge. It didn't make sense, but his own instincts were telling him that this feeble figure before him was a force to be reckoned with. So Sek waited to see if he made an aggressive move, but oddly enough, the unknown man remained quite calm.

"Well, I came here to make sure you don't do anything stupid. Like getting on that plane for instance," was all he said with a knowing smile crossing his face.

"And why shouldn't I get on the plane?" Sek asked with an arched brow.

"As much as I know it's in your nature to be a contrarian, it would be in your best interest to do as my man in your apartment said and stay put. As much as you may believe otherwise, you are our property. Your life belongs to us. Why do you think we went through such great pains to make sure you were in the vicinity of that detonation? You don't honestly think your current situation was a mere accident, do you? We have spent way too many resources pulling your medical records, checking your DNA, and making sure everything would go exactly as planned to just let you fly away. And you should know, I am always watching you. I'm always testing your loyalty, just like now, to see if you would really betray me and get on that plane just because some fool told you to. So, here's what you're going to do. You're going to go back to your apartment and wait for further instructions. There is a shipment of gold heading to your school's research lab tomorrow. I want it, and a man of your intelligence could make good use of your special talents and make it mine, and secure a sizeable bonus for himself in the process," he said with his smile still in place. His words didn't set well with Sek, who was not one for being told what he would and would not do. It was not in his nature to be controlled, and as if sensing the discontent in him, the man went on to say, "Besides, we have put quite a bit of time and effort into protecting you and keeping you well. It would be a shame for you to leave our care and go to someone who would just as quickly kill you as soon as you acted like you would not listen to him. That Brit is a tricky one. He likes to play the game and make you think he has nothing but good intentions, but he's not all that he makes himself out to be. He'd just as quickly take you down as soon as you proved to be a danger to him."

"I don't need your money. And you have a funny way of protecting, mate. I mean, putting me in the way of a large-scale explosion like that isn't exactly the best way of keeping someone safe," Sek responded.

"When you think of it with a closed mind, perhaps. Apparently you weren't listening close enough the first time. We didn't just throw you in the way of an explosion. We did proper research first. Checked all the variables and made sure that not only would you make it through, but you would be stronger than you were before. You can't say that the qualities you gained from the accident weren't beneficial to you, now can you?" He paused briefly. "Didn't think so. Besides, the Brit won't care for your wellbeing outside of your necessary usefulness. Trust me, and go back to your apartment. It's safer for you there."

Sek looked him over for a minute, processing everything that had been said. He wasn't particularly thrilled with the way he continued to talk about him like he was property, but the idea of getting on a plane that could blow up in the air wasn't his idea of a picnic either. As it was, the safest option seemed to be returning to his apartment. Sek was good at playing people, and if need be he could make this guy feel like he had won long enough for him to come up with a better plan. He glanced around the airport thinking it over for a few moments more before looking back at him saying, "I'll keep that in mind."

With that, Sek turned his back on the dog walker and walked away. He didn't stop until he was well out of sight and had finally found a clock just outside the main building. If he really tried, he would still be able to make the plane, but the words of the unknown man bounced around in his head. While he didn't trust either of them, he wasn't sure getting into a flying metal deathtrap would be a good idea, particularly considering his newfound powers he was still mastering. Finally, Sek flagged down a cab and told the driver to take him back to his apartment.

Sek was thoughtful as the vehicle took off and began weaving its way through the traffic. At first, he almost didn't notice it, but just as the car was making a turn, he managed to catch sight of the man again. Sek leaned closer to the window and confirmed his suspicions. It was indeed the same old man walking the dog and there was no mistaking the triumphant smile on his face. Sek was sure that he was pleased his words had been heeded. Leaning back in the seat, Sek contemplated just what was going to be in store for him when he returned to his research. It wasn't long before he was standing outside of his apartment door, turning the key over and over in his hands. Just what the hell was going on?

He shoved the key in the lock and pushed open the door to once again stare at the destruction that was left of the apartment. It irritated him that his own home had been so thoroughly ransacked and he kicked the door closed as he walked over to the kitchen. Even his cabinets had been opened, and various foodstuffs splay across the floor. Yet, there was something off. He scanned the apartment once more and used his newfound powers to have the various metals items around him at the ready in case they would be needed. It was then that the same laughter that came from the shadow man echoed through the apartment once again.

"It was wise of you to come back. Make sure you stay put this time, boy. You guys never get it. You belong to us and we own everything that you are. You're going to do exactly as you're told and not leave our sight. Remember, we will always be watching you. I will always be watching you."

The laughter died away, and the feeling of someone else inside of the apartment disappeared. No matter where he looked or what he did, the invisible bastard was gone and Sek was left standing alone. The only trace he could find that someone other than him had been in his apartment was a shoe print in dirt from a spilled planter near where the voice had come from. In that moment, he wasn't sure where he would be safe, but he knew beyond a shadow of a doubt his apartment was no longer it. He paced back and forth across the carpet for a minute before walking over to the phone and taking the card out of his pocket for the second time. Quickly confirming the number, he punched it into the phone and waited for the Brit to answer.

"Well, I must admit I'm slightly surprised. I thought that you would've been on the plane instead of calling me from your apartment."

"Well, a lot of weird things have been going on and I would like some answers instead of this cryptic crap you're giving me. Just what was your man playing at in my apartment? What the hell is with that out of date old man who's walking all those different dogs? I mean, seriously, putting your dogs in the same old sweater you're wearing is really strange," Sek replied as he looked over the destroyed apartment warily. A small part of him was just itching to put everything back in its proper place, but he was eased that his pot didn't go missing.

There other end of the phone was silent for so long that Sek checked the line to make sure it hadn't been disconnected. Finally, he cleared his throat and that seemed to draw the Brit from his thoughts, "That's not my man and just let me tell you, no matter how unassuming that old man looked, he's not one to be taken lightly. I told you already that there are many different groups that would want to see you as one of theirs. I can't make you choose us over them, but since you're calling me now, I'm going to assume that you realized for yourself that he's not what he appears. He's skilled at spinning a believable web of lies. I can reschedule your plane ticket for a few hours from now, but for the love of god get back to the airport and avoid further contact with him. Do you think you'd be able to do that?"

"Shouldn't be too hard. I'll head back there now."

"Good. Everything will be taken care of. Just go to the front and show them your ID. There will be a package waiting for you at the airport in Indianapolis. I will see you there soon."

Sek didn't even bother making sure the receiver landed back on the base of the phone. Instead, he pulled together the necessary effects that he wanted to take with him, and left the apartment determined this time that he would not be convinced to return to it. He jumped into another taxi and the whole way there, he was looking to see if he would be followed like he was the first time. Surprisingly enough, the ride was uneventful, and not once did he see the dog-walker waiting for him around any turn or standing on any corner. Sek paid the taxi and went into the main terminal, where after giving his ID to the woman behind the initial check-in desk, he was quickly on his way to the gate to wait for his flight. He was on edge, just waiting for someone to approach him and tell him that he was making some grave mistake. As the time for the flight drew closer, the feeling only grew, but no one even looked at him. He shook his head and put his hands in his pockets. It wasn't like him to be so jumpy. Then again, it wasn't exactly normal to wake up from a coma, have an unexplained new power, and have at least two different groups cryptically critiquing his every move either. It was then that the announcement broke over the terminal stating that his flight was now boarding, and he cast one final glance out to look over the planes.

There, standing just out of view of the employees, running back and forth between the planes, was the dog walker. At his side was a rather large dog that came up to Sek's waist.

Sek quickly boarded the flight and in a short span of time, it was off the ground, heading toward its intended destination. For the first hour of the flight, he halfway expected something to go wrong, but the flight was smooth, and he finally relaxed and allowed time to slip by while he carefully went over his situation. He thought over every little thing–from the moment he woke up in the hospital until he sat in his seat on the plane. There was little doubt in his mind that the Brit wasn't going to be the only one waiting for him in Indianapolis. This insane circus he happened to fall into was just getting started, and Sek wasn't sure what exactly would become of it. From what it sounded like, his powers weren't anything surprising for either the Brit or the dog walker, which made him hazard to guess that there were plenty of others with special abilities like him and there were quite a few things going on in the world that, until this moment, he had not been privy to, which begged the question, what else would be waiting for him when the plane landed? Exactly how much danger were these unknown figures expecting him to face without any decent rhyme or reason? Sek wasn't interested in being a hero, and going out of his way to help anyone wasn't exactly his idea of a good time. Whatever these men had planned, Sek was going to make sure they understood just how much of a wild card he really was. He was not a puppet to be pulled by a string, and if need be, he would shock them to their very cores.

The flight was of little consequence. Sek rested and relaxed for the first time since he had woken from his coma. In fact, nothing out of the ordinary occurred until he had disembarked from the plane and was stepping up to baggage claim. He spotted his bag with relative ease, but attached to it was a strange, brown package he hadn't seen before. After glancing around to see if anyone was watching him, he snatched his bag from the rotating luggage claim before walking to sit in a chair far away from everyone else. He looked through the package to find the name of a hotel, a room card, and money enough to pay for a cab to get there. He soon got to his feet and left the main building to where he could get a cab downtown.

    The ride was quiet and Sek didn't see anything out of the ordinary. Instead, he merely looked over the new city he found himself in. It didn't take long for him to get downtown, but he was shocked to find just how congested the streets were and how difficult it was for the taxi to get where he wanted. After sitting through five lights without moving, Sek paid his fare and decided that he would just walk the rest of the way. Apparently, from what his driver had said before he left, there was some big event happening at the convention center tomorrow and there were tons of people not only from out of state, but from out of the country, there for it.

    Walking down the street, Sek allowed his mind to drift, and it wasn't until he was standing near a large building that he remembered he was supposed to be looking for a hotel, but as he glanced around he didn't see any building that resembled a hotel. Although if he had been hungry, he would've found himself in heaven as every corner was a different restaurant and the smells that wafted around him made him almost want to get something to eat. He looked down at the address one more time and then looked around the streets. However, there wasn't anything that even hinted at where he should start his search. He ran his hand through his short hair thoughtfully. It was then that he looked down the street and choked upon spotting a familiar figure that he wasn't expecting to see.

    There was that same godforsaken old man walking that damned poodle and he was heading straight for Sek. This time however, there was something menacing in the air around him. He spun on the balls of his feet and started walking down the street looking for his next way out. Just as he came to the end of the parking on the side of the street his attention was caught by the sight of a relatively nice looking black car parked in the last spot. It wasn't anything special that would cause someone to give it a second look, but Sek was intrigued by the fact that as he approached it, he couldn't sense even an ounce of metal in its makeup. Considering his newfound powers allowed him to turn any vehicle into a deadly weapon, he found it rather strange that while the car looked absolutely normal, it was unlike an vehicle he had ever seen before. He looked back to see that the old man was still walking toward him, and the closer he got the more intense the menacing feeling became. Deciding that the car that wasn't a normal car was a far better bet than sticking around to see what the dog walker had to say, Sek quickly stepped off the sidewalk and stopped beside the car to knock on the window.

The young man inside the vehicle, who at that point had been carefully inspecting a map, gave a slight jump and turned his green eyes to look at Sek warily. Sek gestured for him to open the door and in response, he rolled the window down a little bit to ask, "Can I help you?"

"Yeah. Nice car you've got here. Funny enough it looks pretty normal, but I can tell that it's special considering there isn't any metal in it. How about you let me in and we can talk about it while you drive us somewhere away from this place," Sek quickly said as he turned to look over his shoulder back at the dog walker. He was closer now and the poodle he had been walking before was gone. It had been replaced with a rather vicious looking pit bull that almost seemed like it was just itching to sink its teeth into the meat of Sek's leg. This only made Sek more eager to get into the strange car and get the hell out of dodge as quickly as possible. He tried to the door only to find that it had in fact been locked. All he could think of how was unnecessarily tedious this was.

"Who the hell are you?" the young man asked him incredulously. The mention of the more unique aspects of the car seemed to pique his interest, but Sek could tell that he was in no hurry to open the door for him.

"That doesn't really matter now. What's more important is that I have someone who isn't exactly friendly coming this way and it would be best if we both got out of dodge before shit goes downhill," Sek explained as he gestured over his shoulder to the man walking up on them.

The youth in the car arched his brow and looked around him to see just what he was pointing at. "Right. The old man with the dog is going to attack us I'm sure." At that moment, he turned his attention to the old man to see not only had he had closed quite a bit of distance between them in such a short amount of time, but that the dog had turned from a pit-bull into a much larger mastiff. To make it worse, not only was the dog far more aggressive, but there was a dark gloom radiating from the old man as well as if his dark intent pulsed through the air and knocked the wind out of both their lungs. In seconds, the door was unlocked and he went on to say, "Hurry up and get into the car. My name's James."

"About time. The name's Sek. Now before we talk anymore, let's get the hell out of here," Sek said as he yanked open the door and practically threw himself into the car. He shut the door behind him with a little more force than was needed and turned back just as James was throwing a map into his lap as well as a piece of paper with an address on it.

"I'll drive. You navigate. Get us to that address there for me. We'll figure this all out after that." James threw the car into reverse, and with a quick glance to make sure that he wouldn't hit anyone, practically flew out of the parking spot. They were met with two cars blaring their horns at them and Sek noticed one of the drivers flip them the bird. Being true to his nature, Sek grinned widely and saluted the man back while James focused on getting them out of dodge. In a quick jerk, he shifted it into drive and hauled off as quickly as he could without drawing any unwanted attention from any police officers that may have been in the area. While James was focused on maneuvering through the various lanes to get himself turned around, Sek offered one final glance back to see the dog walker standing there, just watching them go. They sped off, leaving him standing where their car had been.

While a small sense of relief washed over Sek, he knew it would only be a matter of time before he caught back up to them.

Chapter 12: Sek and James, 2016

Sek figured out the streets with relative ease, and after only a few wrong turns, he had James on track to the address on the slip of paper. It was the one-way streets that had given him trouble initially, but he managed to figure out their pattern, and the rest of the drive was quiet. Sek was too concerned about the old man to socialize with James, and James was far more focused on keeping calm as they came closer to the address where he was sure his parents were being held. It wasn't long before they were pulling up to the drive, James's grip on the steering wheel was so tight that his knuckles had turned white. The closer he got to the house, the more he could hear his blood ringing in his ears. Sek looked over the house warily and figured it only seemed fitting that they got away from the dog walker just to drive up to some ominous two-story house that looked entirely too pristine to be true even for him. It was just another occurrence in the sequence of strange and unnatural things that had happened to him in the past two days, and he quietly wondered if this would come to be a new normal. Although, if he was being entirely truthful, he couldn't have cared less – so long as he always had his stash of pot to take the edge off when he needed to.

Finally, James brought the car to a stop and took a moment to collect his thoughts before stepping out the driver's door. Taking the hint that this was their destination, Sek stepped out as well and looked over the house, expecting something to come running out of the front door to attack them. But nothing happened, and when he glanced over at James, he watched him pull out a rather thick looking binder from his bag. Confused as to what he was doing, Sek leaned over the front of the car to see him flipping through various images of armors from games, movies, and other such things. Sek arched his brow and wondered if James was just going to look at all the things he wished he could have before they went barging into God knows whose home. Just as he was about to say something smart, James finally settled on an image and placed his hand on top of it while taking in a deep breath. Sek watched in surprise as James exhaled and the armor started to materialize around his hands and move up his arms as the car they drove in began to disappear. The process was quick, taking only seconds, and James soon stood there in an armored suit plucked straight from one of the most popular post-apocalyptic survival games. It was slick, and there was not a doubt in his mind that it would pack one hell of a punch. Sek couldn't help but think that his new-found friend would be more useful than he originally thought. Seeing his unique abilities in action explained why Sek couldn't sense an ounce of metal in the car that they arrived in. Yet, if things went downhill and he wanted to make his getaway, Sek would now need to find the means to do so seeing as the car was no longer a viable option if he would be leaving by himself.

James hid the binder of pictures away in his bag and turned his attention back to the house. Even with his face hidden behind the visor, it wasn't hard to guess what he was thinking, and the tension in his body indicated he was ready to get what he wanted by force.

"So...why are we here exactly?" Sek asked, looking from window to window to discern if anyone inside was expecting them. From what he could tell, they were uninvited, and as of that moment still unnoticed.

"My parents are in there, and I'm going to get them back," was James's simple answer. He didn't care to elaborate further, but from the way he said it, Sek was under the distinct impression that they weren't there of their own free will.

Having an idea of what he had in mind if no one answered the door, Sek moved in front of James. While it was true that the house was rather secluded with no immediate neighbors, Sek still preferred not to draw any unnecessary attention just yet simply because he was still concerned about the dog walker being close at hand and looking for an indication of where he went. Sek motioned for James to let him try the door first. James shrugged and allowed Sek his shot before he would use force, and instead he looked around the area. Sek walked up to the door and knocked twice, waiting for a moment before stepping back and cracking his knuckles.

"Time for me to make my move, mate," Sek muttered, somewhat pleased with himself, and raised his hand level with the door handle. With a little focus, he ripped all the metal from the door and formed it into a knife laying in the middle of his palm. The door fell open slightly as he stepped back, readying the knife just in case. He then glanced at James, who stepped onto the porch and without hesitation and threw open the door, tossing it into the front yard. They had readied for a rush, but to both of their surprise there was no one there. In fact, the house was eerily quiet as they stepped into the entryway and began to inspect the interior. After walking through a few rooms, it became apparent that, just as Sek had thought, the house was far too perfect for someone to have been living in it. From what Sek could see, it appeared as though the home had been staged, much like they do when they're trying to sell a place. James noticed this as well, and they carefully looked up the staircase near the entry, halfway expecting some unknown figure to be making their way down to them. No matter how hard they listened, they couldn't hear anything coming from upstairs. Instead, the only sound they could hear seemed to be the metallic clanking of pots and pans coming from the kitchen, which was straight down the hall in front of them. The two looked at each other and silently agreed to approach cautiously, quietly slinking down the hall. Sek kept his eyes focused on the doorway that led into the kitchen at the end of the hall and James looked over the walls trying to find anything that seemed out of place.

In the middle of the hall, there was a particular spot on the wall where the wallpaper didn't match up with the rest of the hallway. In fact, it was a perfect rectangle from the ground all the way up to the ceiling where the pattern was off by a mere centimeter. Anyone not paying close enough attention would've easily dismissed it. However, James was so intent on finding something out of place that it was easy for him to spot. He paused at the wall and placed his hands against it in an attempt to find out if there was a reason behind it, and it was at that moment they both caught sight of a rather large iron skillet being hurled from the entrance of the kitchen.
Sek crouched to the ground while James pressed himself close against the wall. The skillet shot past them and buried itself deep into the wall by the entryway. If either had been in the way, it would've taken their heads clean off their shoulders. Sek slowly straightened, his focus on where the pan had been thrown from, and James moved away from the wall, only to feel it shift slightly beneath him. He turned back in surprise and saw that the off-centered piece of wall had sunken in a full inch. A small smirk crossed his face, and he pushed against the wall, willing it to yield beneath him.

Meanwhile, Sek slowly approached kitchen where he could still hear clanking pots and pans, his knife at the ready to defend himself if someone came around the corner unexpectedly. He was pressed close to the wall and glanced back to see James pushing against the wall. Sek turned his attention back to the kitchen. It would be better if at least one of them was interested in whoever launched a skillet straight at their heads before returning to whatever the hell they were doing to make so much noise.

Sek came to the entrance and glanced in. Floating in the middle of the room was what Sek could only describe was a cloud of pots, pans, and other metal utensils that were common in a household kitchen. The floating cooking instruments were jostling around back and forth seemingly without reason. Turning back to James to share his astonishment, Sek found an alcove that had not been there before. Before he could say anything, the clangor of pots grew louder, and when he turned to look, a rather large soup pot, like the ones used to serve over fifty people in one sitting, pushed to the front. Doubling back to the alcove, Sek just managed to make it as the pot soared straight toward them at chest level. Sek pushed James further into the alcove, and they managed to avoid the second pot, which followed the first in burying itself in the wall with a loud crunching sound as the wood gave way. The two could hear the rattling pots getting louder from the kitchen as they crammed themselves into the small opening and into a hidden stairwell. It was a tight fit, and both were in a hurry to find a way out. James noticed a switch near the door and flipped it as he stared down the dark staircase that led into a musty smelling basement. Much to his relief, a strip of lighting that wound its way down the staircase began to glow well enough that the stairs could be seen. Once their way was lit, James started down with Sek following close behind.

    It was quiet. The light from the stair strips wasn't much and as they went further into the basement a very distinct stench wafted through the air. At first, neither of them could place what it was. But as they moved further down the stairs, it they grew wary. Blood, and from what they could tell, there had be a lot of it. It was enough to make them sick, leaving an iron taste in their mouths as they breathed. Soon, the two stood at the bottom of the staircase and noticed a drain that went around the bottom of it. James remembered what he saw in the picture and his mind quickly realized that if someone had to clean the basement after they finished torturing their victims, that drain would make it a lot easier. James's stomach was already starting to turn in knots as he looked around the dark basement, but the lights stopped at the bottom of the stairs wasn't enough to pierce the rest of the room. Though he couldn't see the details of the room around them, their imaginations worked well enough that they could almost see the stains of blood and various other things dripping down the walls and pooling on the floor. Sek and James reached around the walls fumbling for a possible light switch. Finally, Sek's hand brushed the switch on and a few lights along the sides of the basement came to life.

Their imaginations hadn't been exactly accurate, but what they were met with was just as chilling. The floor was streaked with harsh chemical stains from repeated over cleaning. The walls looked similar except seemed not to fair as well as the floors did. As they looked around, they could see various tools along the walls as well as a separating wall that sectioned off a part of the basement further back than they could see. There was no one else in the basement to their knowledge, but the longer James looked, the more he was sure he could hear the clinking sound of a chain link fence moving slightly. The picture of his beaten parents haunted his thoughts, and with his mind set on the task at hand, he walked on through the basement. Sek arched his brow at his comrade and followed behind with his knife raised. They had no idea what would be waiting behind the wall, but they had a feeling it wouldn't be anything they would want to see. Leading the way, James tensed as he approached the doorway, and when he stepped through, his eyes immediately went to the back wall. In the picture his fathers were beaten, bloody, and zip-tied to the chain link fence like they were animals, but the reality was far worse. The sight before him was nothing compared to even his darkest nightmares.

His fathers weren't just beaten. They had been brutalized. They were covered in their own blood, some crusted over and some still oozing from various slashes across their skin, each of them standing a small, drying red puddle. Dark green and blue bruises rose across their pale flesh and broken bones pushed against their skin, but this was not the worst of their injuries. Those things could be expected with the torturous instruments that hung about. James would not willingly admit it, but he had been expecting them to be horrifically mangled and disfigured. What James had not expected though, was the strange deformities that he was faced with. His father, Martin, was moving only enough to show that he was breathing, and the skin around his eyes seemed to have grown so that there was just a layer of flesh where his eyes were supposed to be. It was like they hadn't been there in the first place. His nose was in the same condition, covered with overgrown skin and the corner of his mouth was beginning of the same process. As James looked to his other father, Arnold, he found him quietly moaning in pain and unconscious, the sound muffled by skin that had grown over his mouth, seamlessly sewing his lips together. It was unnatural, and by the stretched look of the skin, probably agonizing.

"What...the hell?" James croaked, unable to comprehend what he was seeing as Sek was at a loss for words. The two were trying to mentally process what they were seeing when they heard a chuckle coming from the doorway behind them. Both spun around, and standing in the doorway was the dog walker. Standing next to him was the Bullmastiff still dressed in that hideous sweater that matched his owner. The dog snarled, its lips peeled back over its teeth, and tensed its muscles, waiting for the order to attack. Meanwhile, the man stood there calmly with a strange smile on his face. It was almost like he was proud of what they had seen.

"What do you think? They're still a work in progress – to be sure, but I am quite satisfied with how they've come along so far," he said as the dog snarled, this time much louder than the first. He looked over the two before him and something flickered behind his eyes.

"You're the one who did this to them?!" James growled as he felt his temper rising. Sek glanced at him and then back at the dog.

"Well of course. Who else could manage such a magnificent feat of sculpting? Mind you it takes time and patience, but I have time enough for it. The conversion is not something that can be rushed," he replied akin to an artist talking about a painting he had been working on. Upon seeing their disgust, the man continued, "Oh don't look so put off. After all, you two will be experiencing this honor yourselves all too soon. Get them!"

The dog lunged forward. James managed to bring his arm up in defense, and the armor he had adorned himself with served its purpose well as the massive dog's teeth clamped down on his arm, and its body slammed him into the table nearby, knocking various torture instruments to the floor with a loud clang. Sek turned his attention to the man and threw his doorknob knife, aiming for his face. Sek was sure he had made a direct hit, but with unnatural speed, the dog walker knocked the blade harmlessly to the side. At that moment, James, who had been struggling to gain leverage against the canine bearing down on him, managed to shove the beast back far enough to deliver a fearsome kick that sent it sprawling away. James stumbled away from the table, kicking a few of the instruments as he did, and heard Martin groaning behind him. He glanced back and saw him moving against the fence.

The dog let out a loud snarl, causing Sek to turn his attention back to it just in time to see the dog plant its feet and charge directly toward him. Where James had his armor to buffer him when he was bit, Sek did not have such a luxury. The back of his heel brushed one of the tools that had been knocked to the floor and he realized that they were all comprised of metal. With a flex of his power, he brought a rather sharp looking implement into the air next to him and sent it soaring into the side of the massive canine. The dog howled and reeled from the blow, blood splattering the ground as it limped back in retreat. Sek turned his attention back to the dog's owner to see the man bearing down on him in an attempt to get a blow of his own. Sek barely managed to jump back in time to dodge the man swinging one of the torture instruments that had been hanging on the wall. The point of a very sharp serrated blade barely missed the tip of his nose, and Sek found his back against the wall close to the fence where the two men were still hanging. James took this chance to draw the dog walker's attention to himself and snatched a wrench from the ground to launch it at dog walker's head. The man seemed to be waiting for this and dodged as if everything was moving in slow motion. He charged straight toward James.

"Shit," James groaned as he quickly pushed the table that was still blocking him out of the way, throwing himself to the side. The dog walker's hand seemed to change as it was swinging through the air where James's head had been. The fingers elongated and the nails were as sharp as any weapon he had seen in the hellish torture chamber. James managed to completely avoid the enemy bearing down on him, sending the enemy's hand into Arnold. The dog walker's weaponized fingers dug deep into the man's face and James was sure he heard them penetrating the bone of his father's skull. This roused his father, and James shuddered as he heard him attempting to scream, but all that could be heard through his grown over mouth was the agony locked in the back of his throat. James stepped back in horror as the dog walker seemed to struggle for a moment as he dislodged his hand, bracing himself against the man's chest before finally ripping his hand free. Blood spurted from his face, and after a final muffled howl of agony, he fell against the fence completely lifeless.

Snapping his attention to the dog, Sek saw that the beast had pulled the weapon from its side with its teeth and had trained its eyes on him. Reflexively, Sek used his powers to float two blades at his side, and as the dog lunged, he sent them flying in response. The dog was in mid leap when the first one struck it cleanly in the middle of the chest, a direct hit to its heart. Seeing how it had moved, he was easily able to slam the second attack straight into the skull of the canine, ensuring that it would not get back on its feet. Sek grabbed the closest thing on the ground to him, a machete, as he turned to see James dodging out of the way of another attack by the dog walker. James rolled to the side, snatching something from the ground and as he did. Sek didn't have time to focus on James as he was trying to get a clear shot at the dog walker without hitting James in the process. After rolling back on his feet, James was likewise lining up his own attack, and the two comrades launched a devastating tandem assault. The enemy didn't see the machete coming at him from behind until it had already been buried deep into his left shoulder blade, and the pain dulled his reaction just enough for James to deliver a heavy blow to the side of his head with a club. The man was sent reeling back in agony as he held his head and ripped the weapon from his shoulder; tossing it to the ground at James's feet. The two took a moment to breathe as the dog walker stumbled back toward the entrance of the room, and they prepared themselves for another onslaught.

"Fine. You two want to play the game like that? I'll oblige you. Why don't you try your hand against this," he growled in pain as he raised his hand and snapped his fingers. The rattling of the chain link fence behind them grew so loud that James spun around unsure of what to expect. Arnold still hung lifelessly on the fence, but Martin was moving. Pained groans escaped his partially-open lips as he struggled against the bindings that held him in place, and with each passing second, his resolve only intensified. The man struggled so fiercely against his bindings that fresh blood started to pool at his feet as his wrists were being cut open from the movement. James slowly stepped back, dropping the club he held, and stared at his father as the tie around his left wrist finally snapped. The ties that held his feet were next, and finally, he snapped the tie on his right wrist and stumbled away from the fence. It took a few seconds for his father to get his footing, but soon he turned his attention to James, and at the beckoning of the dog walker, started his advance.

"Dad..." James choked quietly as he stepped back and his heel nudged the bloody machete, the sound of metal skittering across the floor distracted him for a moment before he looked back at his father. The man struggled to get his body under control, but it was clear to Sek and James that when he was able to, he would attack at the enemy's command. He reached down and swiped the machete from the floor. As he worked his hands over the grip to secure his hold, James looked down the blade, through the space between them and finally to his father. All he could do was whisper quietly, "I'm sorry dad...but I'm not ready to die just yet."

There was a growl as his father finally got himself righted and set his sights on his son. James gripped the handle of the machete so tightly that his knuckles turned white under the armor and he rushed forward in one fluid motion. He didn't give himself time to think. He couldn't think. Instead, James lunged and threw his arm forward in a steady attack. As soon as he felt the jolt of contact shake his arm, he looked away and closed his eyes. James heard the sound of the blade slashing through his father's flesh and the sickening splat of more than just blood splashing against the floor. When he stepped back, there was another dull thud and the sound of gurgling. Then silence. All the time, James kept his eyes closed and tried not to lose his composure. After a moment, he opened his eyes and looked at the dog walker in absolute fury. His enemy however, seemed unimpressed.

"Well, that's rather unfortunate. No matter. Fixing him won't take much effort. You both have only reaffirmed that you two will make excellent additions to my ever growing army," the dog walker said with a calm smile. Sek bristled at the mere thought, and James threw the machete to the ground.

"Like hell we'll be a part of your insanity!" James growled as he shifted into a balanced fighting stance and prepared to rush the enemy.

It was then that Sek noticed James had the dog walker's complete and undivided attention, which meant he had the perfect opportunity to get in a shot without being seen. He flexed his powers and brought two sharp implements to float in the air beside him. He only took a moment to line up his shots before letting them fly. Before James or their enemy knew what happened, both objects had gone clean through the dog walker's shins, pinning him to the ground as they dug into the floor at an angle. He let out a howl of agony, and James darted forward, drawing his fist back. As he closed the gap, James started to charge up some of the suit's power into his fist. When he was finally in range, it started to glow. James planted his feet, and with all the momentum he had working for him, threw the punch into the middle of the guy's chest. As soon as his fist made contact, all of the stored up power discharged and the result was absolutely devastating.

There was a loud crunching sound followed by a wet splashing. James felt his armored fist sinking deeper into his opponent's chest cavity, his knuckles finally breaking straight through the dog walker's back and splattering blood across the wall behind him. The now lifeless body fell to the ground in a heap when James ripped his hand free. There was a moment of silence. Sek glanced at his new comrade and saw through the visor of the helmet that James was struggling to keep his calm. Sek raised a wrench with his powers only to bury it deep into the skull of their fallen opponent. This jarred James from his thoughts and he turned around to absently mutter, "Sorry."

"No worries, mate. So, what do we do now?"

"Hmm," James turned back and looked over the remains of his parents. It was clear that there was a storm in his head, and he quietly walked over. He gingerly went through their pockets and clothing to see if there was anything that he could find. In one pocket, he found a strange identification card and a few other cards which he pocketed to look at later. There was nothing else and he got to his feet. After standing there wordlessly for a few moments, he held his hand out and, using the power of the weaponized suit he had around him, he cleanly shot the father on the ground in the head. Then he looked to the one who was still tied against the fence and turned his head away as he fired off one more shot. James quickly turned back around and said, "Let's get out of here."

But before they could go, the invisible man's voice rang out from the empty stairwell. "This was only a test; don't think you beat the boss that easy. I don't know who you are, armor man, but I know the Limey bastard next to you."

Recognizing the voice from his apartment, Sek responded, "Obviously, I made an impression on you. You followed me all the way here just to watch me work up a sweat showing your boss what a bitch he is."

"I should have taken your head off with those pots upstairs," the disembodied voice threatened. "I doubt you could hold up to a magna-cannon. You're both just a couple of snot nosed punks. It takes more than you two to keep the boss down, and when he's ready, you're his."

As the voice droned on, Sek surreptitiously floated a knife from the floor. He used his power to shoot the blade through what should have been the invisible man's chest, but instead of striking his target, the knife harmlessly impaled itself in the stairwell.

Laughter echoed around them. "Fucking moron. There's a reason I'm the boss's eyes and ears. There's a reason I'm the only one the boss hasn't tried to convert. I'm a shadow. A wraith you can't see, touch, or hurt, but believe me buddy, I can do all that and more to you. So, watch your ass, and don't think you accomplished anything here."

"I bet my ass is exactly what you wanna touch, mate. But I'm not into the prison shower scene," Sek said as he looked over to James. "Let's get the hell out of here."

James quietly agreed, and the two exited the basement without saying anything more. Shadow seemed to have disappeared again, and when they reached the hallway, they were pleased to find that the mass of floating pots and pans were now strewn about the floor and no longer poised to be launched at their heads. James stood in the hallway, looking slightly lost and Sek decided now was as good a time as any to have a look around the place. He turned to his friend and said, "Listen, before we get out of here, how about we have a look around and see if there's anything worth taking? Prepare us for whatever else could be waiting around the corner."

"Sure, whatever," James agreed, not altogether hearing him, but it didn't much matter to Sek as he went about picking through drawers, cabinets and various other hiding places. James quietly went along but hadn't even finished searching the kitchen by the time Sek had completely cleared the top level of the house. He had found a bit of money and a few other ID cards that he would check out later. It wasn't much longer until they were ready to leave, and James doubled back to the kitchen. After tinkering with the gas stove, he turned around to Sek and said, "We should get out of here quickly."

Sek saw no point in arguing, and the two were out of the house and walking toward the drive. James was taking out his binder once more, and after flipping through a few pages, he settled on an image. In a matter of seconds, there was another car sitting right before them, seemingly to have materialized out of thin air. Sek quickly filed that away in his mind for future knowledge. This particular vehicle was a little less conspicuous than the first and could be easily overlooked in a crowd of other cars. Then he watched as James flipped to another page within his binder and changed the hand of the armor he was wearing. The teenager held out his hand, palm facing the house, and without saying a world launched a fireball straight toward it. Sek was quick to put some more space between him and the house. As soon as the fireball shot through the doorway, the house exploded and was fully engulfed in flames. The rush of heat flew through the air and caused Sek to step back reflexively. He glanced back at James, who hadn't moved and was just staring back at the roaring flames; no doubt lost in his own thoughts.

"Maybe we should take our leave. You know, before people start calling the authorities and they want to ask us questions about all this," Sek suggested as he moved to the front passenger door and pulled it open. His voice seemed to call James back from wherever he had gone, and he turned to give a silent nod before he too slipped into the car. They shut the doors and pulled down the drive to leave just as the faint call of sirens could be heard in the distance.

"Where should we go?" James asked as he quickly went through the streets he saw would be difficult for a fire engine to traverse, further diminishing their chance of encountering the authorities as they made their escape.

"Well, I have a room booked for me at a hotel downtown." Sek fished out a paper from his pocket that he had written the name of the hotel on. "The Westin? Why don't we head there and get our heads on straight before we think about going anywhere else. I don't think it was far from where I jumped into your car. Do you think you can get us back there?"

"Shouldn't be too difficult, and it sounds like that's our only option at this point," James conceded and took a few more turns to put himself back on course. The rest of the drive was quiet with neither of them speaking. Sek was thinking through the many times he had seen the dog walker before reaching Indianapolis, and James was lost in thoughts of his fathers. Neither of them was aware of how long they had been driving until they finally pulled up into the parking garage of the Westin Hotel. They found a place and parked haphazardly since the car would not remain there for long. Then they made their way to the front desk to get everything situated for themselves. The young female behind the desk stared at them with wide eyes when James attempted to address her, forgetting that he was still adorned in the armor he had been wearing back at the house. In fact, quite a few members of the staff were staring at the pair.

Sek, stepping in front of him to draw her attention away from James, said, "Sorry about that. We're both ready for a convention and my friend here decided that he couldn't wait to show off his costume. Anyway, I have a reservation. Can you help me out?"

This explanation seemed to calm the desk agent, and she quickly went about finding his reservation so she could get the two of them away as quickly as possible.

Chapter 13: First Meetings, May 13, 2016

Crow stared at the light above the door of the elevator they were in, waiting for it to illuminate the floor they would be arriving on while Amanda amused herself by humming the Battle Hymn of the Republic and rocking back and forth on the balls of her feet. They had been systematically going through the floors of the hotel, looking for anything out of the ordinary. Neither knew exactly what they were looking for, but both figured they would notice if something seemed out of place. Crow was beginning to get anxious as they got closer and closer to the top floor without finding anything. The auction was the next day, and they knew something dark was looming over it, but Crow's instincts wouldn't allow her to turn back. Amanda seemed just as chipper as she had been when she was reunited with her friend, who she viewed as her adopted sister, and if not for her, Crow would've felt far more exposed and vulnerable. Crow knew that if it came down to it, Amanda was one wicked shot, and she would have her sister's back. She may not remember everything they had been through before, but Crow trusted her and wasn't going to lose her friend again.

The elevator dinged, and the light flashed over the doors as they slowly opened. The two calmly stepped out and glanced around at yet another hall of rooms stretching along the whole floor.

Crow sighed and brushed the hair from her face as she muttered, "I'm really getting annoyed with the interior decorating. It's enough to make me stir crazy."

"At least it's warm. Let's get looking," Amanda said as she led them off to the left of the elevator.

Just as they had before, the two went door to door, lingering quietly outside every few feet listening and sensing for anything that seemed like it could be related to the trap they knew had been set for them. It was slow going. This floor was just like all the others, and they reached the end of the hallway to find nothing out of the ordinary.

The duo doubled back to the elevator to start on the right side of the floor. By this point, Crow was somewhat disheartened and looking along the walls at the various works of art the staff had hung to make the hotel seem classier than it really was. Amanda however, was unaffected and ever vigilant.

Amanda heard the elevator ding as they were approaching and slowed down. Crow followed her lead subconsciously, but was far too lost in her thoughts to see what her friend was looking at. If she had, she would've seen the two strange figures emerging from the elevator. The first was a college-looking student, tall and lanky with brown hair and blue eyes. His clothes were slightly disheveled and looked like he had been in a fight with someone. Amanda brushed it off and looked to the figure behind as he stepped out into the hallway. She was surprised to see a shorter figure adorned in full post-apocalyptic armor that seemed like it was pulled straight from her own mental delusions. It was enough to stop Amanda dead in her tracks, and her survival instincts took over. She quickly pressed herself to the wall and carefully inspected the two, noticing that not only did it seem like they had been in a fight, but they were covered in splashes of what looked to be dried blood.

Amanda reached out and pulled Crow off to the side so they weren't seen, motioning her to look at the strange pair. Crow had not been expecting such a sudden change in demeanor from her sister and slammed into the wall. Just as she looked up to see what had come over Amanda, she quickly caught sight of the two new figures and instinctively fell in step behind her.

    The two men didn't notice the girls and went the opposite way down the hall. Amanda motioned for Crow to follow her, and they both quietly slunk through the hall behind them, keeping a safe distance to hide in case the two looked back. They didn't, and the girls watched intently as they stopped in front of a door. The normal-looking one fumbled around in his pockets for a minute before pulling out a keycard and swiping it to open the hotel room door. They went inside, and Amanda watched the door slowly swinging shut. Without looking at Crow, she shot forward and came skidding to stop just in time to place the tip of her foot in the doorway, keeping it slightly ajar. Amanda didn't make a sound as she gently propped the door open a crack with a trinket from her pocket and stepped back to listen in. Crow rushed over to her, taking extra care to remain as stealthy as her sister had, and they listened to the idle chatter. The men were discussing what their next plan of action would be. However, what Crow and Amanda didn't realize was just how aware they actually had been.

    Inside the room, Sek paused after not hearing the door shut, and as he looked back he saw the tip of a shoe retreating after nudging a small child's building block into the doorway. James was focused on drawing the curtains over the windows so no one could look inside. Sek rounded on the door and waited for James to look at him before wordlessly gesturing that they were no longer alone. James tensed, still in his armor, and turned to the door. Crow and Amanda looked at each other when the conversation between the boys stopped. James prepared his armor for a well-placed shot, and Sek adjusted his grip on the cube turned knife. A few tense moments of quiet followed before Sek cleared his throat and said loudly, "Alright, we know you're out there listening. Show yourself. Nice and easy, now."

Amanda kicked open the door and stepped into the threshold as it crashed into the wall. Crow sighed at her friend and slid into the space behind her, unsure what was going to happen next. Crow looked over her adoptive sister's shoulder and began inspecting the armor as best she could. Upon closer look, she realized with some surprise that she recognized what game it looked to have been pulled from, and then she noticed the dark splatters of blood across its shining surface. She turned her attention to the other and saw similar blood speckles over his clothes as well. Whatever they had been doing before arriving at the hotel wasn't peaceful, and Crow wasn't sure she even wanted to know what their story was. Amanda, however, had one thought at the forefront of her mind.

"No! No! No! I know that armor! Bad things follow that armor. Even if you're not the one doing it! Things are good here! We don't need you. We've got this under control. This city is safe without you. You gotta leave!" Amanda said, connecting the armor she saw before her to the world she fell into as her way of coping all those years ago. She knew better than any of them standing there the ramifications of that armor coming to the hotel, and if he didn't get out, very bad things were going to follow. Not only was the hotel in danger, but so was the whole city.

There was a stunned moment of silence as Sek and James exchanged a look of confusion. Neither of them was sure what she was going on about and were unsure how to respond. Crow was in a similar boat, except that even though she didn't understand what Amanda was talking about, she was standing behind her, charging lightning through her hands. She kept her hands behind Amanda so they would not be seen, but she was carefully looking over the many electrical currents running through the room. She noticed an elderly gentleman a few doors down open the door to his room and peek out at them. He narrowed his gaze when he made eye contact with Crow and furrowed his brow at her. He didn't say a word, but he continued to watch them as though he was daring them to make any more noise than they already had. Crow recalled the lighting so that it was no longer crackling around her knuckles but was still surging through her hands.

It was Sek who decided to break the silence as he cleared his throat to say, "You must have us confused with someone else, mate. We haven't done anything and we're not here to cause any trouble."

"Right, and the blood on your clothes is just food coloring. I'm not stupid. You don't want any trouble? Fine. Then leave," Amanda retorted with her hands on her hips. Once again, she received a mystified look from Sek and James. Amanda stared them down seriously, and Crow looked down the hall to see if they were attracting anyone else's attention besides the old man watching. Luckily enough, no one else even seemed to be awake in the hallway.

"Ok, I don't know what you're ranting about, but we're not who you're looking for," James tried to explain, but this only seemed to rile her even more.

"That's fine! Then just leave! We have important work to do and we don't need any help from you. So buh-bye," Amanda exclaimed, raising her voice again in excitement.

Crow heard the old man a few doors down growl something under his breath and stomp away from his door, leaving it slightly ajar. She knew all too well that he would return and when he did, it would worsen the confrontation they were already having. Crow moved to block Amanda from the old man just in time. He was hastily dressed in what would've been a nice suit if they had been adorned properly. He was rather frail looking. He puffed out his chest in an effort to be intimidating, but when he came sputtering up to Crow indignantly, he stood half a foot shorter.

"Do you lot mind keeping it down?! Some of us need the sleep. Respectable people who make a living from events like this auction put in countless hours of travel, and this is the only rest we can get. We don't need it disturbed by delinquents like you!" he fumed and raged a few feet away from an unimpressed Crow.

"Go back to your room and go to sleep then! None of us are stopping you, old man!" Amanda snapped and the man's face flushed in irritation.

"I would if it weren't for children like you in the hallway making enough noise to wake the dead!" he sneered in response.

"Listen, you –"

"Calm down, Amanda. We don't need this getting ugly," Crow interceded, gripping Amanda's shoulder tightly. "We'll quiet down, sir. You won't be hearing from us again."

"Look at his face! It turned ugly the second he came out of the damn room!" Amanda said.

"That's it! I'm calling security!" he howled and stomped back to his room, slamming the door behind him. Crow sighed and pinched the bridge of her nose. Sek stepped aside and motioned for them to come into the room.

"Perhaps we should finish this inside the room," he advised. "I take it you're not leaving, and we've drawn enough attention to ourselves already."

Amanda growled quietly and stalked over to the old man's door. She delivered one swift kick, rattling the door in its frame, and spun around to walk into the room with the other two.
Crow could hear the old man yelling in frustration, no doubt making good on his threat. She stood in the doorway to look down the hallway and turned back to make eye contact with Sek. They stared at each other, and Crow finally conceded and stepped into the room, closing the door behind her.

As soon as the door clicked shut, there was a ripple of movement over James, and the girls watched intently as the armor he had been wearing was wiped from existence, leaving James standing there in a pair of jeans and a gaming t-shirt. Crow arched her brow in interest. She knew the one who had been wearing armor had abilities like her and Amanda. It stood to reason that his friend would likewise have some ability of his own, and this put her on edge. She went from never meeting anyone else with special abilities like herself to being surrounded by them.

"So, why exactly were you eavesdropping on us anyway?" Sek asked. "That's not exactly normal, ya know."

"Oh, but walking around in armor like that is?" Amanda retorted. "Listen, the bad guys are gonna follow you, and we don't need them here. This city isn't perfect, but we've got it under control. What are you doing here anyway?"

James sighed and covered his face with his hand.

Sek turned to Crow and gestured to Amanda questioningly.

"This isn't going to get us anywhere," Crow said. "We're here is because of the auction. It deals with my family and comes from an estate I didn't even know existed. We were trying to find out what was going on when we saw you guys, and you looked suspicious. That's why we followed you. Are you here for the auction?"

"We didn't know anything about it," Sek explained. "I'm here on business. I was supposed to meet someone here and they booked this room for me. When I got here, he and I had a run in with someone who wasn't exactly friendly, and since then we figured we might as well stick together until we figure out what's going on." Amanda snorted in disbelief, but before anything else could be said, there was a knock at the door. The four fell silent and didn't move to answer it. A few seconds passed before there was another firmer, more authoritative knock.

"Security," the knocker said. "We know someone is in there. We have a few questions for you."

The four looked between each other and Crow quietly gestured at Sek to take the lead. He sighed and adjusted his shirt to look a little more presentable before opening the door. Crow moved just out of sight and readied herself in the case things went south. James and Amanda stood in the middle of the room, waiting for any indication that they would need to act. Sek did his best to sound innocent and confused when he opened the door and said, "Can I help you?"

Two security guards stood in the doorway. The smaller one on his right cleared his throat and adjusted his uniform as he attempted to speak with an abrasive tone, "We've had reports of shouting coming from this room. How many of you are in there?"

"Just three of my friends and me. We've been pretty quiet. I think you have the wrong room," Sek answered smoothly.
Crow noted just how easily the lie rolled off his tongue and mentally filed that in her memory. These two that Amanda had stumbled upon were interesting to say the least, and Crow wasn't exactly sure what to make of them.

"Oh, we're sure this is the right room. We had it confirmed quite clearly. We're going to need to see some ID."

Crow decided it was time to try to divert their attention. She quietly slipped her bag to the floor and slid to stand beside Sek. Crow draped her arms around his neck affectionately. She fixed the guards with a pouting stare and purred to Sek curiously, "What's taking so long? What do they want?"

"Apparently, someone complained that we were being too loud," Sek replied, caught slightly off guard by the sudden contact, but quickly realized her plan and rolled with it effortlessly.

"Complained? Oh, it's probably that old guy a few doors down that's been harassing us, since walking past his door is like a sin or something," Crow sighed, trying to seem as innocent as she could while flashing a meek look at the security guards. The first one seemed somewhat distracted by Crow and opened and closed his mouths a few times without saying anything. His comrade however, was not deterred so easily.

"We're still going to need to see ID from you two and your friends."

Sek went through his pocket to fish his ID out from his wallet.

An internal war rose within Crow and she debated whether making a scene to get away was worth it. She had done her best since coming back into Indiana without revealing herself, but now she would have to or start something she didn't want to follow through with at this point. She pondered the ramifications of knocking the guards out and hiding them while she and Amanda fled the scene, but with the two guys in the mix she couldn't guarantee a clean getaway. Finally, she pulled her license from her bag and handed it to the security guards. She had been trying to appear meek and feminine, but as she handed over her ID she drew herself to her full height and fixed each of them with a deadly stare and memorized their faces. She narrowed her gaze on them. They returned Sek's ID and then hesitantly reached for hers, slightly taken aback by the sudden change in her. They seemed further disturbed when they looked at her license, momentarily frozen by what they saw. A look of fear crossed both of their faces and Crow tensed as she arched her brow and inquired, "Is there a problem, gentlemen?"

"You're a Yoshida ma'am? One of the host family?" the first security stammered, growing pale.

At first, Crow didn't know how to respond, but after quickly thinking it over, she drew herself up into a traditional Japanese presentation posture and looked down her nose at the two of them to speak in a tone dripping with disdain and contempt, "Yes I am. What concern is it of you, Gaijin?"

"J-just a moment, please," the second guard said as he quickly returned her license and stepped back with his fellow guard in tow. They stepped a few doors away and huddled together over their radios speaking in hushed tones. Crow leaned closer so she could hear and listened to their almost panicked whispers as they keyed up over the radio, "Front desk?! Yeah this is Mark. Remember that noise complaint you sent us on? Well, it turned out its one of the damn host family for that auction! Do you know how stupid we look right now?!"

The voice that crackled over the second-rate radio sounded equally distressed as the two guards when it replied, "Shit! We don't have record of one of them staying in that room! Are you sure?"

"The license she showed is good. It's definitely one of them."

"Damn! Make this go away. We can't afford to lose face with these people with the amount of money they're spending! Offer her a penthouse suite or free food or something! Just make her fucking happy!"

"Clear."

The two security guards straightened up and walked back over. They both looked like chastised children trying to make amends for their misdeeds, and it was the second guard who stepped up to say, "On behalf of the hotel, we are very sorry for the inconvenience, Ms. Yoshida. The gentleman who complained made it out like there was a wild party going on up here. Clearly that was an exaggeration. As an apology, the hotel would like you to order whatever you want from room service for the remainder of your stay on the house."

Crow smiled in a superior manner and replied, "You're probably right, and as due diligence of the hotel, I would be disappointed if they did not investigate all complaints brought to their attention. We'll be more than happy to make use of your room service. Now if that's everything, I'm sure you have better things you could be doing than talking to us."

"Have a good night ma'am," the first guard muttered quietly as they quickly turned and made their way down the hallway. There were a few gestures at the old man's door from them, and it was easy to gather that if he made any more calls for the night they would be ignored.

"I can't wait for this whole thing to be done and over with. All these Japanese rules of traditional presentation crap are more trouble than it's worth."

"There's going to be all that the pomp and circumstance because the Japanese Ambassador is responsible for the whole auction. At least it will all be over after tomorrow."

The guards turned the corner of the hallway and were out of earshot. Crow leaned against the door, mulling over what she had heard. Drumming her fingers across the wood thoughtfully she muttered, "Hmm. The Japanese Ambassador. Damn, so much for staying anonymous." She stepped back into the room and closed the door behind her.

Chapter 14: Preparations

When Crow turned back to look inside the room, she saw Amanda sitting cross-legged on one of the beds with the phone in her hand dialing hurriedly. James and Sek looked over to Crow warily, who shrugged, not even pretending to know what was going on in her friend's mind. Amanda grinned as the other side answered and quickly said that she wanted to order room service. A smirk curled at Crow's lips. After a few minutes of being directed to the proper person, Amanda set to work on ordering her food. James and Sek thought that she was ordering something for them to snack on while they talked, but realized as she went on that she was ordering enough to feed a professional football team twice over. She finally finished off by telling the operator what room it should be delivered to, but just as they thought she was about to hang up, a bright glint of devious glee shone in her eyes.

"Oh, on top of all that I would like a full course meal be taken to room six-four-two every hour for the elderly gentleman staying in there, and don't tell him who sent it! It looks like he could use some good food, and I don't want him thanking me for it. Yeah. Yeah. Ok thanks!" Amanda hung up the phone with a laugh as she growled, "Sleep now, asshole."

Crow shook her head and crossed her arms over her chest as she leaned against the door thinking over the mention of the Japanese Ambassador. Sek leaned against the wall between James and Crow, taking a position where he could keep his eyes on everyone. Amanda remained seated on the bed quietly humming under her breath, clearly happy with herself.

James ran his hand through his hair, somewhat bemused over the whole situation. Looking between Crow and Amanda he said, "Well, despite how rough we started out, maybe we should restart and introduce ourselves. We might be able to find some common ground. My name is James Vinci."

"You can call me Sek." It was apparent that he wasn't going to offer much more than that, so Crow looked over to Amanda. However, her sister tilted her head toward her indicating that she could take the lead. Crow sighed and pushed off the door to stand closer to the others.

"My name is Crow, and this is Amanda. Like I already said, we're here about the auction. You're supposed to be meeting someone, and James joined you when you got here. It can't be coincidence that everything is happening at this hotel. Who is this person you're supposed to be meeting?" Crow asked looking between Sek and James. The four stood in a moment of silence, each side unsure if they could trust the other.

"Your guess is as good as mine. Some British guy with a scar on his cheek," Sek responded and the other three froze. It would seem that they did indeed have some common ground, but none of them were up to mentioning it. Instead of bringing it up, Crow looked to James and gestured for him to explain himself.

He sighed in response, "I received an envelope that had a picture of my parents beaten and tortured. There was an address, which brought me here to Indiana, and when I got off the train, I met Sek. We went to the address and…" James paused and took a moment to himself before finishing, "By the end of it both of my parents were dead, and we had to fight our way out. Then we came here to figure out what our next move would be."

At the mention of his parents being dead, Crow bowed her head, and for the first time since she had entered the room, James saw genuine emotion flash over her expression, temporarily washing away the calm mask she had been wearing. Eventually, she looked up and said, "I'm sorry to hear that. I understand what it's like to lose your parents. I lost mine too, and by the sounds of it, there was foul play involved in both cases."

"Ok! Enough talking about depressing things already. I think we should tell Hugo everything that's going on and see what he thinks," Amanda chirped as she reached for the hotel phone again, but Sek tensed and using his power caused the metal parts in the phone to bend and twist, making it useless.

"Wait a minute," he said. "I was chased around in New Mexico by a guy who defied all explanation. He followed me here and we ended up having to fight him, and he wasn't exactly a push over. Before you bring someone else we don't know into this, how about you tell us more about what's going on? I'm not thrilled at the prospect of possibly having to run or even fight my way out of here."

While his intentions had not been aggressive, his sudden movement toward Amanda had set Crow off. The lights in the room started to flicker, and she took a warning step toward him with electricity crackling around her briefly. Crow was so focused on staring down Sek intently that she didn't notice Amanda shudder at the electricity coursing through the air.

"I would advise you to step back and leave her alone. Don't try to stop her again," Crow warned him.

There was no doubt she would turn violent in protection of Amanda. While she displayed her control over electricity openly, Sek quickly assessed the changes in the electric currents and the fluctuations in the magnetic fields. He was already planning on how he would have to adapt his power to take her down if it came to it. However, Sek wasn't in the mood for a fight just yet, and gestured for Amanda to continue. Crow's lightning disappeared, and Amanda recovered.

"Sheesh, both of you calm down," she said as she fished a cell phone out of her pocket. "It's just my brother. Besides, he's the one who got us here anyway."

She quickly went about placing her call while Sek plopped down on the bed and leaned back. James sat in a chair by the window, and both of them looked expectantly to Crow. She stared between the two of them warily before sighing and relaxing as she leaned against the wall once again. Amanda hung up the phone, and they sat in silence looking between each other. Nearly ten minutes passed before Amanda broke the silence, "Well this is awkward." No one else bothered to respond to her. There was a knock at the door. She jumped up excitedly and said, "Whoo! Saved by the bell! Well, not exactly, but close enough."

Crow growled something inaudible under her breath as she pushed off the wall and answered the door. She was not at all surprised to see three separate dining carts of food with three somewhat disgruntled employees waiting outside the door. They around the small framed Japanese girl and seemed almost shocked to see just three others in the room. While they stared at her in disbelief, Crow looked over the food and felt grateful she wouldn't have to pay for any of it.

"We have all the food that you've ordered, and we've been made perfectly aware this is all on the house. We hope you enjoy."

"It would seem some things never change," a calm, calculated voice broke from the left side of the door.

All three employees jumped in surprise, and Crow flinched as she turned to see Hugo standing there, looking the same as he did the night she first met him down to the creases in his shirt. He walked up to the three employees, and after handing each of them a generous tip, ushered them away from the room. Then he grabbed two of the carts and said, "Well, shall we take these in?"

"You know, sometimes you scare me," Crow advised as she took the third cart and noticed a small smirk cross his face as she pushed it into the room.

They placed the food in the middle of the room for Amanda to do with as she wished, and Hugo snatched a sandwich before walking over to close the door. Crow followed his lead and took a small snack for herself before Amanda had the chance to devour everything in sight. Amanda jumped off the bed and darted to the food, only pausing long enough to look at the time and then at Hugo.

"Well it sure took you long enough. What were you doing – taking a nap?"

Hugo sighed, "No, Amanda. As I told you before you came here, we are stationed at the other hotel. I dropped everything to come over as soon as you called, just as I always do." Amanda shrugged and helped herself to the food while Hugo adjusted his suit. Then he looked to the guys and continued, "Ah, James Vinci and Arthur Seckel." Sek seemed to bristle at the use of his full name, but refrained from interrupting him. "It is a relief to see that you two are well, despite the circumstances. I had heard you both made it to Indiana, but I was not aware that you had made it to the hotel just yet. At least you both are safe."

"Now, as for you two," Hugo turned his attention to Amanda and Crow. While Amanda was too interested in the food she was eating, Crow cringed somewhat, expecting a lecture. She was not disappointed, "Crow, I understand how you feel about all this, but it would be wiser if you did not attend the auction tomorrow. There are a few things that don't add up, and I'm sure you've noticed it as well. This supposed estate is not one I have found much information on, and it was not connected to your mother or father in any way, shape, or form that I can find."

"So, it really is a trap then? To lure me out?" Crow inquired, taking a bite of the sandwich she had taken.

At this point, Amanda had moved on to her second plate, and the guys realized if they didn't act quickly there would be no food left for them. Each managed to swipe something for themselves without Amanda noticing and retreated back a few steps for fear of her turning on them for touching her food. While they took a few bites, the two eyed Hugo warily, not altogether sure they liked how he seemed to know so much about them but too curious to hear what he had to say to interrupt or question him. Then again, there was so much happening at once, it was almost a relief to have someone who seemed to know what was going on.

"As if there was any doubt. I have agents stationed throughout the hotel, but there are quite a few key points, and the convention center is so large that I haven't been able to properly provide the basic undercover saturation on the short time frame. There are still too many blind spots, and I can't guarantee your safety. Not to mention, we're still trying to discover who was behind organizing all of this," Hugo explained. Crow growled quietly to herself and paced in thought.

"I know it's not the smartest idea, but dammit, whoever is doing this is using my family name, Hugo. I don't have much, especially after what happened two years ago, and if this is even remotely legit – even if there is only one thing connected to my parents – it could be important. I have to try and find out. Besides, if my family name is damaged, I will make them pay dearly for it," Crow explained as she finally stopped pacing and looked at him, hoping he would understand.

"Don't worry. I'll be there if things go bad," Amanda chimed in.

"That's another reason for my concern. Not only is this a blatant lure for you Crow, but all four of you are on radar for more than just the FBI. It was not a coincidence that the four of you would meet in this hotel. If you get away from this, not only will the ones who organized it redouble their efforts in an attempt to capture the four of you, but you'll have drawn even more attention to what you are. It won't be long before other groups try to make their own claims to each of you," Hugo advised them. Even though he spoke to them patiently, his sense of urgency was not lost on the group.

"Hm. Hugo, the other hotel is secured, right?" Crow asked curiously.

"Yes. I was able to secure it and establish a command center there before you arrived to check in. That's how Amanda was there waiting for you. I know everything that goes on in that building. The same cannot be said for this establishment or the convention center, unfortunately."

"Well by the sound of things, we're already targets. We might as well take the threat straight to the ones who marked us," Sek said, deciding to put in his two cents worth.

"If anything, that's the only way to get direct answers about what's going on," James agreed.

"Kids..." Hugo sighed under his breath.

Crow smirked triumphantly. She knew that tone all too well. It was the same her parents had used when they knew they couldn't win the argument against her and would fold. She jumped on her chance.

"It seems we're agreed. We're going to check out the auction. We already know it's a trap, so we have that working in our favor. If things go south, we'll get the hell out of there," Crow said.

"Besides, you'll be close by. If anything goes wrong I'll call you," Amanda smiled at her brother.

While the four of them looked confident, Hugo remained unconvinced. "Just understand, it would take time for us to get to you. At least four minutes. If you're in danger, you'll have to last until we can get there. Keep your eyes open, and watch each other's backs." He patted Amanda on the head and gave her a hug. "You know how to get a hold of me. Do try to keep out of trouble until then." He gave Crow's shoulder a gentle squeeze before leaving. It was quiet for a few minutes while Amanda finished off the food she had ordered, impressing the boys who wondered how a slight girl like her could put food away the way she did.

Finally, after it seemed like Amanda was finished and there was nothing more to talk about, Crow cleared her throat, "We should head back to our room and prepare for tomorrow. From what it sounds like, it's going to be an ordeal and we should get some sleep beforehand. Come on, Amanda."

"Ok," Amanda replied as she bounced up to follow her sister.

"We'll come along too," Sek said.

Crow to froze and spun about as she narrowed her gaze on him.

"What?"

"We're coming with you. It sounds like you girls are in as much trouble as we are, so it makes sense to stay together. Strength in numbers and all that," Sek answered calmly as he gathered up his belongings. He glanced back at James. "Don't you agree?"

"Uh, yeah! Not to mention, her brother just said this place isn't secured. We don't want to get caught off guard, and since all four of us are targets already, we might as well stick together," James agreed and quickly retrieved his bag and other belongings.

Crow looked to Amanda while the two were fiddling around, hoping that she would have a good argument against the boys coming back with them, but Amanda shrugged and walked into the hallway. Crow rolled her eyes. "Fine, whatever. Just don't get in our way."

"Don't worry, princess. We can handle ourselves. So just retract your claws and relax," Sek said as he walked past her and out the door. James watched as anger flashed in her eyes and she stared at the back of Sek's head, no doubt resisting the urge to lash out at him. She mechanically followed behind him after taking a moment to breathe, and James shook his head. With the way they were jumping at each other's throats, their enemies wouldn't have much left to scrounge at.

The four made their way down the hall to the elevators. A few moments later, the doors opened and revealed another employee standing there with a room service cart in front of him. While the other three boarded the elevator, Amanda held her hand to keep it from closing and hung out to watch where the employee was going. She was thoroughly tickled to see him stop in front of the door of the old man who had called security on them and waited to hear him groggily answer the door. He proceeded to scream and rant that he didn't want any damn room service and just to leave him alone so he could finally get some blasted sleep. A satisfied smile crept across Amanda's face, and she finally allowed the elevator to close as she hummed the Battle Hymn of the Republic.

While each of them had entered the Westin while the sun was up, evening had already set and the sun was nearly gone as they stepped outside. Nonetheless, the streets were still busy with cars and the sidewalks were packed with people. Many didn't notice the four young people standing in the middle of the sidewalk and instead walked around them, subconsciously relying on their base instinct to not run into them. Only a few people took notice of them and then wrote them off. It wasn't strange for a group of young people with a few bags to be walking the sidewalks deciding which hotel they would crash in for their stay especially with something happening at the convention center.

The transition from one hotel to the other was done in silence. As they entered the hotel the FBI was staged at, a sense of security washed over them. Each could feel the tension ease, knowing that they had backup hidden in plain sight, and Crow even noticed a few familiar faces from the coffee shop two years previous. When Amanda noticed her sister staring at them, she leaned over and advised her that she "wasn't supposed to look directly at them." Crow couldn't help but smile and shook her head. No doubt that was something Hugo had told her many times in the past.

It wasn't long before they were standing in front of the room that Crow had been given and she watched James and Sek carefully as they walked through the door after she opened it. Amanda skipped in behind them and Crow quickly followed, closing the door and locking it before she went over to her bag. Amanda plopped herself on the bed she had claimed and busily went about messing with things in her bag as well, leaving Sek and James standing awkwardly in the middle of the room.

"So, what should we do now, exactly?" James asked.

"Get ready for tomorrow," Amanda answered as she began spreading things from her bag on the bed around her.

James found an open spot on the floor and pulled out his binder to flip through the many pictures inside. Upon a quick glance, Amanda and Crow realized that it was full of images of armors, weapons, and other things that would be useful to have in a fight. He was flipping through the pages carefully, and Crow managed to catch sight of the same armor he had been wearing earlier that had set Amanda off.

Not sure what to make of it, Crow turned her attention to Sek in time to see him place two strange cubes on the table in front of him and then rummage through his bag some more. Crow sat on the bed she had claimed and noticed that some of things Sek seemed to be messing with could turn volatile if managed incorrectly. She wrinkled her nose and glanced over to see what Amanda was doing. Her sister had pulled five soda cans from the mini fridge in the room and spread them on the bed in front of her. She was picking each one up and giving it a good shake before she put it back on the bed but what struck her as strange was that each can had a strange glow to it after being shaken, and the more she thought about it the more she realized the glow was exactly like discharges she had seen when Amanda shot her guns.

Deciding that everyone was preparing for the possible hell that was in store for them in their own way, Crow decided to comb through her belongings and decide what she would need to take as well.

James, however, noticed the strange glow in the soda cans and stopped to stare in confusion. While he knew that all of them had their own abilities, he couldn't help but question what Amanda was up to and cleared his throat to get her attention when he asked, "What are you doing exactly?"

"I'm making bombs. Duh."

"Out of soda cans?" Sek inquired, arching his brow at her.

When Crow glanced back over at his work it became clear that he too was working on makeshift explosives.

"Well yeah. No one's gonna see it coming. That's why it's perfect," Amanda said as she went back to charging the soda cans with her energy.

"Well, we'll have mine as backup in case things get ugly," Sek said, making it clear that he doubted Amanda's soda cans would serve the purpose she claimed they would.

These plans didn't set well with Crow, and she eyed them both seriously as she growled, "If there are any family heirlooms in that place, you two are going to blow them up before I even have a chance to look at them."

"It's just stuff. You can always get more stuff and besides, her brother even said this is a trap. More likely than not, there isn't going to be anything there other than some guys who think they'll have the jump on us," Sek advised.

"I'm well aware that this could just be a trap and nothing will be there, but I have to try. If there is anything related to my family, it won't be anything I can actually replace. Whatever is at this auction may very well be all that's left from my parents since the house they lived in burst into a ball of hellish fire with them still in it," Crow snapped back. The lights flickered in the room like they were about to go out.

Amanda sighed quietly to herself and shook her head. James stared at Crow warily, trying to decide if he needed to act. Sek, on the other hand, was still unimpressed with the display as he got up and took a few steps, standing face to face with her.

"That's quite the useful trick you have there, although a little less impressive the second time around. Anyway, speaking of stuff, there's actually a few things I have to go get. I'll be back soon," Sek said as he jotted down a quick list of things he would need and then walked past Crow.

"Try not to get lost."

"Of course not, sweetheart. You'd miss me too much."

"Don't let the door hit you on the way out!"

This time, when the lights flickered, Sek laughed on his way out. Crow stomped over to the door and slammed it shut behind him before returning to her own preparations for the confrontation ahead of them.

Sek stopped one of the hotel staff members to ask where the closest gas station and convenience store were located. Once he had that, he was on his way. As he walked, Sek took in downtown Indianapolis and the people who inhabited it. The streets were relatively busy for the time of night, and swarms of people weaved through cars as they were stopped at the intersections. It all seemed so routine, and as Sek walked past them a small part of him wondered if any of them knew of the strange world he had fallen into. No one paid him any attention, though, and Sek went about his business completely undisturbed. It wasn't until he was coming back from his shopping that things took an unexpected turn.

Just as he was walking past the front of the convention center, he noticed movement from the alley off to the side. When he looked, Sek could've sworn he caught sight of a full grown man and a dog. Sek doubled back and stealthily snuck up to the alleyway in an attempt to see the figure once again. Just as he had suspected, Sek arrived just in time to see the dog walker opening a door to the warehouse area behind the convention center and ushering in a new dog in a matching sweater before entering himself and pulling the door closed behind him.

Chapter 15: The Trap

Sek's mind went into overdrive. If the dog walker was in on the scheme of the auction, not only was tomorrow a trap, but it would be one they could have some trouble with. Despite the tension racing through his veins, there was a small sense of satisfaction that he would be able to throw that in Crow's face. He doubled back and pulled out his cell phone. Back at the hotel, the other three were rather surprised when the phone began to ring, and since Crow was the closest, she answered it.

"Hello?"

"It's Sek. Get down to the convention center. The guy who chased me here from New Mexico and fought James and me just walked into the warehouse behind the center where they should be holding the stuff for the auction," Sek quietly explained as he glanced around to see if anyone could've been watching him.

"Clear. We're on the way. Try not to get in over your head before we get there."

"Yeah, I'll see what I can do, sweetheart," Sek replied and hung up the phone.

Muttering a few choice words under her breath, Crow slammed the phone down on the receiver and relayed what she had been told. In a flurry of motion, the three gathered all of the provisions they had been preparing for the fight, and James snatched up what little Sek had left behind. They were out of the hotel within minutes and rushed to the convention center as fast as their legs could carry them. At this point, the traffic had dwindled down, and there was barely anyone out and about. The group passed a few homeless on their way to the convention center, and they seemed not to care where they were going. The group didn't slow down until they caught sight of Sek standing at the mouth of the alley, reassuringly unharmed. Once they had caught their breath, Sek led them toward the back where he saw the dog walker disappear and pointed at the door.

"Hm. This is too easy," James muttered, glancing around as though the trap would reveal itself like the passage behind the wall at the mansion where his parents had been kept. He had no such luck the second time around.

"Agreed," Crow added. She motioned to the cameras they were standing just outside visual range of. It was against her better judgement to have even shown her ID in the first place, but it would be a cold day in hell before she let a camera catch her breaking into a building.

"I'll handle that," Sek said as he reached one hand out and using his power to manipulate the metal bodies of the cameras, caused them to crunch and cave in on themselves. This effectively crushed the lenses and cut all feed coming from them. As the chunks of now useless metal fell to the ground, Sek turned back to look at them with a content smirk.

The four crept forward to the door that Sek pointed out, and Crow silently opened it. Much to their surprise, there was no one inside, and no alarms alerting anyone to their presence went off. It was absolutely silent aside from the sounds of their breathing. They found themselves in a hallway with various doors leading to storage units the convention center used, and some of the old overhead lights were flickering. The dog walker was nowhere to be seen.

As was her nature, Crow took the lead and moved down the doors, reading the ones that were marked as she looked for some sort of indication of where he could've gone. Amanda was close on her sister's heels, and the boys followed in tow. Soon Crow stopped in front of the door marked "Warehouse 9," which also had a temporary tag under it: Yoshida Estate Auction.

Gritting her teeth, Crow looked back to Amanda and said, "After what Hugo said, what do you think the likelihood is of our not-so-dead-dog-walker being in there?"

"Only one way to find out," Amanda responded as she pulled out her paintball gun. Before going to the door, she observed a side hallway next to the warehouse in question and walked over to it cautiously. Without exposing herself, she peeked around the corner and saw that there was a second entrance to the same warehouse on the side. Looking between the two doors, Amanda waved the other three over and said, "Well, we shouldn't all barge in through the front."

"Agreed. The question is who should go through which door?" James piped up.

"Well, this was meant to draw me in. If anything, they're expecting me to come through the front door, and they're not expecting a fight. To throw them off, I'll go through the side door," Crow decided and looked to Amanda, who wordlessly assured her that she would be watching her back.

"Alright. So, James and I will be front and center for all to see and all to take aim at," Sek said.
Crow threw him an unfathomable expression. "Yes. You'll be the surprise, and we'll sneak in from the side to give you cover. With Amanda's aim you guys won't have anything to worry about. Just don't purposely go and try to get yourself killed," Crow said in dead monotone.

Sek and James looked over to see Amanda adjusting the site on her paintball gun. Neither was reassured.

"Well, we've fought this guy once already and won. This shouldn't be any different," James said, sounding like he was trying to convince himself as well as Sek.

Though they looked calm, the boys would not admit that they didn't exactly appreciate the girl's plan. The girls made their way to the side door as the boys approached the front. Each team waited a moment before opening their respective doors, prepared for an attack. Yet, the sight they were met with was strange, confusing, and altogether didn't quite make sense with the dimensions of the warehouse itself.

Though none of them had seen the inside of the storage unit beforehand, they could guess the size of it by the outside. The outer walls looked to be the length of a regulation basketball court and the width to be just a bit longer than that with raised ceilings that looked to be near three stories tall. It seemed as though this was one of the larger storage units, and by the talk that Amanda and Crow had eavesdropped on while running recon of the hotel, it should've been at least half full. After all, there were rumors of great treasures to have been discovered among this mysterious Yoshida estate Crow had no idea existed, and it called quite a few prestigious collectors from all over the world jumping at the chance to get their hands on anything they could.

Instead, each team was met with a strange, plain white hallway that wide enough for two people to stand side by side. There were no other discernible markings in the halls, and the only thing they could see was a door at the end of the hallway, which seemed to lead to what would be the middle of the storage unit. Neither team could see the other as they stepped into the eerily quiet halls, closing the doors behind them. Amanda and Crow stared at the walls, almost expecting them to change or for something to crawl out of nowhere, but nothing happened. So, they carefully advanced. James and Sek slowly made their way toward the door as well, checking over their shoulders regularly to make sure nothing was attempting to sneak up from behind. Each was aware of the deafening and unnatural silence that surrounded them and it put each of them on edge. Once reaching the end of the hall, they paused before opening the doors. They strained all of their senses in an attempt to pick up on anything waiting for them on the other side, but all they heard was silence. Each team took a breath before throwing open the doors with their attacks raised and ready for what was waiting.

Stepping through the threshold, the four all found themselves standing together in an empty room. There was nothing and no one else. They looked around in an attempt to find any sort of explanation for what was going on. Suddenly, the doors slammed shut behind them and seamlessly melded into the rest of the walls. There was no way out. The team stood in dumbstruck awe. At that moment, ominous maniacal laughter echoed through the air; bouncing through the large warehouse unit they stood in.

The trap had been sprung. Amanda raised her gun and steadied herself, ready to start lining up her shots. James instinctively reached for his binder and without looking flipped to the various pictures of armors. After a quick glance, he touched his hand to one particular image, and instantly the armor began to materialize around him, making it seem as if he had stepped out of yet another very popular first person shooter game. As he was replacing the binder in the bag, Sek produced his two cubes, and using his power, raised them to float in the air by his head while taking the form of knives. Crow flexed her hands at her sides, allowing electrical currents to discharge and snap between her fingers.

"Seems like Hugo gets to say I told you so next time you see him," Sek noted, looking over his shoulder at Crow with a satisfied smirk.

"Yeah, yeah. When we get out of this you can yuck it up with him," Crow growled.

"If we get out of this, you mean,"

"Oh, get over it already. We'll get out of this just fine. Just make sure you keep up," Amanda said.

The room around them changed once again. The walls wavered and began to disperse as though they were waking from a dream. Light began to come up in the warehouse and as they looked around they found that the dimensions had been restored to what they should've been, but the sight that revealed itself was far from comforting. The unit was full of at least sixty strange, intimidating figures dressed in identical black leather jackets and black motorcycle helmets with visors down, hiding their faces from view. Each figure was lean and muscular and standing at attention; almost as though they were poised and waiting for war. They didn't move. They didn't even appear to be breathing. They stood still as statues: intimidating, powerful, and exactly the same from each muscle definition to the exact buttons on the leather jackets they all wore. The four fighters stood right in the middle of them, surrounded on all sides.

"Crow, if these guys were the family heirlooms you were talking about, your parents were weird," Amanda said matter-of-factly. She carefully scanned her possible targets, planning how to clear a path to get them out of dodge.

"Here we go," Crow growled, looking among the unknown soldiers awaiting their marching orders.

Before they even stepped foot in the convention center, they all knew it was guaranteed to be a trap, but it wasn't until she stood there, staring at all the possible combatants, that Crow realized just how out of her league she was. She would never admit it, but there was a part of her wishing that she had listened to Hugo and not been so stubborn to investigate it herself. She was counting her blessings that she had three others standing at her side to take on the threat. There was a ripple of movement among the group directly in front of them, and a few stepped aside to allow an older looking man walk out before they fell back into place. James and Sek recognized the dog walker, and it seemed as though his "death" at their hands hadn't slowed him down in the slightest. In fact, he seemed to be looking just as chipper as he did before.

"Whoa, whoa, whoa. I'm pretty sure we killed you already. Don't you know that you're supposed to stay dead? That's how this kinda thing works, mate," Sek said.

Amanda took aim, her gun sights poised to shoot the old man straight between the eyes, and prepared to take the shot until Crow's hand darted out to cover the barrel of her gun. She released a small sigh that almost sounded like a hiss and maintained her aim, but removed her finger from the trigger.

The older man merely laughed. "Oh Arthur, a smart-ass to the very end. I thought you Brits were supposed to be bound by that irritating, unspoken code of politeness. Although, it doesn't matter. You will meet the same fate as your friends regardless," he said.

"First off, the name is Sek. Remember that for however many lives you may have left. Second, who the hell are you exactly? You're trying to sound big and bad, but it's hard to take you seriously with that ridiculous sweater you're wearing."

"Take a look around," he said as he stepped back and gestured with both hands to the beings standing at attention. Then a change came over him. It was instantaneous. His arms dropped to his sides, and his facial features sank into the skin. They watched in horror as the skin fused together over the bone structure to look as though a seamless, flesh-colored cloth had been pulled tightly over his face. They could even see the stretch marks reappear on the skin as the old man's features faded away. His body fell into the same position as the rest of them. Then one of the figures to the left of the group suddenly jumped into motion and reached up to raise the visor of its helmet, revealing the dog walker's face. He leaned forward with a vicious smile as he spoke.

"I am them."

He flicked the visor down, and the soldier fell motionless once again. Then directly across from that one, this time on the right side of the group, another figure moved to flick up its visor, revealing his face on it as well.

"They are me."

Almost immediately, the group heard movement behind them and then his voice growling deeply like a threatening beast.

"We are one, and I am many."

A gravelly, deep throated laugh broke from in front and they quickly spun to see him return to his original body and gestured at his soldiers as he declared, "I am Legion!"

"Take your hand off the fucking barrel," Amanda growled through grit teeth, doing her best to keep steady aim despite her friend's interference.

"Not yet, Crow replied softly as her gaze was flicking between the various bodies that surrounded them, counting just how many were in the front ranks.

"The four of you will be wonderful additions to my horde." He looked up at them and took notice of the horror and disgust on their faces. "Oh come now, don't act so surprised, especially after all the trouble I went through to lure you all here. I handpicked each one of you for your abilities, and I did my research. I pick nothing but the perfect candidates. After all, the process of making my minions is both time consuming and expensive. Although, to be perfectly honest, the time and effort don't bother me in the slightest."

Legion motioned for one of his minions to walk forward, and it stopped at his side with the simplest gesture. He turned and raised his hand to gently caress the side of the creature's face as he continued, "Each of you will join the ranks of my Faceless."

Legion calmly pulled the helmet off the head of the minion, giving the group a proper look at the monster he called the Faceless. The seamless flesh that had been pulled over the face actually went around the head completely. Its smooth surface was disturbing and unnatural. Just by looking at it, they sure that whatever it took to become a Faceless was agonizing and horrific. Now Legion had his sights set on the four standing before him.

Anger and disgust swelled in James' chest in memory of his fathers.

Crow released her hold on Amanda's gun. As soon as her hand was out of the way, Amanda only needed a fraction of a second to readjust her aim and then let her energy shot fly. True to her skill, the shot was clean and left a deep hole in Legion's flesh right between the eyes.

"Finally! Crow if you do that again, I might just shoot you first!" Amanda yelled as the lifeless corpse fell to the ground, but once again Legion's maniacal laugh broke through the entire warehouse.

James and Sek quickly focused on the door they had come from and found that the ranks had closed to trap them in place. James aimed his arm and steadied it with the other just as a gun raised itself from the armor. Amanda quickly produced one of the charged cans from her bag and launched it into the mass of Faceless blocking their way. At first, it hit the ground with a dull thud and rolled across the concrete floor. Then there was a sudden explosion of superheated carbonated syrup and shrapnel from the metal can ripping through the thick of those surrounding it. The explosion was volatile enough to knock the immediate enemies to the ground, and satisfied with the damages, Amanda fell back with the others. Working together, Sek and James cleared a path to the door and with the help of Amanda's precision shooting, kept the Faceless from getting between them and the exit.

Crow slowed and turned to the Faceless advancing on them from behind. After taking a few hurried steps back, she planted her feet and focused on the electric currents running through the warehouse lights, concentrating on pulling it down around her. Once she felt it surging through her fingertips, Crow threw her hands out just as they were nearing arms reach and discharged the electricity in a crackling semi-circle.

Her lightning burst effectively knocked the closest Faceless in pursuit to the ground in twitching heaps. However, without hesitation or consideration for the fallen, a second wave started closing in, stepping over the Faceless on the ground as they reached for Crow. Five clean shots were fired over her shoulder, and she looked to see Amanda put a bullet in between each of where their eyes should've been, effectively stopping them from getting a hold of her sister.

Crow dashed back to the other three as they threw open the door to the warehouse. All four spilled out into the hallway and took off toward the door leading to the alley. As they ran, they heard other warehouse doors open and the thunder of boots marching behind them. It wasn't long before they spilled into the alley they had come from, but to their dismay the Faceless were waiting for them.

Sek and Crow dodged out of reach from the outstretched hands grasping at them as they exited the building into the alley, but Amanda and James were both caught unaware. One took hold of Amanda by her hair, and another snatched James up in a headlock. Amanda growled in frustration as she attempted to pull away, and James yelped as he was pulled off balance. Both Faceless tightened their grips on the two and attempted to drag them back into the ever growing horde.

"Screw this!" Amanda hissed as she reached back to grab the hand wrapped in her hair as she brought her gun up. Before it had time to react, she fired her shot — blowing off the creature's hand just above the wrist. The Faceless stumbled back, and Amanda scrambled over to Sek and Crow. James let out a muffled growl as he struggled to break free but found that his enemy had a far better grip on him. It tightened its grip around his neck, and James began choking. The Faceless dragged him closer to the mass, and Sek realized he had to act. After looking over the alley to assess his options, he took notice of the air conditioning units positioned on the side of the convention center.

Sek focused on the air conditioners and with a little force managed to use his control over the metals to rip them clean off the side of the building. His movements were a little uncoordinated at first, but as he got used to their mass, he was able to maneuver them as if they were a part of his own body. He had them floating in the air as if they were hung on suspension wires and slammed the corner of one unit down on the creature's head. The blow was jarring enough for James to escape the creature's grip, and there was a very audible cracking sound that broke through the air. James spun around as Sek positioned the two units for another attack and watched as the helmet on the Faceless that had been holding him cracked in half. The pieces started to fall to the ground and when James caught sight of the smooth surface of its face, he froze in absolute horror.

While the Faceless' skin was just as smooth as the others before it, there was a five-point scar in the middle of it, which James recognized as the exact five points where Legion had buried his fingers into the face of his father back at the house. He couldn't move as he just stared at the monster that had once been his father. Apparently, he hadn't done the job well enough back at the house to spare his father's body any further perversions from Legion.

"Get out of the way, mate!" Sek commanded loudly. James threw himself back to land beside Amanda in time for Sek to launch both units into the thick of their enemies.

Amanda stepped back and pulled her cell phone from her pocket before furiously dialing a number into it. James stepped to block her, and they all watched as more and more enemies filed out of the various doors along the alley. The group had their back to the street and slowly stepped back. Crow heard the sounds of semis driving nearby and started to surge more electricity through her fingers in preparation for another attack.

"Damn it, Hugo! Where the hell are you?!" Amanda growled angrily as she put her phone back in her pocket.

"That's not good," Crow muttered as dread began to knot in her stomach.

The four realized how severely outnumbered they were, and with Hugo not answering the phone, their last lifeline had been cut. Each wracked their brains in an effort to find some way out, but nothing came.

"Ey! Down this way, you lot!" a familiar British voice called from behind them.

They spun around to see a tall, muscular figure at the end of the alley waving them toward him. As they looked between the newcomer and the growing horde, he was clearly the safer choice. Amanda and James were the first two to retreat, and as they doubled back they saw the new figure brandish a long, elegant sword and skillfully cut down a few Faceless that stood between them. Sek ran back as soon as he was sure the air conditioners had barreled down the tightly enclosed space, breaking a few spines as they flew. Crow, once again, lingered a little further behind the others to wait for the inevitable marching Faceless to walk over their fallen comrades to pursue them.

It wasn't nearly as quick as it had been before, considering the air conditioners Sek had thrown had knocked nearly all of them back, and Crow was sure to keep walking backwards as she began charging more and more electricity in her hands. She didn't stop backing up until they had gotten too close for her comfort. Then she took a breath and sent out all the stored lightning straight toward the horde, not only shutting down the frontline Faceless's nervous systems, but managing to stun the ones behind them as well. Without waiting to see how effective her attack was, Crow turned heel and ran to her comrades just as they reached the end of the alley. The British man stepped aside to allow them by, and upon seeing his face, each of them realized where they had seen him before.

Amanda recognized him as the social worker Hugo sent to take care of her when he couldn't and kept her from having to go with "the people."

James recognized him as the psychologist who worked him through much of his trauma and told him where his fathers were being kept.

Sek recognized him as the release doctor who got him out of the hospital and was the one who got him all the way to Indiana.

Crow recognized him as the physical therapist who went out of his way to make her laugh at least once every time he saw her.

He was the one person all of them had in common.

Chapter 16: The Chase

"Good to see you lot are alright, considering the circumstances. Now we need to get you out of here and to safety. Do any of you have a car?" the Brit asked as he walked over to stand in the entrance of the alley, blocking any enemies that might try to come through. He was dressed in a khaki-colored suit with a red tie and a few pins that the kids did not understand. They were at a loss for words, and after a few moments, he looked back sternly with his eyes catching each of theirs as he asked, "Well?"

"Uh, I do, but it's in the garage at our hotel," Crow answered. She looked past the man and saw the creatures were starting to recover from her shock treatment, stepping over those that hadn't.

"I can make us a car," James offered and set to work.
The Brit looked over his shoulder at them with a smile. "Very good! Once you sorry lot load up, you'll be heading to the airport. There will be a plane on the international strip waiting to take you to safety, and the best pilot I know will take care of you," he explained as he rolled his shoulders and stretched for the fight ahead. He calmly took off the suit coat and loosened the tie around his neck. After a quick look around, he decided there wasn't anywhere to put his coat and simply dropped it on the ground followed by his tie.

"How will we know which one is ours?" Crow asked.

He laughed, "You won't be able to miss it."

"What about you?" Crow asked, tensing as she heard a strange sound behind her. She glanced back to see an armored car that looked like it had been pulled straight from a gaming magazine, and Sek was stepping into the back of it. James was looking it over carefully to make sure it was flawless. Amanda, however, was waiting for Crow.

"Don't worry about me, young lady. I will be holding them back," he said with a dismissive wave. "Now piss off and get to safety,"

Amanda looked between her sister and the man and said in an unusually serious tone, "Thanks for the save, Charles. You always seem to know when to show up, but I don't think you know just how many of those are coming and I doubt they're going to be friendly when they get here."

"Once again, piss off!"

While the sudden change in her sister's demeanor unnerved Crow, the trucks she heard before were louder than ever and saw they had pulled up at the opposite end of the alley. There were two, and they had backed up so the rear loading doors were easily pulled open by the Faceless. Just inside each of the trailers were a couple dozen motorcycles: more than enough for every creature and then some to pursue the group.

The Brit stepped further into the alley and turned toward the horde as he drew a second, shorter blade to accompany his long one. Crow knew beyond a shadow of a doubt that he would not make it out of this fight alive. By the way the Brit squared his shoulders as he looked into the alley, she was sure he knew that too.

"Thank you," was all Crow could whisper. She wanted to make him come with them. She wanted to come up with something that would force him to abandon this suicide mission, but they would need someone to hold them back while they ran. She looked to Amanda who looked just as conflicted if not more. Crow sighed, and hoping Amanda would follow her lead, turned and climbed into the car.

"Who should drive?" James asked, looking between the other three.

"I've got this. Load up!" Crow took control as she jumped into the driver's seat. Sek looked out from the back while James took the passenger seat. Crow turned on the car. Then she glanced out to see that instead of getting into the car, Amanda still stood outside, staring down the sight of her gun, aiming down the alley past their friend. Crow tightened her grip on the wheel and called out, "Anytime, Amanda!"

"I'm working on it," she called back, adjusting her aim just a hair before letting off the shot she had been carefully charging. The bullet of energy streaked down the alley, rocketing past the Brit's ear, but astoundingly enough managed to miss every enemy squeezed into the tight space, and it seemed as though Amanda had completely missed her mark until the bullet of energy made contact with the inside gas tank of one of the semis holding the motorcycles. It erupted in a ball of flames and shrapnel as the truck was decimated in the explosion. The force of the blast threw the second trailer onto its side – taking the motorcycles and the Faceless that had been inside trying to unload them with it. Satisfied, Amanda spun and was about to jump in the back of the armored car when they all heard the sound of something heavy hit the hood.

"What the hell?" James yelled in surprise. A small shot of pain seared through his right temple.

"I told you boys you would be seeing the boss soon, but you dummies didn't want to listen," a disembodied voice said as it slid across the front of the car.

"It's that bloody voice again," Sek sneered angrily. "I told you mate, you can't have my body. It's off limits!"

"Your body belongs to the boss!" the voice said from the alley side of the armored car.

The Brit charged into the alley. At first, he had done well keeping the horde from advancing forward, but Crow had noticed the Brit step backwards several feet the longer he fought. The Faceless bodies were piling up in front of him. He came to a stop in the entrance to the alley. His head cocked to the side as he looked into the Faceless as they struggled to clear the debris and fallen bodies. His blades were dripping, and he seemed oddly distracted. Crow stepped out of the car and pointed to him as she called out "Amanda!"

As all four of them looked back to the alley, they heard the Brit chanting quotes that Crow would later identify came from the ancient swordsman Miyamoto Musashi, "Perceive that which cannot be seen with the eye. Do nothing which is of no use."

He seemed to be waiting for the Faceless to charge again. Then, an invisible force slashed across the back of his left leg, severing his Achilles tendon in a spray of blood. As the four screamed in fear for their friend, the Brit spun as he fell, an angry growl on his lips, and brought his weight down on both blades.

A female voice screamed out in agony as a body flickered into view. She was dressed in all black with the Brit's blades impaling her through her upper back. The sleek black suit that she was wearing had a few stray currents of electricity spark around her as the systems hidden beneath it started to short circuit from the damage. Coughing blood onto the Brit's suit, she croaked out, "How did you.... I was.... How?"

"Shadow! Ya silly git, I shoulda known!" the Brit barked out. "I'm not just a pretty face. You forgot I'm a fucking spotter," he said, his wounded leg sliding out from under him awkwardly as he leaned in to speak in her ear. The four could barely make out the words of his low growl, "It weren't enough for ya to betray Sarge, ya had to betray all of us!"

The words sparked venom in her eyes, and she spit fresh blood in his face. The Brit smiled at her, violently twisting his blades in opposite directions. She shuddered trying not to give him the satisfaction of another scream. But the pain was too much, and she let out a dampened whimper.

"I shoulda left ya in the brothel I found ya in," he said. Then, looking up to the group as the Faceless horde behind him reached out, their powerful hands grasping his shoulders and pulling backwards, the Brit screamed, "What part a piss off don't you get?!"

Crow watched as Amanda screamed, reflexively shooting blast after blast into the Faceless. A manhole cover flew over their head from Sek's direction. There was another blast shot off from James' suit. Crow was the only one who stood there without moving. The Faceless who weren't struck down by the stray attacks continued to drag the Brit further down the alley. The last they saw of him was his blades flashing under the dim streetlights as the horde engulfed him. Just as Amanda moved to pursue the Faceless in an attempt to save him, Crow heard his voice ordering in a pained shout, "Drive, you silly git!!"

Snapping out of her daze, Crow reached out and tugged on Amanda's arm, saying her name softly. Amanda spun, she looked between her sister and the alley for only a moment longer before turning on her heel and diving into the back of the car beside Sek. She quickly situated herself and prepared her gun before looking up to Crow to say, "Hit it!"

As Amanda slammed the door behind her, Sek called up to Crow, his voice tighter than usual, "You heard the man, mate. Drive!"

Crow didn't need to be told twice and didn't have it in her to respond with a smart retort. The car jumped as she gunned it out of the alley, and the tires squealed as she pulled into the street. The sound of the tires seemed to echo and bounce between the buildings in the night as she corrected her course and peeled off toward Washington Street.

"Why are the streets empty?" Crow said out loud as she noticed the lack of traffic.

The other three looked back, and Amanda nudged Sek as she noticed several of Hugo's men blocking intersections with their cars and ushering pedestrians off the street. One nearby agent saw them pull away from the alley, and his left fingers darted to his ear as he began motioning to the others on the street first to the armored car and then in the direction of the alley by the convention center. Amanda followed his motions and saw Hugo standing on top of the warehouses. Once he was certain they were not going to stop, he looked down into the alley and raised his right hand over his head first with his hand open then making a clenched fist. As he did, FBI snipers stood up into view, lining the rooftops on both sides of the alley walls, and began raining machine gun fire into the horde.

The car jerked as Crow cut a sharp corner to get them on Washington Street from Capitol Avenue and slammed the gas pedal to the floor. Sek called forward "I know why the streets are empty. Big Brother is watching."

"Just avoid any long black cars you may see blocking streets, ok," Amanda added.

With a nod, Crow stepped harder on the gas. They continued picking up speed, and Crow faintly registered seeing the police car sitting on the side of the road as she barreled past it. She wasn't surprised to see its flashing lights in the rearview mirror. Crow growled and continued speeding down the street as she exclaimed, "Looks like someone missed the memo. Hang on guys! I'm not stopping until we get to the airport. Let's just hope we make it. I thought Hugo's guys were blocking for us!"

"He's blocking the streets and traffic!" Amanda called back indignantly. "What more do you want? He's the FBI, not the Police!"

"Well, it looks like the cop called for backup," Sek noted as three more police cars joined the pursuit.

"We'll be fine unless they try to force us to stop," James said as they continued barreling down the road. A few more police cars joined the chase, and the cars in front started inching closer.

"Shit," Crow said as two police cars pulled out from the streets in front of her and attempted to block their way. But they unwittingly left just enough space that she could get the armored vehicle between them with barely bumping their fenders. Exhaling with a hiss, Crow adjusted her grip on the wheel and rolled her shoulders. "This is going to get a little rough."

Sek looked back at the approaching cars and moved to brace against the back of the seat. After watching the cars intently, he reached out with his powers toward the cars. He could feel the magnetic field of the metal, and with a little focus, he was able to flex, bend, and invert the axels of the three cars leading the chase. Two quickly spun out harmlessly on the sides of the road, but the third lost control and clipped a fourth car attempting to dodge around it. The remaining two police cars backed off, and Sek smirked at the quick work he had made of their pursuers. Crow was approaching the space between the two police cars in front of her, but just as she was about the clear the gap the group heard her frantically curse in Japanese.

"What?" Sek asked, but before she could answer, the armored car jerked and four loud pops went off as the tires burst out from under them. The car started rattling as the rims began grinding against the pavement, and Crow barely kept them from spinning out of control. Amanda and Sek struggled to keep themselves from being tossed around in the back while James held tight to his seatbelt, groaning somewhat in pain. All the while, Crow continued hissing under her breath furiously in Japanese but refused to take her eyes off the road before her or loosen her grip on the wheel. She quickly adjusted her speed to keep from losing control, but still pushing the vehicle as fast as she could.

"Stop strips," James muttered as he glanced out the window to look over the damage.

"I can't do anything evasive on four flats and those officers aren't letting up!" Crow snapped as James looked up to see the four remaining police cars regroup and rejoin the chase full force.

"I'll take care of the tires," James said, placing his hands on the dash and closing his eyes to block out everything so he could focus on the car. As he did, the veins on his forehead seemed to bulge slightly, and sweat was beading at his forehead. Meanwhile, Sek and Amanda redirected their attention to the cars behind them.

"We'll handle the cops," Sek advised just as one closed the distance fairly quickly and seemed to be gunning for the rear driver side tire.

"He's trying to hit us!" Amanda called as James was envisioning with his mind's eye all four tires re-inflating. Her exclamation caused him to lose focus just as he was calling on his powers to manifest what he saw. Three tires inflated instantly, but the driver's side rear tire didn't, and the police officer took his chance in an attempt to pit the armored car. Crow miraculously jerked the car to the side just enough to avoid the first attempt, and James took the precious seconds she gained to get the last tire inflated. The officer drove forward to pit again, and this time he didn't miss.

"Damn, damn, damn," Crow hissed as she skillfully corrected the vehicle despite the vicious jolt and, after a few tense seconds, dislodged the two cars while still managing to keep control. Crow gunned it again and pulled off from the officer as they started to round a turn. She returned her full focus to the road ahead of her, and what she saw made her heart skip a beat. While the chase was still relatively new, the police had coordinated unusually well, and a mile or so ahead there was a roadblock of five police cars in the middle of the street and dozens of officers poised and ready just before the main entrance of the Indianapolis Zoo. After muttering a few choice words in her native tongue, Crow looked at James saying, "I don't know how strong this thing is, but something tells me we're not going to make it through that!"

"Nothing can be easy, can it?" Amanda growled as she leaned out the window and shot the front tire of the police car that had struck them. It spun out of control, and the other officers had to slow down to avoid striking their comrade. Amanda readjusted her gun and aimed out the window as the cars were working on recovering from the sudden diversion. She didn't even look up when she said, "I've got these guys. See what you can do about the ones ahead of us."

"Got it," Sek replied as he turned and adjusted himself so he could see between the driver and passenger seats. Crow shifted nervously in her seat.

"What should I do?" Crow inquired quietly, trying to keep her tone level and calm.

"Just drive straight. I got this."

"I hope you do,"

James tensed in the passenger seat and did all he could to keep his focus on the car. All he could hope was that Crow would continue to keep driving like she had been trained to do this and Sek would once again pull an ace out of his sleeve to get them out of this.

Sek took a breath and stared at the roadblock. He only woke up with his power almost two days ago, and it would be the most he had asked of it yet. If they were going to get out of this with as few casualties as possible on both sides, he couldn't falter. Crow maintained her speed and course as he had told her. Amanda was keeping the cars behind them at bay. James was keeping the car around them.

As they drew closer, Sek extended his own magnetic field, stretching it out to the cars ahead. He felt the metal sing as soon his magnetic fields touched the cars, and an ominous idea came to him that would no doubt leave quite the lasting impression on the officers squaring off against them. Instead of crippling the cars as he had done before, Sek strained his powers and meticulously lifted the two police cars that were in Crow's direct path. It was shaky at first, and the police officers let out cries of terror before diving to the side to get away from the inexplicably floating cars. The sheer weight of the cars was enough to make him continually readjust and redouble his efforts to keep the cars steady. Sek was soon able to lift the empty police vehicles twenty feet in the air and separated them by sending one car to each side of the road. After making sure that there was no one in the way, Sek promptly released his hold on the cars and let them crash unceremoniously to the ground. Crow floored it and easily drove through the empty space where they had once been. Sek fell back against his seat sighing heavily.

While Sek and Crow were intently focused on getting away without hurting any of the officers, James and Amanda were able to see the wide-eyed looks of terror on their faces as the officers looked between the armored car barreling past them and back to their own cars that had just defied all logic and explanation. With a slight flex of his power, James changed the radio in the car to a scanner so they would be able to listen to the officers' traffic. Just as he did, an officer had keyed up to speak in a trembling voice, "C-control...they...got through the roadblock..."

"Subjects have made it through the roadblock," a female control operator echoed calmly. Though she remained calm, there was unmistakable surprise in her voice.

"Edward three-o-one control, terminate the pursuit. We've passed the point of safety for civilians," an older, more experienced voice grumbled, sounding rather peeved that they would be unable to capture the four suspects in the armored car.

"Clear. Attention all units, authority of Edward three-o-one terminate the pursuit. Authority of Edward three-o-one terminate the pursuit," control echoed as the sound of furious typing could be heard crackling through the radio.

"Thank god," Crow sighed relaxing her shoulders. Then the radio crackled back to life.

"Officer down! Code one! Washington and West!" an officer keyed up screaming into the radio in pain. The four jumped slightly and looked at the scanner. If they weren't the ones who caused this officer to drop into emergency status, who was?

"Shots fired, control! Shots fired!" another officer howled over the radio, and gunshots could be heard raining around him in the background. Control didn't even have a chance to respond as she had before as the situation only deteriorated.

"Stop! Stop or I will shoot! St–" the first officer was violently cut off, and there was the sickening sound of flesh being ripped by his microphone. There was the sound of liquid gurgling and then a dull thump as the radio and microphone that was transmitting hit the ground. The radio remained keyed up as other officers could be heard shouting in the background and the gunfire intensified. Then there was a roar of motorcycle engines, and the radio cut off.

"Edward three-three-two to the roadblock! Get out of the roadway! Repeat. Get out of the roadway! Five subjects in black jackets and black helmets on motorcycles incoming fast! They're not stopping, and they will strike anything in their way!" The officer's speech was tight and strained to remain as calm though he could not stop from screaming into his radio.

Amanda caught sight of the motorcycles approaching the roadblock they had just passed. Any hopes that the five motorcycles were unrelated flew from her mind as she saw the Faceless quickly closing the gap. The officers seemed to shy away from them as they passed, and James turned off the police scanner. Amanda settled in and stared down the sight of her gun again as she shouted, "Floor it!! We lost the cops, but now we've got the freaks on our ass!"

"Got it!" Crow called over her shoulder, and she slammed her foot on the gas again. As they flew down the road, Crow thanked Hugo and every power above that the streets were abandoned and no civilians were getting caught in the crossfire. The path to the airport was clear.

Slightly recovered from his prior strain, Sek bounced back to brace himself at Amanda's side and watched as the Faceless approached. Amanda had already picked her intended target and was waiting for him to get within range. Seeing this, Sek looked over his options and picked his target so there was a Faceless in between his and Amanda's.

The motorcycles roared as they flew across the pavement and followed the armored car. Crow was blowing through the stoplights and picking up speed on the straight stretch of road. The Faceless, however, were slowly but surely closing the distance. Amanda waited long enough only to make sure she had a clear shot before letting her bullet fly, and Sek waited until she fired to make the front tire of the motorcycle invert on its axel. Amanda's shot hit the tank of her target's motorcycle, and it burst into flames as it veered to the left. Sek's target jerked to the right and threw its rider into the street as it barreled toward the middle. The rider between couldn't avoid both in time. In an explosion of flames, smoke, and shrapnel, three Faceless were taken out of the fight. The surviving two accelerated and moved to pull up on either side of the group's car.

Sek was too worn from moving the police cars to stop them. He grit his teeth in annoyance, and he realized that he was reaching his limits and would need to rest to recover. Soon enough, the disturbing creatures came level with the driver and passenger side windows just as the car reached the intersection of Washington and Tibbs. James tensed, keeping his focus on maintaining the car around them and looked between the windows, trying to guess at what the monsters had in mind. Crow caught sight of the Faceless out of the corner of her eye and refused to look away from the road but charged lighting in her fingers in case the creature reached in to get at her. It came as a surprise when, instead of attacking them, the creatures each threw something into the windows to land in the laps of both James and Crow and then slowed so they were no longer even with them. James was the first to look down at what had been tossed into his lap and let out a surprised yelp when he saw a severed arm. A closer glance at the custom-tailored sleeve revealed that it had belonged to the Brit. Crow glanced over in time to see James fumble the severed limb to the ground at his feet. She then looked down to see what was now resting in her lap. She nearly choked when she found herself staring into the eyes of the Brit who had worked as her physical therapist, and she could feel blood oozing into her pants as his severed head rested in the middle of her legs.

Crow's mind nearly blanked in horror, but just as she was beginning to focus on the blood seeping and dripping down her legs, she heard her parents' voices calling her name. Hearing them ringing through the thoughts in her head snapped her back, and Crow tightened her grip on the wheel so forcefully that her knuckles turned white. She took a steadying deep breath. She never looked away from the road, but James could hear her faintly whispering, "Remember the fire. Remember the fire. You've seen worse. You've felt worse. Remember the fire."

James noticed the Faceless on each side in the side-view mirrors steady their motorcycles before suddenly leaping straight into the air and landing simultaneously on the roof of the car. The car continued barreling down Washington Street at nearly eighty miles per hour, and Crow warily looked up when she heard them land. James unfastened his seatbelt.

"I'll get them off the car."

"Just make sure they don't take you with them!" Amanda chirped, causing him to sigh.

"Thanks for the vote of confidence." Screwing his courage to the sticking place, he wiggled halfway out of the window and sat on the door to brace himself as he reached for the roof. When he was sure his grip wouldn't slip, he heaved himself the rest of the way out of the window and was halfway onto the roof when he looked up to see the two Faceless effortlessly standing on top of the moving vehicle. He wrinkled his nose and called down to Crow, "Try to shake them off!!"

She did, and James focused on two grips to appear on the top of the car to hold on to so he would not be tossed to the side. She picked up speed to try to get rid of the Faceless. After a long stretch of high-speed driving and some tactful maneuvers, which caused the Faceless to secure their spots on the roof, the car was finally turning onto the strip of the Indianapolis International Airport, and they could see in the distance the plane that was waiting for them.
James glared at the creatures and said with a confidence he didn't altogether feel, "You guys aren't going to stop us."

The closest Faceless slammed his boot down on his left hand in response. The second pulled a gun from his jacket and leveled it at his right hand. James didn't have time to react and howled in agony after the shot rang through the air. His armor took most of the blow, but due to the point-blank range, the bullet still made it through to his flesh. James's right hand fell to the side, and the other Faceless reached down to grab him by the neck before releasing his left hand from under his boot. In a display of inhuman strength, the creature lifted the teenager over his head with one hand, and in a devastatingly fluid motion slammed him down headfirst onto the roof. The sharp blow dazed James and caused him to lose focus over his power. First with armor disappeared and then with a quiet pop, the group realized just how quickly his manifestations could disappear. The car was gone, leaving all six of them hurtling forward at eighty miles per hour through the air down the landing strip.

Chapter 17: To Psion

The loss of the car shocked them. The wind whistled as they flew through the air, and they approached the ground at an alarming speed. Crow and Sek acted instinctively. Crow's training in Ninjutsu and Sek's in Kendo allowed each of them to safely tumble and roll across the ground without sustaining any major injuries as they went. Although, it did take them a few tries to gain control and get themselves righted. Amanda was utterly caught off guard and didn't have enough time to tuck her gun against her to roll safely. She hit the ground hard and was propelled forward, flipping head over heels for thirty feet past Sek and Crow before coming to a stop. Covered in scratches, scrapes and bruises, Amanda laid on her back, staring up at the sky while trying to see if she had broken anything. Astoundingly enough, she escaped any serious injury, but her body screamed in pain. All the while, she still kept her gun clutched tightly in her hand. James, however, was still far too dazed from the blow to his head to protect himself, and he crashed unceremoniously to the ground. His limp form flipped a few times before skidding across the ground to stop a few feet behind Amanda, unconscious but breathing.

Meanwhile, the Faceless faired far better. Each had gone limp as soon as they were sent flying and bounced along until they gained enough control to stop. Crow and Sek were standing and dusting themselves as they noticed the creatures start to get up as well. They didn't seem affected by the impact at all. Though if one looked close enough, there was evidence of their road-rash evident in the leathers they wore. Sek and Crow noticed that the creatures stood between them and Amanda, James, and the idling plane waiting as the Brit had promised them. The Faceless were focused on the two standing, no doubt determined to keep them from getting to the plane and assured that the other two were too injured to make it on their own. It reassured Crow. If she could work with Sek and keep the enemies focused on them, it would keep them away from the others, who weren't moving. It was the only thing that kept her from trying to rush to Amanda's side to make sure she was ok. Crow glanced over at Sek and he seemed to be on the same page as she was. Crow took a deep breath and seized the moment of surprise. She darted forward a few feet sending out two surges of electricity powerful enough to bring both of them down temporarily.

The Faceless closest to her was unable to get out of the way in time and crumbled to the ground the second the lightning touched him. The other seemed to anticipate such a reaction and leapt into the air to land closer to the two of them.

Amanda had pushed herself up, wincing in pain as she did. Glancing back to where she heard the crackling of lightning, she managed to see one enemy go down before she looked over to see James lying on the ground motionless. Despite her own body screaming in pain, Amanda got to her feet and stumbled over to him. She had a clear path to the plane, and if she could get James there safely, Crow and Sek had two fewer people to worry about. If they were still fighting by the time she got to the plane, she could safely shoot from afar without having to worry about the Faceless closing the distance before she could defend herself. So, she grit her teeth and slung his arm over her shoulder as she started dragging him toward the plane.

Crow and Sek turned their focus to the unharmed Faceless as it straightened up and reached for something it had been holding tight at its side. It was a sword – the same sword the Brit had been using to cut down its brethren in the alley. The Faceless raised the weapon so that the light glinted menacingly off the blade, and it promptly drew its arm back and launched the sword straight ahead. The sheer strength behind the throw drove it through the air at such an astounding speed that Crow didn't have time to react as the blade buried itself deep into the muscle of her right shoulder. The force of the impact knocked Crow clean off her feet with a yelp, and she landed flat on her back. She choked on the wind escaping her lungs and struggled to catch her breath. She had to try to keep the pain from completely hazing over her mind and keep the panic at not being able to breathe at bay.

    Sek looked between the two Faceless and then back down to Crow. An idea was taken form and he planned to act on it quickly. He moved to Crow's side and wrapped his hand around the hilt of the sword. With a quiet word of apology and his advising her to hold her breath, Sek ripped the weapon free from her shoulder doing his best to cause as little damage as he could. Crow let out a short howl of pain, and Sek spun around to focus on the Faceless still stunned from Crow's lightning attack. He lunged forward and severed the creature's head in one clean sweep. He adjusted his attack and attempted to do the same to the second one, but the Faceless was ready. It reached up and effortlessly caught the blade with both hands, pinning Sek in a deadlock. Each of them pushed against the other, but neither would give an inch.

    Crow gingerly pushed herself up and knelt on the ground hissing under her breath as she clutched her injured shoulder tightly. Her lungs finally stopped spasming from the blow, and she was able to draw in deep breaths. She could feel blood oozing between her fingers as she looked around to see Amanda dragging James closer to the plane. The last enemy had Sek gridlocked, and with the amount of blood she was losing she would only be useful for a limited time before she would be too weak. Crow staggered to her feet and turned her attention to the sky. Taking a deep breath, she felt every charged particle in the air and held both of her hands out to her sides palms facing up. After a few moments, Crow pulled together every ounce of energy she had and started to form all the currents in the air into one devastating bolt hidden behind the cloud cover. "Heads up, Sek! I'm frying this asshole!"

    Sek sensed the magnetic fields shift in the space around him, and he looked up to see the clouds opening to reveal lightning just above his head. Sek shifted his weight to one side and pulled back in tactful retreat, managing to take the sword with him as he went. He rolled away as the bolt of the lightning crackled and came crashing down on the top of the Faceless's head. The smell of charred flesh wafted through the air and when the blinding flash dissipated, the creature was lying on the ground motionless. Sek looked back to find Crow sitting on the ground looking dazed as she shakily tried to stem the bleeding in her shoulder and noticed she was looking pale. He walked over to the fallen Faceless and pulled the sheath from the crisped enemy. It was damaged, but would suffice for now and returned the sword to its proper place. With his weapon was safely secured, Sek gingerly helped Crow to her feet and they made their way to catch up with Amanda and James. Once at her side, Sek took over carrying James, and they approached the plane.

    Just a few yards from the plane, they saw something that made their stomachs turn, and they quickly averted their gaze. When the car had disappeared around them, Crow was far too focused on righting herself that she hadn't paid any attention to where the Brit's head had been thrown. Apparently, it had been sent bouncing and skidding across the ground and was now covered with scratches across the face and peeled back skin in some places. The skin around one of his eyes was torn making it appear as though the eyeball was bulging out, and a small trickle of blood was dripping from the corner of the eye like a tear. They all kept slogging along toward the plane in hopes of forgetting what they had just seen.

    As they drew closer, the side panel door on the plane opened, and a figure stood in the entrance. The three stared at him in awe as his presence left quite the first impression. He was a tall man, standing about six foot ten, and though he was not overweight by any means, his body was thick with muscles of manual labor. His complexion was that of a man who enjoyed spending his time in the sun, and a bit of red sun-burnt skin peaked out from beneath the thick handlebar mustache resting on his upper lip. He was wearing worn boot-cut jeans, cowboy boots, a white button up shirt, and a large, white ten-gallon hat resting just above his eyebrows.

Upon setting his dark brown eyes on the group, a large smile broke across his features and he called out, "Good to see you kids! I was worried ya weren't gonna make it. Guess I shoulda known better! The name's Tex, and I'll be yer pilot tonight. I'll take yeh somewhere safe from those uh, things."

Crow and Sek looked between each other uncertainly, but Amanda grinned, saying, "Oh, thank God!" Then she looked back to Sek and Crow saying, "You guys don't get motion sick, right? Cuz if you do, you're gonna have a bad time. You might wanna locate the barf bags."

Tex walked to the bottom of the stairs and effortlessly took James and carried him into the plane. Amanda followed him a little less bouncy than usual, leaving Sek and Crow standing at the bottom of the stairs. Crow boarded the plane with Sek following close behind. Tex shut the door behind them while they moved toward the seats. Crow saw Tex looking over James carefully and saw that he was administering basic first aid. Satisfied that he would be taken care of, Crow moved toward Amanda. She handed her adoptive sister some bandages from her bag and then sat down a few seats away so she could set to work on handling her own shoulder. Sek sat down near James and watched Tex finishing stabilizing the teen. Then he tipped his hat at them with a wink and made his way to the cockpit.

The team was quietly lost in their own worlds of thought. So, it came as a surprise when they heard the toilet flush from the back of the plane and they froze in their seats. Tension and distrust were thick in the air as the lock clicked and slowly opened. There in the doorway stood Hugo. A communal sigh of relief was heard as the four kids relaxed in their seats. He looked between the three of them and seemed almost amused by their wary stares.

Amanda piped up first, "How the hell did you get here first? I saw you on the rooftop."

"After I made sure everything was taken care of and we had a clear path to get you here, I took the helicopter. Your sudden departure from the hotel threw our timeline out the window, and I needed a backup plan. I think I did well to have this plane waiting and someone to help you kids out. Speaking of, where is Charles? I assumed he evacuated the alley and was in the armored transport with you?" Hugo asked as he went over to Amanda and began tending to her wounds in true older brother fashion.

"If you mean the guy who owned this sword, he's dead," Sek answered bluntly.

This revelation seemed to surprise the FBI agent, but he was quick to hide it and listened as Amanda told him in no uncertain terms how annoyed she was by the fact that he hadn't answered his phone when she called him for help. She recounted their journey running from the Faceless and her being skipped across the pavement like a rock across the surface of water. Sek lounged back in his seat and soon was nodding off to sleep. Crow went back to cleaning out her shoulder and wrapping up the wound.

"Alrighty then," Tex announced over the intercom. "We're gonna be takin' off here soon. Get yerselves settled and enjoy the flight. We'll be arriving in D.C. in just a few hours," The engines roared to life. The initial movement of the plane taxing across the runway was a jolt, but as it gained momentum, things smoothed out. After the easiest take off imaginable, they were in the air.

Crow watched as they left the city behind and sat back after finishing her shoulder. She growled under her breath in pain at the slightest movement and fell into her thoughts over everything that they had been through. Someone cleared their throat, and she snapped back to see Hugo standing there with large white pills in one hand and a small bottle of whiskey in the other. She arched her brow at him with a smirk and asked, "Horse tranquilizers and whiskey to wash it down? Is that an FBI trick?"

"Trade secret. Besides, it will tide you over until we can get you properly taken care of when we get where we're going," Hugo said as he gestured to Amanda, who was also nodding off to sleep.

"Well if it's good enough for you, I'll take it, but before I get too loopy I have a few questions for you."

"Go on."

"First, when we were at the Westin hotel, before you came, we heard someone say that the auction was being held by the Japanese Ambassador. Who is he?"

Hugo took a minute before responding.

"The Japanese Ambassador's name is Saiato Nakamura. He's an ally of the group I'm taking you kids to now. You'll be able to meet him soon, I'm sure. As for his possible involvement with the auction, I doubt he knew anything about it. Legion is known for his dirty tricks and isn't afraid to drag people through the mud to get what he wants. However, I will look into it, and I'll be able to find out more when we land."

"I know you said our sudden departure threw off the timeline. If it hadn't, would you have been able to remove police involvement?"

"Initially that was our hope, but I was unable to get in contact with them soon enough to still be there in time to help keep the Faceless from overtaking you."

"So, how bad did the police get hit?" Crow asked meekly, remembering the radio transmission of the officer being injured.

"Even IMPD hasn't fully assessed the situation yet and may not have a full damage report until we reach our destination. I will be sure to keep my eye on it. Until then, take a moment to relax. You all have earned it," Hugo said her with a gentle pat on her good shoulder before he went back to Amanda.

Crow couldn't shake the chills that raced down her spine at the mention of the ambassador's name and the guilt for the harm that came to those officers doing their jobs. Sighing, she lounged back and took the medicine Hugo had given her with just enough whiskey to let her relax.

In the skilled hands of Tex, their flight was uneventful, and they arrived in D.C. with no problems. But when Crow checked the time, she was positive they had made it there faster than any public flight could have hoped for. Tex was the first to disembark, and Hugo made sure that James – who was finally conscious and hurting – was ready to travel. He told the rest of the team to sit tight for a minute and stood at the bottom of the stairs. The group all looked out the window to see Hugo talking on his cell phone. Shortly after he hung up, a long black limo pulled up to the side of the plane. Hugo walked over, and after exchanging a few words with the driver, waved the group to join him.

James whistled and looked over his team saying, "We're going to be riding in style."

"It's not that big a deal. I ride in limos all the time. And police cars," Amanda said.

Crow smacked her forehead with the palm of her hand at her sister's tone. "Frequenting police cars isn't a normal thing, Amanda, especially if you're riding in the back."

"Oh, well that's not my fault," Amanda shrugged and lead them down the stairs.

"At least this vehicle won't disappear on us if you get knocked out again," Sek said with a smirk. James shot him a death glare, and the two women quickly made their way down the stairs to meet Hugo. Sek laughed as he walked past James, "Come on now. Don't get your panties in a twist. They're waiting on us."

James growled under his breath as he disembarked the plane.

"Alright kids. We're expected. Load into the limo, and Tex will take us there. Soon, we'll be in safe territory, and we can get your injuries looked at," Hugo said, holding open the door of the limo for them.

As they climbed inside, the group took a look around at the empty tarmac, aware that their plane was the only one on the landing strip. It didn't seem like there was anyone else there, and they were pretty sure they were on a private airstrip.

"You may want to buckle up," Hugo said. "Tex is the best driver alive, but he tends to surprise and unsettle people who aren't used to it."

They heard the limo doors lock as it shifted into gear and they shot into motion like it was a bullet being fired from a gun. James and Sek barely managed to fasten their seat belts in time and held on to them for dear life. Crow's head smacked against the headrest, and she grasped tight at the door to keep from falling forward. Only Hugo and Amanda were left unfazed, sitting perfectly calm in their seats. The group was just managing to recover from the initial shock when Tex took a turn sharp enough turn to lean the limo on two wheels. When it landed back on all four tires, they sped off like the devil himself was chasing after them.

Sek looked at Hugo incredulously and asked, "So, is he trying to kill us or what?"

"I would never put you kids at risk. I have half a mind to be offended you'd even think that, youngin. I just thought you might wanna get somewhere you can rest yer head and heal up sooner," Tex said over the intercom.

"Yes, that would be nice, but it'd be even better if we get there without having to scrape ourselves off the inside of the limo."

"Don't you tell him how to drive his car!" Amanda interjected protectively.

"For the record, Tex, I think your driving is amazing," Crow said, grinning. "I might ask you to teach me a few things."

"Well thank you kindly, little lady. When you get settled in, I'll show you a few tricks I've learned. Now if y'all will just sit back and enjoy the ride while I make this old girl get up and dance for yeh. We'll be at Psion in close to an hour."

"Psion?" James repeated questioningly.

"You'll see here soon," Hugo said with a smile.

The rest of their drive was quiet, albeit unsettling for the newcomers. Tex navigated through the populated streets as if he were the only one on the roads, and on multiple occasions it seemed like he timed it perfectly to just catch the changing of a light in his favor. It wasn't long before the city was left behind and they were barreling through the open Virginia hills. Amanda rolled some of the windows down, and they enjoyed the fresh open air. Around forty-five minutes into the drive, Hugo leaned forward and pointed out the window across from him.

"There it is. That's Psion."

Chapter 18: Settling In

  Sek, Crow, and James scrambled to the window while Amanda opened the sunroof to look out. All of their eyes grew wide at the vast estate that stretched out before them. It was the most expansive grounds any of them had ever seen, and that was saying something in Sek's case since his parents had quite ornate estates in London as well as various other countries. The tall fence that towered along the edges of the land was gorgeous. There were cameras every so many feet and clear security systems all along it, but for the most part it seemed completely serene out in the empty hills of Virginia. Inside its perimeter was beautiful green grass and lush foliage with trees and flowers growing freely. There was a long drive heading up the lawn to an enormous building rivaling the size of any castle and seemed to have been designed to resemble a decorated plantation house. Tex slowed his approach, giving them time to take it all in as he reached the front gate. A minute passed before the gates shakily jumped to life and slowly opened before them.

  Amanda perched herself on the roof of the car with her legs dangling in through the sunroof while the other three moved to get better views. There were dozens of people scattered across the lawn tending to various things. There were even some children playing happily, but they all seemed to stop at the sight of the limo. Well, most of them did. At that moment, all four heard a loud, excited scream from a child and turned to see where it came from. Off to the left about a hundred feet from the road was a small boy around ten years old, running as fast as his legs could take him, clothed solely in his underwear. His smile was wide, flashing his white teeth as his bare feet raced across the ground. As he ran, the group noticed small flares of fire trailing in the grass behind him. The boy's laughter rang out around him as he brushed the short brown locks from his face, and they noticed that while most his hair was short, there was a long tail of hair that ran from the back of his neck all the way to the middle of his dark-skinned back. His brown eyes were alight with flames, and he ran even faster. As he went, the tail of his hair seemed to catch as well and left fiery wisps in the air behind him. He threw his arms out to his sides. The next time he let out a call, it sounded like the screech of a bird. In an astounding display that none of the group had ever seen before, the boy jumped into the air mid-run and burst into flames before their eyes. The blaze rose further from the ground and quickly took the shape of a bird as his wings spread wide on either side and skimmed across the nearby treetops.

It was at this moment, the group noticed three adults running behind him.

"I said stay in the training circle!" the one leading the charge called loudly as he held his hands out before him. With each flick of the wrist, the man sent out a strange burst of mist that killed the fires dancing across the blades of grass. Though he seemed intent on keeping the damage minimal, there was a good-natured smile on his face.

"I'll get him. Such a free little spirit, isn't he?" The woman was buttoning a strange coat tightly around herself as she ran and then pulled on a pair of thick looking gloves to match the pants and boots she was already wearing. She finished by putting a protective mask over her face before suddenly taking flight herself and soaring after the child cawing back happily.

"Stay away from the trees, Thunderbird, you're going to set them all on fire again!" the third shouted quickly after dousing the singed trees with spouts of water.

Sure enough, the boy skimmed the tops of a few more, setting them alight, before the woman flying after him plucked him out of the air. She brought him to the ground gently and held him in a firm embrace while the third went to take care of the burning trees. The child reverted back into his human form still laughing and whooping in excitement.

"It seems like he's the same ball of energy he's always been," Hugo noted calmly. Crow looked back at him with an arched brow and he shrugged, "You'll see quite a few things like this especially when it comes to young kids who are just coming into their powers and learning the limits of everything that they can do. I have someone to introduce you to who will explain it much better than I could."

Crow bit the corner of her mouth and looked back out the window. Those who weren't watching the fiasco with the fire child were instead intently watching the limo as it slowly pulled closer to the enormous building at the center. She sat back in her seat and growled in displeasure, "My, aren't we popular already. Even a child bursting into flames isn't as interesting as the new meat riding in the limo."

"It ain't often we get new arrivals, and y'all gained a reputation facin' off with Legion and coming out mostly unscathed. Not many newbies coulda dun that," Tex advised.

"Indeed. You've outdone yourselves this time," Hugo said, eyeing Amanda intently.

"That's not my fault!" Amanda cried defensively as she dipped her head down through the sunroof.

"No, it was a combined effort on behalf of your group," Hugo replied calmly.

"Is that our Welcoming Committee?" James asked.

Everyone snapped their heads to the front of the building. A new figure stood at the entrance of the grand building. He was tall – about six-foot-four, likely in his late fifties, and dressed in a suit with creases so sharp it looked like it could cut straight through the metal of a car. His light brown hair was kept short in a military crew cut. Even through the suit, it was obvious that, he had the body of a twenty-year-old in pique condition. His muscles were subtle but nonetheless apparent, and his body language was that of a highly trained soldier. However, what that caught all of their focus was the pair of pitch-black sunglasses that wrapped around the sides of his temples that were so dark it was impossible to see his eyes behind them. He waited at the entrance with a relaxed smile.

"Yes, he is. He's the one who oversees this facility," Hugo answered.

The group looked between Hugo and back through the windows to stare at the new figure. Though they had not met in person yet, his presence even from afar was still enough to make all of them sure he was a force to be reckoned with.

It wasn't long before Tex stopped the limo in front of him, and Hugo was the first to step out. He gestured for the rest of the team to follow him.

Crow's instincts were telling her to get back on the road and run, but she glanced to Amanda and felt it get squashed. She didn't have the means to run anyway. She wouldn't have gotten far. Tex walked around the side of the car and walked up to the new figure with Hugo. Each was embraced warmly in welcome, and there was a brief exchange of words before he turned to look over each of the new arrivals. He smiled at Sek and James and gave a respectful nod to each of them. His eyes lingered on Crow for a few seconds and then even longer when he looked to Amanda. Nonetheless, he still kept the same smile on his face. His expression was masked by the dark lenses, but the girls knew there was something he wasn't sharing.

With a small shake of his head, he extended both of his arms out in welcome and said, "It's good to see you all made it here safe and sound. We've been expecting you. Welcome to Psion."

"Kids. I'm honored to introduce you all to John Ironhawk. He's head coordinator here at Psion and will be taking care of you while you're here. There's no one I would trust more," Hugo explained with a look of calm he hadn't had the whole time they were in Indiana. However, the team was not convinced.

"And what is Psion exactly?" Sek asked with a glance around.

"I'll be happy to explain, but before we go into it too much, perhaps we should make a stop at the infirmary. Once everyone's injuries are seen to, I will give you the grand tour of the place," Ironhawk replied, looking between James, Amanda, and Crow. James looked over his severe case of road rash, Amanda looked at her own bumps and bruises, and Crow gingerly reached up to her wrapped shoulder caked in her own dried blood. Sek stood off to the side very aware that he was the only one who did not need to be looked at and seemed quite satisfied.

"On that note, I must take my leave. You're in good hands. I'll be back after I handle some business at the office," Hugo said. He wrapped Amanda in his embrace and gave her a gentle pat on the head. She pouted slightly, but he whispered something that quickly put her in a better mood. He then gave the rest a reassuring look before walking back to the car. Tex tipped his hat and then held the door open for Hugo to get in.

Ironhawk opened the doors and gestured for them to follow him as he stepped inside. They exchanged a look before following on his heels. Once inside, they were struck with how magnificent it truly was. The entrance was massive and covered in beautiful décor and had large paintings of many people and battles. There were plaques under each, and members of the group each made separate mental notes to come back and look them over when they got the chance. From first glance, it was obvious there was more to them than met the eye.

"Psion is one of the many safe havens in America for parahumans like ourselves. We all have our abilities, and this is a safe place sanctioned by our government for us to live without being persecuted. In return for this arrangement, we attempt to keep the rest of the parahuman population within the United States peaceful. Our missions involve reigning in rampant misuse and abuse of abilities as well as protecting those who can't defend themselves, normal and parahuman alike," Ironhawk explained as he gestured around to the adorned walls. "We take in as many as we can and help teach discipline for those who have not yet mastered their powers. I'm sure you noticed the many training areas on our grounds. Inside, we have rooms for everyone, a large kitchen and dining hall to feed everyone here, and dozens of meeting rooms to plan for our missions. That's just what's above ground. Oh, and I can't forget the infirmary, which I will be taking you to now."

"So, there's a lot of people with abilities like us?" James asked wincing slightly as the sedatives were beginning to wear off. His torn flesh felt like it was catching fire beneath his clothes.

Ironhawk chuckled, "More than you can imagine. We may still be the minority, but more and more are discovered with each passing day. More are born every day to parahuman parents and those who had no idea any special abilities existed until they see them manifest in their children. The willing are rescued and brought here. This facility just broken over a hundred members before your arrival, and our sister facilities are growing as well, although ours is the largest as of now. There are many skilled trainers here that are meant to help gain control over one's abilities and hone raw potential."

After a few more turns, they entered a clean hall in smelling of antiseptic and medicine. Their host opened the door, and they stepped into a grand medical wing. It was immaculate, and Crow was reminded of the hospital where she worked alongside her father. There were rooms lining the sides of the hall with beds and IVs and monitoring stations. In the middle of all the rooms was a nurse's station, set up with books, tools, and various other things someone would need to handle minor medical procedures in a pinch. Crow found herself remembering working with her father in the hospital and conversing at stations just like that one. Her heart ached at the memory and she bowed her head.

There was an elderly woman standing at the nurse's station with two children hand-in-hand in front of her. Her skin was as dark as the night sky, and her eyes were focused on the two children before her. Her black hair was pinned up loosely, and she wore a multicolored scrub shirt. Despite her age, there was an air of energy about her that filled the room, and the new arrivals felt themselves relax as they drew closer to her. She had her hands on her hips in a motherly sort of fashion as she said, "Well, you can't fix it?"

The two children standing in front of her looked to be identical twins with matching shaggy brown hair and freckles lining their chubby cheeks. They had light brown eyes that almost looked gold and appeared to be a little younger than ten. They were dressed exactly the same and had the same scratch across their left cheek. In perfect unison, the two boys shook their heads and said, "We've tried! We really did!!"

Nurse sighed, and with a small smile and shake of her head she said, "This is the fourth time this week, Mito. I'll fix it this one last time, but next time you have to figure it out yourself. Fair?"

A smile spread across the boys' faces and they nodded excitedly, "OK!!"

Nurse clicked her tongue good-naturedly and held her hands out to place one on each of their heads. The boys closed their eyes, and after a moment their bodies almost shimmered in front of them. Then the boys started moving closer together. It took a minute for the group to realize that they were actually melding together, but soon they became one person with both of Nurse's hands on either side of his head. As soon as the process was finished, the shimmering receded and the scratch on his cheek was healed. He opened his eyes and smiled as Nurse looked him over.

"Better?"

"Uh-huh!!" he nodded emphatically.

"Alright, get on then! And remember next time you gotta fix it on ya own," Nurse said, patting him on the head, and he rushed out, running past Ironhawk and the group without paying them any attention.

Ironhawk cleared his throat to announce their presence and said, "Kids, I would like you to meet Nurse. Nurse, we have new recruits."

The old woman was on her feet with an agility that didn't match her age. Rolling up her sleeves, she shook her head and said, "It looks like our new recruits have already been initiated. Poor dears. Don't worry, though. This old woman has her uses still. Besides, this is usually the first stop for all the new people here. Now let me get a look at you babies and see what I can do."

She motioned for James, Amanda, and Crow to come over and took stock of their injuries. As she did so, another figure emerged from one of the rooms a few doors down. He was five-foot-three and his short, black hair was slicked back with shaping gel. There was a thin mustache on his upper lip, and his brown eyes were only a few shades lighter that his tanned, Latino skin. He too wore medical scrubs, however, his sleeves were rolled up and his shirt was slightly opened to reveal a white sleeveless shirt beneath it. He looked to be around his mid-twenties, and though he did not have a scrawny build, he was not nearly as muscled as Tex or Ironhawk. He was holding a medical book in front of him and glanced up when he heard Nurse talking. He glanced over James, Sek, and Ironhawk without much thought, but when his eyes fell on Crow and Amanda, he stopped dead in his tracks, dropping the book to the floor. There was a slight accent when he said, "Oh fuck me. Not them."

Nurse bristled. "Watch your mouth and hush child. And pick up that book while you're at it. I taught you better than that, and get back to your work. We need that paperwork done before the next orders get sent out."

"Y-Yes ma'am." He quickly scooped the book up from the floor and shuffled off into one of the rooms.

Nurse shook her head and looked back at them with a slight smile. "That's my boy, Medic. He came here an orphan, and I took him under my wing. Later I found out he had a talent for healing and taught him everything I could. He takes care of the night shift, and I take care of the day shift. Anyway, let me look over you babies," she gestured for them to step up.

While Amanda and James let her look them over, Crow lingered back, glancing around carefully. When Nurse turned her attention to her, Crow hesitantly lowered her hand from her shoulder so the elderly woman could see. Nurse made a small, thoughtful noise in the back of her throat and she stepped back.

"It looks like you've got enough medical know how that you stabilized yourself sweetie. So, I'll take care of your friends first, and then I'll take care of you."

Crow nodded while Nurse gestured for James to sit in the chair just behind the station. The woman looked over his injuries one more time before she extended her hands out and slowly began running them over him. James felt a slight discomfort at first, but soon enough his skin was healing beneath her touch like she was seaming it back together. After a few minutes, he felt renewed and was pain-free as she put the finishing touches to healing him. Nurse sat back with a smile and gestured for Amanda to take James's seat as he was walking back to stand with Ironhawk and Sek. Amanda sat down, kicking her feet back and forth in a nervous sort of way, and Nurse fussed at her not to fidget so much. In the same order, Amanda was healed and bouncing up to inspect the old woman's handiwork with a smirk. She looked to her older sister, and Crow grudgingly sat down where Nurse had the other two sit before her. The old woman carefully unwrapped the bandages Crow had put around her injury. Before she went to healing it, Nurse inspected the wound and sighed quietly.

"What?"

"Nothin' child. You did a good job on taking care of this wound by yourself. Especially not bein' able to stitch it closed."

"Oh, my dad taught me how to handle things. He was a doctor," Crow began, but trailed off weakly at the mention of her father.

Nurse ran her healing hands over her shoulder and the younger fighter just watched in interest. "This brings back memories," she chuckled under her breath as she glanced at Ironhawk with a smile.

"What do you mean?" Crow asked in confusion.

"Oh nothin', honey. Just an old woman talking to herself. There we go now. You're all taken care of. Don't be afraid to drop by any time if you get yourself banged up. Medic and I are more than happy to take care of you kids." Nurse stood up to give Ironhawk a firm embrace before she stepped back and looked at him saying, "You show these kids around now. There's way more exciting things for them to see than just this place."

James, Amanda, and Crow thanked her for taking care of them, and they followed Ironhawk as he led them out of the hospital area. As they walked, Ironhawk explained the intricacies of the facility. While many of the people residing within Psion were in their twenties or later, they worked very hard to find and take in as many orphans as they could who were cast out of various situations due to their abilities. They had classrooms and teachers educating them and trainers to teach them how to control their powers. There were dorm suites for everyone residing there, and they even had rooms set up for the four of them on the west wing of the building just above the infirmary. In the center of the building on the ground floor was an enormous mess hall, and above it were various meeting and conference rooms. Ironhawk even showed them his office, where he spent a lot of time working with the government and coordinating missions. It overlooked the entire front of the grounds and the training sites outside. The east wing had multiple conference rooms on the ground floor and above those were classrooms for the children and other teachings. There were other buildings on the grounds separate from the main one they found themselves in, and the group was told that they could explore those later at their leisure. Ironhawk smiled as they stood in the main hall again. "We are still growing and relatively small in the grand scheme of things, but we have a wide range of trainers and teachers that can assist you with any skill you could imagine – anything you need to help you grow and develop and any skills that would be useful on missions in the field."

"What kind of missions?" James asked.

"A little bit of everything, honestly: information gathering, rescuing parahumans that would be facing death otherwise, tracking down those that are causing trouble and abusing their abilities to terrorize the general populace. As it stands now, the existence of parahumans is a well-guarded secret that the government wants to keep mass panic at bay. When people can be more accepting of us and we can coexist with them without lording our powers over them, this will be a different story. Until then, we work for the government to keep the peace and have access to resources that many don't. The Senior Team handles the more dangerous and grander scale missions. The Junior Team handles missions that are no less important, but of a different caliber."

"So, while we're here, we're going to be the government's dogs," Crow muttered darkly.

Ironhawk fixed his gaze on her thoughtfully for a few moments before speaking again.

"We're sanctioned by the government. We're protected and given a place of safe haven. In return, we handle problem parahumans that they aren't equipped to handle. If you wish to view it as being their dogs, that's your prerogative, but realize, they have given us a chance to build a place for our kind in society and grow where we can be much more than fugitives. This is the road for us to be seen as ordinary people, just like the rest of the population," Ironhawk's tone was calm, but there was an unspoken message lying underneath it that Crow did not miss. This sudden change, no matter how slight, in his demeanor was enough to quell her rebellion and he went on to say, "I understand that this is a lot to take in for you all, and you haven't had time to process much of it. Why don't you each take an hour to yourselves, and we'll meet back after that in briefing room five?"

The four nodded in wordless agreement, and Ironhawk excused himself to leave them to their own devices. They could hear the playful screams of kids in the east wing of the building, and there were even the sounds of laughter from the mess hall.

Amanda glanced back to the dormitory area and wandered off without the rest realizing she was gone until she was already out of sight.

Sek was the second to split off from the group without a word, leaving James and Crow standing alone in the entrance hall. James sighed and ran his hand through his hair as he said, "Well, what should we do now?"

"I don't know about you, but I'm going to do some thinking and decide if I even want to stay here," Crow growled and promptly walked away to leave him alone.

James sighed, "She's just warm and fuzzy, isn't she?" He turned to the entrance and went out to sit on the front stairs to think.

Chapter 19: One Hour

    Amanda walked down the hall housing the living spaces for residents. Although she couldn't explain it, something was calling her to the hall where the Senior Team members lived; the strange thought in the back of her head didn't altogether make sense. As she walked down the hall looking at the doors with the various names written across them, something was nagging at her. She didn't understand why, but the names were ringing bells. She paused at each door, staring at the names as she passed. "Tex," "Eight-Millimeter," "Billy," "Ironhawk," and the names went on. She slowly paced the hall from one side to the other. She did this repeatedly. Back and forth. Back and forth. All the while she stared hard at each of the doors and the space between them. She walked along each side, tracing the walls between the doors with the tips of her fingers. When she grew tired of tracing the walls, she went down the sides of the hall rapping her knuckles on the walls in between the doors.

    There was one spot where she kept stopping. Every time she passed it, she would stop and stare at it. It was between Ironhawk's room and Billy's room. Ironhawk explained that each room was more like a grand suite, which explained why there was so much space between each door. However, between Ironhawk and Billy's rooms there was an abnormally large space that didn't make sense. Finally, she stopped walking and stood in front of it. She placed her hand against the wall, looking over it carefully. She couldn't explain why it was calling her back. She couldn't explain the nagging in the back of her head. After thirty minutes of this, she finally sat down in the middle of the hall and stared at the wall as though the answer would suddenly appear in the paint before her.

After sitting a while more, Amanda bounced back to her feet and pulled out a pocket knife. She flicked the blade out with her thumb and carefully inspected the wall one last time. After a few knocks with her knuckles, she held her arm out as far as it would extend and stood on her tiptoes as she buried the edge of her knife into the wall. With confidence and a steady hand, she drew a straight line horizontally into the wood. The first time wasn't pronounced enough, so she went over it again. And then one more time for good measure. Once she was satisfied, she carved two vertical lines down to the ground. Amanda went over these lines as well, and when she stood back to inspect her handiwork, there was a makeshift door carved into the wall matching where a door should have been following the pattern of the others in the hallway. She went over to the wall across from the door and sat down staring at it once again.

There was some memory trying to break through her consciousness. She wrinkled her brow in thought and turned the pocket knife over and over in her hand. She stuck her tongue out slightly between her teeth and tried to figure out why this one wall was causing so much discord in her mind.

Amanda didn't move. Not even when people walked by her. She remained still and fixated on that same wall.

Sek made his way down the halls of the various suites and dorms. As he went, he checked the doors to see if any were open. He could use his powers to open the doors if he really wanted to, but he could be more intrusive later if needed. In the meantime, he would focus on those who were a little more trusting. Sek noticed Amanda but realized she was too far in her own thoughts to even notice him there, so he continued and finally found an open door with the name Eight-Millimeter written across the middle of it. Sek glanced back and forth to make sure no one was watching before slipping into the room and silently shutting the door behind him.

No one was inside the suite, and there was a shudder that shook his spine at the disarray the room was in. There were piles and piles of cases holding DVDs and various other storage devices marked with dates and different locations. Some were clearly in different countries and some went as far back as the early eighties. But none of that interested Sek. Instead, he inspected the room and carefully began searching through places that were common to hide things. His first place to look was under the bed and he was not surprised to see a small chest looking box sitting there. Sek slid it out carefully and flipped it open. Just a stash of porn – both magazines and DVD's. He flicked it shut and pushed it back under the bed in one fluid motion. Sek then stood, and while pouring a generous amount of hand-sanitizer on his hands, walked over to the closet.

It was just as cluttered as the rest of the room and still full of more DVDs and various surveillance devices. He moved these things out of his way and came to stacks of containers and boxes. As he sifted through, Sek only found more DVDs. But when he stood to search the top shelf, he noticed a container similar to what his grandmother stored baked goods in. He took it from the shelf and lifted the lid to be met with a familiar smell. A satisfied smirk crept along his face as he realized that he just discovered Eight Millimeter's stash of pot brownies. He set this container on the bed and replaced everything where he found it. Then he took the container of brownies and left to go enjoy his newfound stash.

James sighed as he sat down on the front steps of Psion and looked out over the grounds. Business there had gone back to what he assumed was normal, and the residents were focusing on other things. He could see one woman tending the flowers of a nearby garden to his left and, to his right were two men sparring with each other in some form of martial art he had never seen before. The child who had burst into flames had been reined in by his trainers and was now playing with a group of other children with a soccer ball. Everything seemed so peaceful and so routine. It was the complete opposite of what his world had become over the last few days.

As he thought over the events leading him to where he sat now, he couldn't keep the questions at bay anymore. How had his fathers been captured in the first place? Why had Legion singled them out, and why hadn't he attacked James before the convention center? Speaking of the convention center, how were the others handling everything? What would his rag tag team do now? What kept them together? How would they work together?

Sek was far too focused on himself to care about anyone else, but he had amazing control over all things metal. Amanda seemed out in a world of her own that no one quite understood, but the bolts of energy she could shoot were no doubt powerful. Crow was cold and almost robotic unless it dealt with anything involving Amanda, but she had astounding control over lightning and electricity. Then there was him. If he was being honest with himself, he wasn't sure there was anything he could offer to the group. The most he could do was take images from pictures and make them real so long as he wasn't knocked out in the process. If there were no images for him to pull from, he was practically useless aside from the few things he had picked up being the son of two decorated military men. All of them were so strange, and as it stood, he wasn't sure they would stay a team for very long.

A shuffling sound ahead of James drew him from his thoughts, and he looked up to see Tex slowing to a stop. The old Texan smiled and tipped his hat.

"Well hello there, young'un. Where's yer team at?"

"I don't know," James sighed with a shrug. "Ironhawk gave us an hour to process everything, and they all split up the second he walked away."

"They left ya on yer own, eh?" Tex asked as he sat down beside him.

He fixed his gaze on James, and there was so much warmth in his expression and the way he held himself that James relaxed somewhat. Everyone he had met up to this point, new teammates included, were so bizarre and Tex was the first one that seemed even remotely normal.

"Basically."

"Don't take it personal, kid. Don't let it get to ya. You kids have been through a lot, each of ya. Most your age wouldn't be able to take on someone like Legion, but you did, and you left with a bang. Yer teammates have a lot to take in, and no team starts out smooth and happy. Lord knows ours didn't. What makes a team is workin' together despite your conflicts and takin' care of each other. Just give it some time. Each of you have yer own demons to fight, but you kids will get there. I know that for a fact."

James shook his head. "Can we even be considered a team?"

Tex laughed, "Oh trust me, James. Ya'll a team, alright."

James shrugged and looked back over the grounds. He wasn't entirely sure that they would stand up to Tex's trust in them, but then again, it seemed like he was speaking from experience. He glanced over at him to see that he was smiling. Tex clapped the youngster across the back once again with a strong hand. James coughed as the sudden powerful force, and Tex laughed. Then he leaned back on the stairs and started to explain to James the various things going on around Psion.

Crow took her time walking the grounds. She spent some time at the gates, looking down the road they had come from. She faintly wished she had her father's car so she could drive and feel the wind through her hair. She wanted to forget what happened in Indiana. She wanted to be back on the road. She wanted to keep running. At least then she could move when her thoughts caught up with her. The only thing that kept her confined behind those fences and inside those grounds was that Amanda was still there. She wouldn't leave her. Not after finally getting her back. So, she stayed.

The building made her uncomfortable. She couldn't explain it, but the fact that she knew it was full of people like her, parahumans, made her feel strange. It was safe to show her true self around them. None of them would freak out, but she was faintly concerned as to what abilities others had. What could Ironhawk do? What could the Senior Team do?

She walked the grounds and saw others out using their powers like it was normal. She even witnessed a woman bring flowers back to life that a crying child had accidentally crushed. As she continued her walk, she noticed some places where there were large circles drawn along the ground, and while an older looking person stood watching, younger people stood in the center of those circles seeming to be practicing. Crow watched a few and saw that in some places they were trying to do accomplish certain goals with their powers and in others, they were trying to imitate the amazing feats the elder showed them.

Though she was intrigued, she continued walking. As it was, she wasn't up to interacting with anyone just yet and was doing her best to avoid it. She waited until she found a circle away from everyone else and slowly walked up to it. Just standing along the edge of it, she held her hand out in front of her and allowed lightning to surge through her fingertips. She played with the currents and caused them to spark out with simple flexes of her energy. Satisfied that her powers were working at full capacity, she stepped into the circle and felt something come over her. Holding her hands out in front of her, Crow focused on all the energy in her body, but no matter how hard she tried she couldn't get the smallest spark to manifest. This went on for several minutes, and she stared at her hands. Crow then slowly stepped just outside of the circle and flicked her wrist sending a controlled burst out to her left. Wrinkling her nose and inspecting the circle on the ground closer, Crow muttered, "Well that's interesting."

"Extremely useful too. Especially for teaching and making sure no one gets hurt while people are trying to get the hang of their powers. It gives many the chance to learn to control themselves and the abilities they have," a voice spoke out from behind her.

Crow jumped in surprise. She spun around tense and saw a thin man who looked like he had come out of a western movie. There was a red bandana loosely tied around his neck and his old, dusty coat had a few big pockets along the sides. His jeans were worn but still in good shape, and his boots had a certain shine. He had thin, long, brown and gray hair that fell around his face, and Crow immediately noticed the older style guns in holsters on either side of his hips. He looked to be in his mid-sixties, but his stride was that of a confident younger man ready to take on the world. Crow stepped away from the circle quickly, and he laughed.

"Don't act like I caught you doing something wrong, now. It's ok to be curious, but let me introduce myself. The name's Henry McCarty."

Crow stopped and tilted her head to the side, "McCarty…that sounds familiar."

"Perhaps you know me by the other name I went by: William H. Bonney."

"That's ringing a few more bells," Crow said slowly as her brow furrowed in concentration. She swore she had heard that name before, but couldn't place where.

"My friends call me Billy, though," he said with a small smile.

"Nice to meet you," Crow said thoughtfully and bowed in traditional Japanese fashion. As she straightened up, she eyed him carefully and said, "My name is Crow. Are you one of the trainers here?"

"I sure am. I show people here how to shoot the enemy instead of their own feet. See those targets over there?" Billy indicated just over her shoulder. When she turned around, Crow caught sight of the targets. He pulled one of his guns from his hip and leveled it with one of the targets. With the gun out of the holster,

Crow was able to see that it was indeed a very old style of pistol. In fact, it looked so old that it stood to reason that it shouldn't work anymore, but when he fired his trained shot, the bullet whistled as it soared out of the barrel of the gun. The target burst into pieces all over the ground. She flinched at the sound of the destruction and watched with wide eyes as he returned the gun to its holster.

He grinned back at her stunned look and said, "Like I said, my specialty is handling guns and these beauties are my treasures. However, I am good with all types of guns. Happy to teach anyone who's willing to learn."

"Are...you..." Crow trailed off, not sure if she should finish her thought. His display brought a historical figure to mind, but realistically it couldn't have been. "Are you THE Billy the Kid?"

He just grinned as he said, "That I am. Now some stories you have heard may have been slightly exaggerated for dramatic effect. Anyway, I'm not as young as I used to be, but I still haven't met anyone who handles a gun like me."

"You can't be. Age wise that would make you..." Crow trailed off and stared at him warily.

"Now that is something you'll learn about in time. Trust me," he chuckled with a wink.

"A-Are all the circles power neutralizers?" Crow, asked changing the subject.

"To a degree. Each circle is keyed to a specific trainer. They respond to the trainer who can, more or less, allow power to flow within it. We are able to monitor whoever is inside and give them more power as they are ready to control it," Billy explained as he walked into the middle of the circle. Crow noticed the outline grow bolder and more defined before going plain once again. She looked back as Billy said, "All of us on the Senior Team have these. Some are better suited inside while some us of need a wider range. And some aren't even in circles like this one is. Some are as large as football fields and some are contained to multiple rooms."

At that moment, a car entered the front gates. Both looked up to see a long black limo coming up the drive, and as it drew closer, Crow distinctly saw foreign dignitary flags flying on the sides of the hood. Crow watched as it pulled up to the front stairs. After stopping, an older Japanese man stepped out of the driver's seat. He was dressed in a nice suit and walked back to the passenger side of the vehicle. Crow moved to get a better view as he opened the door and watched as an unusually tall Japanese man stepped out. His expression was just as impressive and sharp as the angles of his face. His eyes were dark and seemed to stare holes in whatever he saw as he looked about the grounds. He wore a mixture of an expensive business suit and a high quality Ninjutsu Gi. Over top the suit, he wore a long coat decorated with an ornate Japanese dragon spiraling across the back. Chills raced down her spine as his piercing gaze fell on her, and she found herself locked in place only able to stare back at the intimidating man. The world seemed to freeze as every nerve in her body tensed at the look in his eyes. Crow knew beyond the shadow of a doubt this was the Japanese Ambassador she had spoken to Hugo about.

He broke eye contact, and the world crept back into motion. He shared a few words with his driver and then spun around to ascend the stairs with his long coat flaring out around him as he walked. Someone at the door ushered him inside.

Crow crossed her arms tightly over her chest as she muttered, "I assume that would be the Japanese Ambassador?"

"Yep. That would be Saiato Nakamura. He and Ironhawk will be meeting with your group here soon."

"Wonder what would happen if I just didn't show up," Crow mused as she glanced to the entrance of the compound grounds. She was faintly debating on leaving and going back on the run, but her concern for Amanda kept coming back. She doubted that she would even make it out the front gate.

"Listen sweetheart. I know you're not exactly thrilled to be here, but maybe you should at least give it a chance. Go to the meeting, and don't make them wait. It's hard to get Ironhawk angry, but it's not wise to try," Billy advised with a reassuring hand on her shoulder.

Crow stiffened at the contact but sighed and tried to shake her nerves. She couldn't understand what it was, but she sensed an unspoken challenge in the ambassador's eyes when she looked at him.

Chapter 20: Junior Team

    Tex stood and held his hand out to James to help him up. As they walked into the building, Tex reassured him that things would eventually work themselves out if he just gave it time. He led James to the room, clapped him across the back, and whispered, "You kids have a lot of potential. You included, son. Don't sell yerself short. You'll come into yer own in time." He tipped his hat and took his leave.

    James felt a little better as he stepped in and saw Ironhawk greeting him with a warm smile, but they were not alone. Standing beside him was a tall, intimidating Japanese man who inspected James coldly for a moment before looking back to Ironhawk disinterested. He was clean-shaven, and the look in his eyes seemed to wound well enough without weapons. His expression was an unfathomable mask. He adjusted his expensive suit beneath the flowing coat and smoothed the wrinkles on his sleeves.

    "Go ahead and sit down James. When the rest of your team gets here, we'll begin," Ironhawk advised, gesturing to any of the seats at the long table.

    James chose a seat near the middle and looked around. There wasn't much other than a screen pulled down on the wall behind the two older men, and sitting on the table in front of the Japanese man was a suitcase open to reveal files and papers. James had a sneaking suspicion that his team wasn't going to like what they had to say.

Sek was the second to arrive, and he plopped down in the chair across from James to prop his feet up on the chair next to him. He calmly finished off a brownie and glanced over at his friend with a satisfied smirk. Just by looking at him it was clear that he was high and not paying any attention to the second man standing beside Ironhawk. His condition did not go unnoticed by the older men, and while Ironhawk shook his head with a slight smirk, the Japanese man stared down his nose at him. Sek, however, didn't seem to care.

Five more minutes passed, and Amanda appeared in the doorway. She was lost in thought, and she came to a stop at the closest chair to the door. Leaning back and kicking her feet up on the table, Amanda glanced from Ironhawk to stare down the inscrutable man standing next to him. He looked at her with disinterest, and she stared back at him, daring him to say something to her. This stare down went on for another ten minutes until the Japanese man decided he was tired of waiting. He cleared his throat and turned to Ironhawk saying, "We are waiting on one more, am I correct?"

"Yes, we're waiting on Crow," Ironhawk sighed. "Do you know where she is, Amanda?" The tone of his voice sounded slightly annoyed and yet not surprised in the slightest.

Amanda shrugged, "I'm not her keeper."

"She's your sister, right? Aren't you two supposed to be inseparable?" Sek asked.

"What do you want me to do? Crawl up her ass and go with her everywhere she goes?"

"That won't be necessary. I'm here."

James jumped in his seat. Everyone turned their attention to the door and found Crow leaning against the wall just inside the room with her arms crossed tightly over her chest. It was like she had appeared out of thin air. Like the mere mention of her name had summoned her.

Crow's dark eyes were focused on the Japanese Ambassador, and he returned her stare with just as much intensity.

"Now that everyone is here, we can begin. Usually, we would give you kids a few days to get used to how everything works around here. But unfortunately time is of the essence, and we don't have that luxury. Thanks to our friend Saiato Nakamura, we've been alerted to a plot that's too close to home and would be a good chance for you, as the new junior team, to sink your teeth into," Ironhawk explained.

"When did we become the new junior team, exactly?" Sek asked, raising his hand.

"Don't you remember? That's the fine print on the welcome package. To live in a government sanctioned building and be protected and taken care of, we have to be their lap dogs," Crow said.

"Oh, carry on then," Sek advised as he leaned back in the chair.

Ironhawk sighed and pinched the bridge of his nose, pushing his sunglasses up slightly. Meanwhile, the ambassador eyed Crow with something akin to interest and a hint of amusement.

"Let me start with your individual qualifications," Ironhawk said in a flat monotone. "We have been watching you four for quite a long time. Sek, you are a superb swordsman and two-time national Kendo champion in your age division. You also possess a brilliant scientific mind and a quick wit. Even though you hide it behind a constant stream of sarcasm and self-servitude, you have a general desire to see that the right thing is done, as is evidenced by the many campus reports listing you as the good Samaritan. All of which occurred before the incident which endowed you your powers." Ironhawk paused. "James. Even though you have a tendency for self-doubt and seem to question your talents needlessly, you have developed a high-level command of your abilities faster than most. And since I knew your fathers, I am well aware of what they taught you."

"What do you know about my fathers and me?" James demanded.

"I know they taught you academy graduate level tactics and stratagem – both individual and unit-based. I know they taught you hand to hand combat, at which you excelled. And I know they were fiercely proud of your accomplishments and loyalty to those you care about. "

"How do you know what they taught me?" James asked curiously.

"Because they charted your progress closely and used the records to keep the courts from committing you to an asylum against their will. As I said, they were fiercely proud of you and would have fought for your best interests."

James offered him a tight smile and nodded his head for Ironhawk to continue.

"Crow," he said as he turned his mirrored gaze to her. "Youngest female ever to achieve black belt in traditional Ninjutsu. Youngest female to ever win the international title in your age division. You also demonstrated your cunning and survival skills while you were on the run. If this weren't enough, your medical knowledge makes you even more of an asset."

Crow glared back, but kept silent, unsure how to react to the praise wrapped in such a punishing tone. This response caused Ironhawk to smirk slightly, and even Nakamura seemed amused by it.

"And finally, Amanda – " Ironhawk stopped short, realizing the girl had gotten up from her seat while he was speaking and seemed to be rearranging books and knick-knacks in the meeting room.

She turned around. "Yeah, what about me? I want to hear! And someone messed up the decor in here, nothing is where it should be. Fire the maid."

"I am very familiar with the training you have received. That's all that need be said."

"No, you see that's not how this works," Sek interjected. "You just waved our knickers about for everyone else to see, and she gets a pass? I call foul."

"The point is," Ironhawk continued as he pointedly ignored Sek's complaint, "The four of you are highly skilled and highly trained for your age. You lack field experience, but you more than make up for it in ability. Not to mention your natural abilities to use chaotic situations to your own advantage."

James leaned forward on his elbows and addressed Ironhawk with a contemplative look, "We get it, you feel all of us have the skills. But since the whole point of this place is to train people like us, why don't you have some of your students make up junior team? For that matter, why don't you and senior team do the mission? And what makes you think we can even work together as a team? What if last night was a fluke?"

"All valid points Mr. Vinci," Ironhawk responded. "So, let me address them. First, our people pulled all of the police camera, security camera, ATM video, and every other video of last night's battle. We spent the entire morning studying it. You four mesh like a well-oiled machine. That type of squad work normally takes years to build, and you four had it in moments. That is no fluke. Second, even after years of training, none of our residents other than senior team are ready for combat. I doubt they would have survived last night. And finally, the window of operations for this mission is only hours long; indeed, we are wasting time already, and as soon as junior team is deployed, senior team is flying out west to face down a Class 1 Parahuman threat."

"A what?" Amanda asked with a sarcastic tone as she plopped back into her seat, seemingly satisfied with the changes she had made around the room.

Ironhawk stared at the things she had moved with a small, surprised smirk at the corner of his mouth. "A parahuman whose powers endanger the entire state he is tearing apart. Our local agents are barely keeping the media blackout intact, and we have lost contact with two of them already. So, if there are no further questions about our decision-making abilities, can we continue before more lives are lost?" Ironhawk inquired pointedly.

"You're the one that felt the need to explain yourself mate, I told you to go on five minutes ago," Sek said nonchalantly.

"Anyway, kids, as I said, our friend here, the Japanese Ambassador Saiato Nakamura, discovered this vital information, and without it, who knows how long this would've gone before we found out," Ironhawk said gesturing for his friend to finally speak. Nakamura bowed in traditional Japanese fashion and cleared his throat. "It is an honor to meet you all. James Vinci. Amanda Wilson. Arthur Seckel, Ren Yoshida. Your reputation precedes you."

"My name is Crow." She responded icily.

"My apologies. Ms. Crow," he amended, "I'm well aware of what transpired in Indianapolis. In fact, your group left quite an impression on the city before you departed."

"What do you mean?" James asked in confusion.

Ironhawk reached down to the table in front of him and held up a newspaper so they could read the headline: ARMORED CAR GANG LEADS IMPD IN HIGH-SPEED CHASE. There was a grainy picture of a large armored car speeding along the road with three police cars running red lights and sirens behind it. He flipped open the paper and read the article aloud, "In the late hours of the night, the Armored Car Gang broke into the convention center, and after destroying a semi-trailer filled with heirlooms to the Yoshida estate, led the police on a dangerous chase through downtown Indianapolis. IMPD followed but was forced to call off the pursuit after seven police cars were put out of commission and speeds exceeded well over eighty miles per hour down Washington Street. At this time, there are no leads, and authorities are still looking for the getaway vehicle. Any information on the four unknown subjects is welcome to the IMPD tip line."

Crow bowed her head in an attempt to hide her smile and shook her head. Amanda openly grinned and leaned back in her chair proudly. James hid behind his hands. Sek only shrugged and replied, "Well, at least we made an impression. Judging by the shit quality of that photo, they won't be able to link anything back to us."

"Be that as it may, in the future your team may benefit from a lesson in subtly," Ironhawk advised.

Amanda rolled her eyes. "That's not our fault. Besides, we didn't hurt any of the cops that followed us, and we wouldn't have had to do that if that asshole Legion hadn't brought a bunch of his freaky guys to fight us. What were we supposed to do? Trying to fight them wasn't a good idea. They threw Charles at us in pieces for it! Pieces!"

James shuddered at the memory. Crow's smile was stricken from her face.

"Charles was one of us for a very long time," Ironhawk said, shaking his head. "He was what we called a Spotter. He was able to see parahumans and was one of our recruiters. There are many here that he single-handedly saved from bad situations. His death is a terrible loss, but knowing Charles, he was proud to go down in a fight protecting young talent like you kids."

Amanda remembered how he would take care of her until Hugo was able to pick her up. James remembered how caring he was when he reassured him that he was important and had so much to offer. Crow remembered how he always reached out and tried to make her keep smiling when that was the last thing she wanted to do. Sek silently thanked him for getting him away from the dog walker and his minions.

"I have a question, Ironhawk…"

"Yes, Crow?"

"When we were running, we did everything we could not to harm any of the officers, but at one point we heard one of the officers being attacked by the Faceless over the radio. It was too far back, and it happened too fast for us to be able to do anything. Do you know what happened?" Crow spoke almost timidly. The change in her demeanor drew Nakamura's tapered interest.

Ironhawk's expression became somber and he took a breath before saying, "The officer you are referring to was killed by the Faceless. It punched straight through his chest and then was shot down in a hail of fire from his fellow officers. The department is still trying to decide how they will explain his death. From what I have heard, it will be explained to the media that the Armored Car Gang and another gang and one of the many motorcycle gangs in the area got into a turf war, which in some way involved the items from the auction, and the poor officer was killed in the line of duty protecting his city. From everything I have seen, though, he will be buried a hero."

The group went quiet again, and Ironhawk gave them a moment to absorb what he had said.

"Damn, Legion! That twisted asshole is gonna pay! For Charles, that police officer, and everyone else he's hurt!" Amanda exclaimed.

"Yeah," James said, and both Sek and Crow nodded in agreement.

"Charles was a good man," Nakamura said. "He was honorable and reliable in battle. We have found an opportunity to strike back at Legion. I have reports and reliable intel that one of his facilities for making the Faceless is here in Washington D.C. Your team will infiltrate it and bring back the artifact he's using to keep the base running without him there."

The screen on the back wall came to life behind him, showing pictures of two people. Nakamura glanced down at the suitcase that was sitting on the table and made sure that all of the documents he had brought were intact. Then he turned, and with a flick of his wrist, the various reports and papers spread out along the table for the group to see.

Crow slowly approached and looked over Amanda's shoulder to see a map with their target location circled in red.

"Forgive my rudeness, but how do we know we can trust you?" she asked, meeting Nakamura's gaze. "After all, that mess of an auction in Indiana was held under your name and title. Now you conveniently have information on one of Legion's bases? What guarantee do we have that you're not a part of his plan? You could be marching us right back to his grasp and using your reputation with Ironhawk to get him to go along with it."

"I can appreciate your position," Nakamura replied. "Your group was thrown into a fight against people the likes of which none of you even knew existed. Legion planned for you meticulously. Especially for you, Ms. Crow. He wanted to make the auction irresistible to you. What better way to do so than having a Japanese Ambassador, a man of status and title, put up an unknown estate belonging to a well-known Japanese family? Our enemy is no fool, but I promise you I had nothing to do with that auction."

Ironhawk cleared his throat and added, "Besides, this would not be the first time Legion has used our names in his schemes. After all, he once was a trusted friend and knows us well."

"With friends like that, how do you sleep at night?" Crow muttered darkly.

"Quite well, actually. Legion is formidable, to be sure, but he would not dare assault Psion. That would be a fight he would not fare well from," Ironhawk responded.

"If I may continue," Nakamura said, looking at Crow. She stared back in defiance but didn't say another word. Satisfied, he went on, "It has been through the great effort of many agencies working together to find out everything we possibly could of Legion's many labs in dozens of countries across the globe. We have discovered one close to home and the two men he has hired to stand guard over it."

"It's a popular hamburger restaurant in the middle of D.C.: The All American Burger, a place that I myself have frequented," Ironhawk said. "It's owned by an old Korean war veteran and his wife. It's unknown at this time if the owner is actively a part of Legion's schemes or an unwitting pawn, but your team will be tasked to infiltrate the business and destroy Legion's base.

"In a few of our reports, it's mentioned that the only way into the base itself is by means of teleportation. If this is true, it explains the hired mercenaries he has guarding the place," Ironhawk explained. On the screen behind him, there were mug shots of two men and beneath them reports and listings of various charges filed against them. "These are the Bayou Brothers: Porter and Gator. They don't care about doing dirty work for people so long as they pay the right price. They have an extensive rap sheet ranging from violent assaults, murders, robberies, and violent acts against children. What makes them valuable to Legion is that they're both parahumans with control over teleportation. Porter is able to teleport himself within certain limits, and Gator makes teleportation gates which he can step through or allow others to step through."

"Once you have gotten into the base, you will need to retrieve the artifact that runs the lab while Legion is not there and bring it back to us," Nakamura said as he reached down and placed a large, square case on the table in front of him. It seemed to be military grade with a high-tech locking mechanism and a protective lining that would effectively seal the contents inside from the outside world completely. "It is imperative that you recover the artifact first and then destroy the base. Bring it back at all costs."

"Two questions," James said. "One, what does this artifact look like? Two, I don't mean to offend you, but why exactly are you trusting us with this? We've only been here an hour, and this seems like a pretty important mission."

"You will know the artifact when you see it. As for trusting your team, I have asked the same thing," Nakamura responded coldly.

"As I've said before, it takes talent to face off against someone like Legion and his Faceless," Ironhawk explained, looking at the team and Nakamura pointedly. "You kids not only faced him and got away, but you foiled one of his highly calculated plots. That's quite a feat and makes your team a prime choice for handling this mission." He smiled. "Each of you possesses skills and abilities that have proven to be powerful assets. Psion wants you to join us in making a place for our kind in this world. We want you to join as part of your Birthright."

"Birthright?" Amanda's eyes widened in wonder. "Is that like some inheritance thing? Do I get money from some dead uncle I don't know about?"

Ironhawk sighed and shook his head; a small vein pulsated in his left temple, "Not quite."

"I never get free money," Amanda deflated as she pouted slightly.

"Let me tell you a little story: There was a time in history when parahumans were rounded up and imprisoned simply for being who they are. They were experimented on and treated as though they were lab rats because they had abilities the rest of the population did not. There came a time when the prisoners banded together to make their escape, and once they were out, they did not want anyone to suffer as they had. They started a movement that eventually grew into organizations such as Psion. These great parahumans decided that it was their Birthright, as people born with such fantastic abilities, to create a world where humans and parahumans can coexist in peace. That is part of your Birthright and why we extend this chance to you as those who came before did for us,"

The four were quiet. While it was no surprise to any of them at this point that they had been watched for some time, it was almost disturbing that these people were so sure of their capabilities and even more their moralities. What was more astonishing was how many people seemed to have abilities and kept them hidden from the general populace. While it was such a common thought that art since the dawn of time depicted it, the reality of it was ludicrous.

"Fine. Let's go kick some ass and piss this guy off," Amanda said, breaking the silence.

"Might as well for now anyway," Sek shrugged.

"We are here, and you guys are taking us in. Seems fair," James conceded.

Everyone looked to Crow. She sighed, "Fine."

"Good. You will leave in a few hours," Ironhawk said.

Crow snorted. "We don't even get a day to settle in?"

"Strike while the iron is hot," Nakamura said.

"Precisely," Ironhawk agreed. "Not to mention the possibility that Legion could realize we have found out about this base and attempt to clean it out before we can get to it if we wait. You kids were far more cunning than he initially planned for, and he will not make that mistake a second time."

"So, what's our plan?" James asked.

"That's for you kids to figure out. Also, there will be a new addition to your team for this mission as well. One of our non-combatant agents will be accompanying you for information gathering purposes," Ironhawk said.

"So, we're babysitting while running headfirst into danger. That's fun," Amanda said.

"That is the way it is done. Our team has gone into far more dangerous situations than this with multiple non-combatants for every combatant. If you are unable to handle those conditions and bring your team back safely, then you are not fit to be an agent of Psion, junior or otherwise," Nakamura growled.

Crow bristled at his accusation and leaned over the table with lightning sparking through the ends of her hair. "I never said I was an agent of Psion, and if I'm not mistaken, you are the one who needs us to get your artifact back for you, not the other way around."

"I question your fitness to even join Psion," Nakamura replied. "Your attitude is likely to get not only yourself killed but your teammates as well. However, we have little choice in the matter, and you are who we have."

"I would never put my team in danger, and I would be more than happy to show you just what this attitude is good for, Ambassador," Crow hissed.

"Okay, okay, okay. Cool it, Crow!" Amanda snapped. Crow withdrew, biting her tongue and taking her lightning with her. Amanda turned her attention to Ironhawk, "We already said we're gonna do it. We don't need him being a dick about it!"

Ironhawk placed a hand on Nakamura's shoulder. Crow stepped behind Amanda and was biting the inside of her cheek so hard she drew blood.

Ironhawk turned back to the group and then looked up to the door with a smile. He gestured to the doorway behind them and said, "You kids are more than qualified and capable of handling this mission. Now, it looks like your fifth has just arrived."

Chapter 21: Equipment in R&D

The four turned to their attention to the new figure standing in the doorway. He was just a bit scrawnier and only a few inches taller than Sek. His short, black hair flared wildly around his face, and his pale, gray eyes seem magnified by the coke bottle glasses he wore. As he blinked, there was a strange flutter that went through his eyes, but it stopped once he had looked each of them over. He pushed his glasses further up the bridge of his nose and adjusted the oversized military jacket he was wearing. He wore a plain black shirt under it and blue jeans, but the shoes he wore were custom tailored and looked fairly expensive. After clearing his throat skittishly, he looked back to Ironhawk and said, "I'm not late, am I?"

"No, you're right on time," Ironhawk said. "I would like you all to meet Shutters. He's part of research and will be the mission's Intel officer. Shutters, why don't you take them down to research and development to get their equipment? Then you can come back up here and set your strategy."

"Uh sure. Whenever you guys are ready, I'll show you the way," Shutters said, shrugging.

James, Sek, and Amanda looked between each other to see who would take the lead. Crow sighed and was the first to walk over to the new arrival. Sek wordlessly followed, and James thanked

Ironhawk before he followed suit. Amanda was the last one to stand and left when the others had already stepped out of the conference room. She strolled out at her own pace and then doubled back to lean against the wall just beside the door while the rest of her team continued.

"They are an interesting group of children, my friend, but they are still just children. I'm not sure how they will handle being a part of all this," Nakamura mused.

"They have great potential. They remind me of us when we were young and impetuous. Back when we thought we knew best. Although I must admit, you were strangely harsh on Crow, even for you," Ironhawk said.

Nakamura scoffed, "That child fancies herself a ninja, but she lacks the necessary discipline, sense of self, and wisdom. She has much to learn, and I will not coddle such an impudent girl."

"They all have a lot to learn, but then again so did we," Ironhawk replied.

Amanda decided it was time to leave before she fully lost track of the others or was caught. She left and found the team without much effort. They hadn't even noticed her disappearance. She slid back into place behind them just in time to hear James ask Shutters, "So how many missions have you been on?"

"Well, actually, this will be my second time in the field," he answered.

"So, you're as green as us. Isn't that nice," Sek noted with a sigh.

"We'll be fine. We took on Legion after all," Crow muttered absently as she looked down the various halls they were walking past.

Amanda arched her eyebrow but didn't say anything.

"At least you're confident. It's highly unusual for a team to be made official and then sent out on a mission the same day. You guys must be serious business." Shutters looked between each of them expectantly.

"So, what are your abilities?" James inquired curiously.

Shutters grinned. "I'll show you when we get our equipment."

A few more turns in the halls and they arrived at the elevator to the basements of the facility. Shutters explained that there were five levels below the enormous building. The first level was research and development, which also happened to double as the armory. Most of the scientists preferred to stay on the first level, and Shutters warned some were very particular on how things were done and could have unique personalities. The second level was the prison where criminal parahumans were kept. Shutters quickly assured them they only had a few people there, and that they weren't overly dangerous. The third level was the storage part of the facility. There were dozens and dozens of units filled with things from people who had come and gone from the facility as well as other things. The fourth level was the underground cave system discovered when Psion was being put together, and below that was a top-secret level only senior team knew anything about.

Sek was curious as to what they would find in the research and development. Amanda was curious about the cave systems and what could be found there. James wondered just what kind of people were kept in the prison block. Crow was more focused on her altercation with the Japanese Ambassador and proving that he was a fool to assume anything about her.

Shutters pressed the button to take them to research and development, and the elevator jumped to life. When the doors opened again, and they stepped out, the junior team was met with quite a sight. The halls were white and brightly lit. The level was lined with rooms all along both sides. There were laboratories where developers could experiment and build things and storage rooms in which their creations had been placed.

Shutters let them stare and gawk at the various inventions as he walked straight back to a large room at the far end of the hall with brightly flashing lights. He shared a quick word with the occupant before the rest of the group caught up to him, and he gestured them inside with a smile.

The group stepped into the room. Massive computer towers and wires ran along the back wall. Large monitors took up the entire wall were full of information, some of which the group couldn't even begin to decipher. They could hear the electricity coursing through the room.

Junior team heard a furious tapping of keys on a keyboard and quick clicks of a computer mouse. Astoundingly, the entire set up was manned by a single person who was sitting in a chair at the center of it all with one keyboard and one mouse in front of him.

He spoke in a slightly aggravated Indian accent. "Well? Are you going to tell me what you need or are you just going to stand there slack-jawed and silent?"

"Everyone, this is Mainframe, a computer genius and one of the best hackers in the world. He handles all of our digital security needs. He also works closely with the head of our research and development teams, the world-famous scientist Johnson Stone, to help design and create everything you saw in the rooms we passed. With the two of them working together, our R&D division is top notch. Although, he doesn't get out much." Shutters introduced them with a sheepish smile.

Mainframe spun around in his chair to face the team. His skin was dark, and his black eyes focused on each of them in turn. He wore a long-sleeved button up shirt with a few pens in the pocket, khaki pants and regular dress shoes. He seemed rather unassuming, but the sheer intelligence reflecting behind his eyes was clear. A man in his mid-forties, Mainframe seemed to have found his niche and flourished in it. The irritation was clear on his face as he looked between the new junior team and back to Shutters.

"Yes, yes, yes. They call me a recluse and are afraid it's contagious. What they don't realize is the only virus to be caught here is a computer virus. Besides, this environment suits me just fine. Anyway, why do I need to get out? I have control over all in my domain and I see everything just fine from where I am. Not to mention I can find out anything that I need to know, and I know who each of you is, Amanda, Crow, James, and Sek. I also know that you four have been given the mission on that burger place Nakamura says Legion is hiding out in. You four are going to need your basic equipment. Hold on."

Mainframe went back to the terminal and began furiously typing across they keyboard. A strange humming sound came from the side of the room, and machine opened up with a conveyer belt to a table. It was clear that this one machine was connected to every room on the floor. Soon, four bags rolled out onto the conveyer belt.

"Well, go ahead and take them," Mainframe said. "There's one for each of you."

In the bags, each was given a collar communication device they could easily hide around their necks. There was also a K-bar survival knife with a belt attachment, a super high capacity flash drive, tactical flashlight, a standard police-issue Glock Forty with three extra clips, a map of D.C., and a bus pass. Mainframe seemed to have known which bag they would grab because each member pulled out an identification card for each of them. In the cases of Sek and Crow, they even had their preferred names instead of their legal ones. At first none of them spoke and looked at him in astonishment. Mainframe went from a small, amused smile to slight irritation at this.

"You kids like staring like deer in the headlights, don't you? That's not all you can get here. You want something else for the mission? Just ask. I can give you maps and layouts of the buildings. Tell me what weapons you need. I'll have them brought here so you don't go searching through the rooms."

"So, say I needed a sheathe for my new sword?" Sek inquired.

"Pft," Mainframe scoffed and hurriedly typed something into the computer behind him.

There was a hum as the machine came to life, and a few moments passed before a combat sheathe rolled out in front of him. Sek quickly took it up in his hands and went about making sure it fit.

Mainframe looked over his shoulder as he leaned back in his chair slightly saying, "What else?"

"I could use a set of throwing knives, good balance and sharp enough to cut through almost anything, and some C4 too," Sek said, getting wary looks from both James and Crow.

"Now, that's more like it," Mainframe laughed and turned to type away once again. Just as before, the machine hummed and a set of five high-quality throwing knives and four pounds of C4 came out on the conveyer belt to stop in front of him.

As Sek gathered up his items to safely put in his bag, Amanda stepped up. "I need the street maps ten blocks around the burger place and the building schematics. Also, any changes that may have happened in the last ten years," she demanded and within a minute they were on the conveyer belt. Amanda snatched them up and hid them away in her bag before turning back to look at Mainframe with glee as she said, "Now, for my guns."

Mainframe winced. He gave a quick glance to Shutters, and he looked just as concerned as to what she had planned. Amanda told them that she needed a working canister launcher, two specific toy guns that Mainframe had to confirm through a toy catalog, and a pack of six soda cans. It took a minute for him to find where everything was in the system – and ultimately got the soda from the refrigerator he had hidden under his main console – but was able to supply her with everything she requested. He eyed the canister launcher warily as she turned it over in her hands with a satisfied smirk.

Seeming eager to move on and get them out of his hair, Mainframe focused on Crow, "Ok, so what do you need for the mission?"

She blinked back at him in surprise and then stammered, "Ah...well I could use some Bo Shuriken, Makibishi, Happoo, and some rope. Then I have a request for a custom sword if that's possible."

Mainframe whispered, barely audible, "Never thought I'd see the day I would be grateful for the prick Nakamura browbeating his language into my head." He cleared his throat and began speaking to her again, "I can give you five throwing knives, custom to your style of Ninjustu. As for the caltrops, I can give you three right now and you can come back for more if you need. As for the flash bombs, I can give you four of those, just be careful so you don't blind your teammates. You'd be surprised with how many accidents we've already had with flash grenades. Hazards of the job. Now what are you thinking for the sword? Clearly, you'll be wanting a Japanese style of some sort by the sounds of it," Mainframe pulled up a program with such dizzying coding that the others in the group stared at it in awe.

"Uh...a Tachi. It's slightly longer than the normal katana. I want the blade to be made out of something strong but not metal, and I would like it to be able to have my lightning travel through it," Crow explained as Mainframe went to typing away as she did.

"Strong as steel without the metal... So, ceramic blast plating. As for the electro-conductivity, some slight modifications to the hilt and the blade. We'll have a prototype when you get back so we can account for your style, grip, and other things before we get to the finished product. In the meantime, your other weapons will do." Mainframe dismissively waved her off. "Alright, I've set the rest of your teammates up and I already know what Shutters needs. How about you?"

"Well, I pull things out of pictures. I mainly use armors from games, but I use guns and stuff too."

"Where do you keep the pictures?" Mainframe asked.

"My binder," James answered as he pulled it out of his bag.

"You have a decent variety there, but I have a few armors and guns that might catch your eye. Also, carrying that whole binder into the field isn't the best idea. I suggest a smaller binder with some reinforcement so it doesn't get damaged. I'll make it so the images are interchangeable for the demands of each mission"

Upon seeing James approve, he soon had the small binder out on the conveyer belt just like all the others.

"Thanks," James said, as he looked through the binder.

"Now, your turn, Shutters," Mainframe turned around and the conveyer belt buzzed to life once again.

Junior team watched in interest at what he needed for the upcoming mission. They were all slightly surprised when a strange thermos rolled out for him to pick up and nothing else. Shutters turned to see how they were all staring at him and smiled.

"You guys wanted to see what my powers are, right? Stand together now," Shutters said as he unscrewed the cap and took a sip of the strange silver colored liquid inside. He grimaced a little from the taste, but then looked back at them to say, "Smile!" His glasses seemed to flash, and when he blinked it looked the shutter motion of a camera flicked over his lenses. He was then still for a few seconds with his eyes closed and he shook his head a little as his lips moved almost strangely. There was a slight protrusion in the sides of his cheeks that had not been there before and he opened his eyes once again. He reached up to his mouth and with a strange look on his face pulled out a thin square object that resembled a Polaroid picture. Shutters gave it a small shake and presented it. "The new junior team!"

Chapter 22: Breaking In

"Wow," James said.

"Eww," Amanda muttered under her breath.

"Producing the pictures themselves takes a lot out of my physically." Shutters said as he stashed the thermos in his bag. "So, our researchers created this for me. It doesn't taste the best, but it's the right mix of essential vitamins and things to keep me healthy and producing good quality images. It's not much in comparison to the things you guys can do, but it's what I do."

"At least we'll have proof of everything we see," Crow mused.

"That's the reason I'm going. So, shall we get planning?" Shutters asked.

The others agreed and filed out of the room with quick words of thanks to Mainframe, who shrugged them off. Just as Shutters moved to follow them, Mainframe cleared his throat.

"You're going to need all the luck you can get with that mission, kid. Make sure you don't do anything stupid. You stay behind them and don't get caught in the crossfire. They're the combatants, not you, and we don't want a repeat of the last time," Mainframe warned as he narrowed his eyes.

"I'll watch myself. See you later," Shutters said with a shake of his head, and he left to catch up with the others, who hadn't heard a word. They returned to the meeting room and found that neither Nakamura nor Ironhawk were there. However, the case that was intended for the artifact was left behind as well as the other papers that the ambassador had gathered. The files of the Bayou Brothers were still shown on the screen against the wall.

It was agreed that being dropped off in front of the location would be too brash and decided that they would come from four blocks away on foot. They planned on arriving a full hour before it closed so they could get a sense of the area with all the streets and alleys. It would still be a fairly busy area even after it was closed around six thirty, but they would wait until the restaurant itself was empty before infiltrating and seeing what Legion was up to. The foot traffic outside the business after the doors were closed and locked would decide how they would enter. The case for the artifact would be left in Shutters' possession until they needed it, that way the fighters could have use of both hands and free range of motion.

Shutters' raised his hand, "Question."

"This isn't a class, mate. Just ask," Sek rolled his eyes. His high was wearing off, as was his patience.

"So, essentially, we don't have a real plan other than to wait for most people to clear out and then wing it from there?" he asked in confusion.

"Basically. It worked for us the first time. Just make sure you don't lose the case," Amanda shrugged.

This answer seemed to shock Shutters even more, but as he looked to the others, he saw that they agreed with her so he fell silent once again.

Someone in the door behind them cleared their throat. Junior team turned to see Medic standing in the doorway, waiting to be acknowledged.

"Good, you haven't left yet," he said. "Nurse wants all of you to stop by the infirmary before you leave. Standard operating procedure is to have a clean bill of health before you go out on a mission. When you get done here, she'll be waiting."

"Ok, but she just healed us like two hours ago," Crow said.

"Well, she healed you guys. I was perfectly fine," Sek gloated, leaning back in his chair.

"I'm just telling you what I was told, and I don't question it when she says she wants something. You kids would be smart to do the same." He turned on his heels and left.

When they decided that their plans were finished, they made their way to the infirmary as they had been told. Nurse was in the same spot she had been when they first met her, and when she heard them walking up, she was on her feet greeting them with a warm smile.

"There you are, my dears. Since you're gonna be going out on a mission, I wanted to give you one more look over to make sure nothing will sneak up on you. Come here dear, you first," Nurse said gesturing for James to come over to her.

She led him down a little from the others and then reached out to gently but firmly cup his temples between the palms of her hands. Her hands glowed slightly and warmed his head as the power filtered through him. She smiled and told him everything was fine and sent him back as she called Sek over to her then Crow then Shutters. Each who had been touched by Nurse's powers was left feeling calm and almost peaceful as they waited for her to finish her work. The anxiety of the impending mission was washed away, and they were confident that they could get the job done.

She finally motioned Amanda over for the last check. As her hands began to glow, she leaned in close and whispered in a voice so low only Amanda could hear, "You all look out for him, ya hear? He ain't like the rest of you. You are used to fighting and born to do it. He isn't."

Amanda nodded in understanding, and Nurse smiled, "You're a good girl, Amanda. Now you're all right. Clear and good to go."

Nurse walked back to her station as Amanda joined the rest of the team, and the old woman wished them luck on the mission and reminded them to stay safe. They faintly heard a snort from a nearby room and saw Medic duck inside just as Nurse fixed him with a stern gaze.

With everything finished and ironed out, they walked outside to find Tex waiting for them with the limo. As he slipped into the driver's seat, the rest of the team climbed into the back seats and quickly went about fastening themselves in before he could turn on the car. Tex took off, and as soon as they were out of Psion's gates, he drove down the roads like they were running from the Faceless all over again.

In record time, they were at their drop location and getting out of the limo, they saw Tex already standing by the driver's door. Sek faintly wondered how a man of his stature moved as effortlessly as Tex did but refrained from asking.

James walked over to him and said, "Are you going to be close by in case this goes bad?"

A large grin broke over his face and he grabbed James's shoulder reassuringly saying, "Course I will. Me and a few boys'll be close by, but don't ya worry. You kids are more'n capable a handling this on yer own. We're here just to take ya home when all's said and done. Now, get goin'."

Junior team thanked him and set off. Thanks to Tex's expert driving, they arrived an hour and forty-five minutes before closing and had plenty of time to get their bearings. They were able to get a layout of the streets around the restaurant and the other businesses that surrounded it. Foot traffic began to dwindle around five thirty, and it seemed like after closing time it would be fairly quiet. As for the restaurant itself, it was busy and simple. The old Korean couple that owned it worked hard, and their customers left happy. From what the team observed, there were plenty of repeat customers, and other than seeming to almost have the food in front of their customers as soon as they sat down, nothing seemed out of the ordinary.

When six o'clock came, the old couple took their time cleaning and organizing their business for the following day. Finally, they locked up, set the alarm, and left just as the streets were starting to empty out of other people going home in the surrounding buildings.

Junior team stepped into the street, and Amanda crossed her arms saying, "Well, what now?"

"Well, I'm sure their alarm system is monitored. If I focus, I should be able to manipulate the electricity so we can open the door without setting the alarm off," Crow said.

"Sounds like a plan. We should go through the back so we don't draw any attention to ourselves," James added.

"I'll take care of any surveillance cameras and the door," Sek said as he started to head that way.

Crow followed behind him while James and Amanda lagged just enough to make sure they weren't being watched. Shutters walked in between them, carrying the case as carefully as he could. Sek made quick work of the cameras in the alley behind the business that could catch them, and Crow stepped up to the building, placing her hands on the wall. She closed her eyes and took a breath as she focused on the electricity still coursing inside of the building. It took her a few minutes, but she found the pulse leading to the alarm system. Sek set to work on manipulating the metal in the lock so they could open the door.

Once they had it open, Amanda and James had their guns at the ready as they entered and checked the Bayou Brothers. Sek slipped in behind them, and after making sure her electricity wouldn't falter, Crow darted in right after Shutters as the door closed softly behind them.

Shutters clutched his bag with one hand and the briefcase with other. His fingers were so tight on the briefcase that his knuckles were white.

"Just stay behind us," Crow said. "You'll be fine. Promise. Besides, as it is, the Bayou Brothers are more likely that not are going to be more focused on trying to beat our heads in than yours."

The inside was oddly as simple and unassuming at the outside. The kitchen was pristine and stocked full enough to feed an army. The office was messy and full of important documents and pictures of the owners and their family as well as some of the husband in military gear and a few medals in some of the desk drawers. Various folders and boxes were strewn about the small room, and the group struggled to make sure they didn't accidentally damage any of it.

As the group moved to the dining room, they found it was just as plain. The worn carpet and faded booth seats and chairs were a testament to the steady flow of customers they had received. The only thing that stood out as strange to the group was that while the business had a rather high-tech register at the host stand, there was an abacus bolted tightly on top of it. When Sek inspected it, it was obviously used frequently as some places the paint was chipped and worn away.

They decided to split up in order to search every inch of the building while Shutters took pictures of it. Yet, no matter how hard they looked, there was nothing amiss.

"Did they get their information wrong?" James voiced the question running through all of their minds.

"Probably. I mean, it came from the Japanese Ambassador. He probably translated it wrong. English isn't easy for those people. Right, Crow?" Sek asked. He came out of the office wearing the same military coat the husband wore in the pictures. "I think I'm going to keep this. Looks good on me."

"You go around stealing people's things often?" Crow said. "No, don't answer that. I don't want to know. Anyway, I sincerely doubt the ambassador's grip on the English language has anything to do with this, you prick. A more likely option is that Legion is a sneaky bastard and we're missing something." She turned to Amanda. "Are we sure we've searched everything and everywhere?"

"Yes," Amanda huffed in annoyance.

"Well, except one place," Shutters suggested. He shifted back and forth on his feet. "The walk-in cooler."

"Go figure. Let's go see what we can find," Crow sighed and led the way after patting Shutters on the shoulder.

Amanda was close behind, and the others fell into step. Everything was quiet, and as they approached the cooler, junior team couldn't help but tense. They reached the door, and Crow paused just as her hand touched the handle. The others prepared themselves for a possible attack, and Crow pulled open the door ready for something to leap out at them.

The only thing that came out of the cooler was cold air and the mixed smells of the various perishable foods stored inside. Food lined the shelves, and in back was a separated part dividing off the frozen section. All in all, the cooler looked just as bland as the rest of the place down to the worn tiling. In the interest of being thorough, the five stepped inside just to be sure. James and Sek searched through the boxes on the left while Amanda and Shutters searched through the boxes on the right.

Crow went straight to the back of the cooler and opened the freezer. Some of the wind escaped her lungs as the frigid air hit her chest. Despite the uncomfortable drop in temperature, the five were searching diligently through things when they heard laughter coming from behind them. All of them spun around just in time to see the main door to the cooler slam shut. James rushed over, but no matter how hard he tried, the door would not move.

Chapter 23: The Bayou Brothers

"Get behind us," Amanda ordered, and Shutters scrambled past her as fast as he could.

Crow shut the freezer door, and Shutters leaned against it, fumbling in his bag for something. James stepped away from the door and, using the faint light from above, looked through his small binder for a suit to change into. In seconds, he was adorned in yet another suit pulled straight from a gaming franchise. He and Sek took up the front lines while Amanda and Crow stood protectively blocking Shutters.

"Well lookie what we done caught, bro. A buncha kids way in over dey heads," one voice barked from the other side of the door.

"Whooee. Looks like Legion was right. Dey done walked right inta dat one. I was expecting more of a fight. Ain't very bright now, are dey?" a second voice cackled.

"Only two against four. At least this time the odds are in our favor," James noted.

"For now," Amanda growled as she pulled out a can of soda and her canister launcher.

"Seems like we found Gator and Porter. Let's try to take them down fast and hard. We don't want to give them a chance to teleport," Crow said. She held out her hands on both sides and electricity crackled through her fingertips.

"Alright. My turn," Sek mused. Flexing his power, he focused on the hinges on the door. After peeling them away from the frame, he held his hand out and activated his magnetic field to send the door flying out from the cooler violently.

It shot across the hall and slammed into the wall with a loud crash. Each member of Junior team hoped one of the brothers had been injured by the flying door, but when it fell to the ground after denting the wall, they were disappointed to see there was no one behind it. Two figures on either side stepped out to reveal themselves.

"Well den, looks like dese kids don't wanna play nice then, do dey, Gator?" the one on the left whooped with a shake of his head. He stood five-foot-two with a fairly muscled physique that came from physical labor, and his dirty, torn clothing only further attested to it. His hiking boots were caked in dry mud, and his worn out khaki pants had tears at the knees. The t-shirt he wore had dozens of stains that were so set in they could be dried mud, blood, or even grease. Around his neck hung a large bulky necklace that had unnaturally large, sharp teeth that looked like they were pulled from an alligator. His tanned skin was covered in scars along his arms, and his long, dark hair was held back by a black bandana tied at the base of his neck. His grey eyes flicked between the five figures standing in the cooler, and a dangerous smile curled the corners of his mouth.

Gator wore scuffed black boots and blue jeans stained almost black. He had a dirty, white, shirt under his open black button-up with the sleeves rolled to his elbows, and he stood a few inches taller than his brother. He was equally muscled but seemed to have far more scars running along his arms. He wore a large hat with a sun-blocking rim, and lining the middle of the hat were the same teeth as Porter's necklace. His eyes were such a pale green that they almost seemed yellow, and he grinned viciously as he locked his eyes on

Shutters, "I reckon you be right, Porter. Let's show 'em some manners. Bayou Brother style! This is gonna be fun."

"Take 'em out!" Amanda ordered, and James instinctively leveled his Glock at Porter's head while she loaded her can into the canister launcher. James quickly squeezed off four rounds in Porter's direction, and Amanda fired the soda can right at Gator's head. Their attacks were aimed perfectly. The brothers stood still as statues like they would take the blows head on.

Their reactions were so sudden that Shutters was the only one who managed to see what happened as he captured them in his pictures. Porter disappeared a fraction of a second before the first bullet would've laid into him and reappeared a second after the last bullet passed by, leaving him completely unharmed as the wall behind him was riddled with four holes. Gator fixed his gaze on the can flying toward his head, and out of thin air a strange rift opened in front of him and swallowed the can before closing. Before any of them had a chance to react, another rift opened directly behind Amanda and the can spiraled out of it to smack into the middle of the back of her head with a disturbing thud. The force behind the impact was strong enough to daze her and knocked her to the ground in a heap. The can rolled across the floor to stop in the middle of them, and they all saw that it was still glowing brightly, but now seeming to flash like it was about to explode.

Sek sent the can flying across the floor just behind the Bayou Brothers, who were thoroughly uninterested in the can itself as it went. Just as it rolled to a stop, the energy in it exploded, but only succeeded in spraying soda all around the hall. The sound of it caused the Bayou Brothers to turn, but when they realized that it was harmless, they turned back to face the group and laughed.

Sek focused on the door that was lying on the floor, and while the Bayou Brothers were focused on the team, he set to work on pulling the metal from the door, turning it into bits of shrapnel that he would use as an attack from behind. All he needed was the perfect distraction. Crow slid forward with her hands flared out at her sides and threw her surge forward, catching Porter dead center, dropping him to his knees. Gator looked at his brother in shock, and Sek turned the metal from the door into a small cloud of shrapnel. With a flick of his eyes, he sent it flying straight at them. Gator glanced back in time to see the cloud coming right at them. Porter, on the other hand, was still too stunned from the shock to move. All he could do was howl in pain as shrapnel tore through his torso, spraying blood all across the walls and floor. Gator narrowly avoided the same thing by disappearing again. He returned to land on his feet and looked over to his brother who was bleeding all over the ground and slipping in and out of consciousness.

"Damn! Let's go brotha. We'll get dese kids later," Gator snarled ferociously as he charged across the hall and grabbed his brother by the shoulders. With a slight shake, Porter grabbed Gator by the arms. In the blink of an eye and a teleportation gate appeared beneath them and then they were gone.

"Shit!" Amanda hissed as she managed to stagger back to her feet in time to see the brothers disappear from sight. She put the canister launcher in her bag as she rushed out the door and caught the side of the frame as she pulled out her Glock. Bouncing off the doorframe, she barreled into the dining room to give chase, and Sek dashed out behind her. Crow ran to follow but stopped in the doorway and looked between James to Shutters.

"Shutters stay back and keep safe. Let's go James! We can't let them get away!" Crow commanded and then ran down the hall.

The same strange rift they had seen before opened up in front of the main window. Innocent bystanders paused outside and stared to watch as the two brothers came crashing out of the portal to land on the ground with a hard thud. The rift closed, and more people began to congregate as Gator rolled away from his brother to get to his feet. He seemed jarred from his sudden transportation and was shaking his head vigorously. Porter remained in a heap where he had fallen, and traffic was quickly blocked by the spectators.

"This just got interesting," Sek noted as he counted twenty civilians already on the scene as more filtered in. "I can already see our casualty count growing by the minute."

"Not if we take these guys out before they hurt anyone. We can figure the rest out later!" Amanda said. She took aim at Gator.

"I can work with that," Sek smirked and leveled his gun at Porter.

Crow looked at the people joining the crowd. Lightning sparked between her fingertips. There were too many people in the danger zone. In order to keep casualties to a minimum, they would have to throw everything they had into it. Keeping their abilities a secret had already been compromised and too many people were at stake.

Sek and Amanda opened fire on the brothers, and the sound of glass shattering joined the volley of bullets whistling through the air. Porter was only just beginning to regain himself, but Gator was fully aware of the onslaught making its way toward them and swiftly opened a gate in front of both him and his brother to catch the bullets. Another rift opened just behind them, and the bullets flew straight toward the people watching. Screams echoed through the air as people scattered to avoid them. Luckily, everyone managed to get out of the way in time, but the tires of a school bus passing by were riddled with holes.

"Misdirect this, asshole," Crow hissed as she raised her hands to the sky and began calling all the lightning in the clouds above them.

A bolt of lightning came streaking down from the sky. Gator heard it crackling above him and turned around just in time to see it come crashing down on top of Porter's head. His scream ripped through the air, and the metal bits of shrapnel glowed in his skin from the live current coursing through his body. The smell of charred flesh wafted through the shattered window back into the restaurant, and they could see the metal melting into his flesh. Porter slumped over, dead. Gator stood in shock. Time seemed to freeze just for a minute as everyone – junior team, Gator, and the crowd watching – looked over the scene, all holding their breaths.

"You gonna pay for dat girlie…oh trust me you gonna pay. You kids gonna wish you neva messed with the Bayou Brothers. I promise you that," Gator swore as he stared pointedly into Crow's eyes before he spun around and ran.

As he barreled through the crowd of people, he diverted his path toward the school bus that had been effectively disabled. Just as Gator kicked open the door of the bus, Amanda leapt through the broken glass window and was running toward him with her gun at the ready. Terrified screams echoed from the bus, and many of the spectators moved away from the vehicle to give Amanda a clear path. Gator ran down the aisle of the bus, threw open the back emergency door and jumped out. Having cleared the thick group of people with relative ease, he ran down the street with nothing to slow him down. He quickly put distance between him and the restaurant, and Amanda continued running after him.

"Damn it," Crow muttered, looking to Shutters, who was focused on Porter's corpse, and then back to Amanda. She ran her hand through her hair, unsure of what to do.

"I'll switch into a suit that flies and back up Amanda," James said.

Athletic as she was, Crow knew she wouldn't be able to physically catch up. She conceded with a nod that it was the best course of action.

"Alright, we'll stay behind and figure out how we're going to get into Legion's lab. Although, we might be limited on time after this scene. Take him down quick," Crow said.

Sek was already inspecting the floor in the middle of the dining room. He stood and started rummaging through his bag.

"So what's the plan?" Crow asked.

"I'm going to blow through the floor. The lab should be right under us, so some C4 placed right…about…here will do it," Sek explained. He moved a table and a set of chairs out of his way.

"Does he know what he's doing?" Shutters asked in undertone.

"I hope so," Crow said.

James flipped through his binder until he found an armor with flight capabilities. It flashed around him, and he secured the binder safely before shooting off to back up Amanda.

As soon as they had broken free from the crowd, both Gator and Amanda had picked up speed and put quite a bit of distance between them and the restaurant. It surprised James how swift a man of Gator's size was, and he was even more surprised at how Amanda seemed to close the gap. James flew down the nearly abandoned street after them and noticed that everyone was so focused on the commotion at the restaurant that no one seemed to pay them any mind at all. James pushed the flight capabilities of his suit close to the limit when he realized that Gator was smiling and pulling away from Amanda. He seemed to be opening portals in front of himself as he ran and using them to teleport ahead several feet at a time. Amanda was starting to get winded.

James realized that at the speed he was flying he wouldn't be able to slow down enough to help Amanda. He did, however, see an opportunity to catch Gator off guard and ducked his head as he barreled straight into his target's back. James wrapped his arms around Gator's torso as they skittered across the pavement and shut off the thrusters of the suit.

The impact knocked Gator's feet out from under him, and they painfully tumbled to the ground after skidding a few feet. James positioned Gator below him to take the brunt of the skid. But despite his best efforts, the impact dazed James as well, and after coming to a stop, Gator was able to dislodge himself from his grip. He staggered to his feet as James laid sprawled on the ground trying to regain himself.

"Bring it on, boy! You gonna regret takin' me on. Yer friends killed my brotha, so now I'm gonna kill you."

He flicked his hand and opened a gate aimed at James' side. The gate was only two inches wide, but it went straight through the meat of his side and took all of the flesh that was in its way when Gator closed it. James howled in pain as flesh and muscle was ripped out of his body, and he rolled to his side, trying to stem the bleeding as the pavement stained crimson.

"Just you wait boy. I'm really gonna make you squeal." Gator pulled out a poaching knife and advanced on James. The blade of the knife had flakes of dried blood still on it, and James did not want to see what the serrated edge could do to his flesh. The shock was starting to wear off, and James struggled to get to his feet but was too weak from sudden blood loss to do anything to stop Gator. He enemy raised the blade, and all James could do was wait for the blow to land.

A shot rang out as a glowing bullet cut through the air. It flew into the Gator's knife hand and blew it into a bloody spray of chunks. Gator howled in agony as he stumbled back, clutching his bleeding stump. James looked around him to see Amanda still aiming her gun at Gator, slowly advancing as she waited to take another shot.

James called on all his strength to deliver one powerful punch to Gator's head with his armored hand. The blow was enough to knock him unconscious, and Gator sprawled out across the pavement.

Amanda continued her careful approach, and lowered her gun as she looked at James's side. "You ok?"

"Yeah. I think so. Thanks," James grimaced.

Amanda keyed up on the collar-com. "We need a pick up. We killed one of the guys back at the restaurant. We've got the other guy here, and James is hurt."

She glanced back down the road and bounced on her feet anxiously. Gator had managed to get a mile out from where they had started and it would take her some time to get back there. It would take even longer with James in tow.

"We'll be there in a just a few minutes, little lady. Just hang tight," Tex responded.

They arrived faster than either of the two junior team members thought possible. Three agents got out of the back of the limo and set to work on securing Gator. Tex carefully stepped out of the driver's seat, and Amanda adjusted the bag she was carrying.

"I'm going to head back. Tex, the other brother is dead in front of the restaurant. You might want to get people over there before the police try to take over," Amanda advised. She looked over to James. "Stay safe."

She dashed back toward the restaurant as fast as her tired legs could take her. James watched in amusement and shook his head as Tex walked up to him. He smiled and held out bandages to the teenager as he said, "That's the best I can do fer now. We'll get this guy taken care of and then we'll be back around to take care of you kids. Can you handle yerselves till then?"

"We'll see what we can do," James laughed taking the bandages and set to work on wrapping up the wound so it would no longer bleed freely.

Amanda was rushing down the street to get back to the restaurant as fast as she could, and she faintly heard sirens approaching. She cursed under her breath and reached into her bag to pull out a hat that she quickly jammed down on her head. She stuffed the coat she had been wearing into the bag and re-secured it on her back.

More people had started to gather outside the restaurant past the school bus. Police had arrived at the scene, and Amanda used all the people standing around to blend in. She advanced further through the throng of people and found that it was thicker around the school bus. Curiosity got the better of her. As she got closer, she could hear people wailing in shock and horror. She squeezed through the group of people in time to see a young police officer staggering away from the back of the bus and barely threw himself against the front of his cruiser as he doubled over puking.

Everyone was distracted, giving Amanda the chance to slip past the police line without anyone noticing and moved to the front of the bus. With a quick look over her shoulder, she stepped in the door Gator had kicked open. She hopped up the steps of the bus and paused at the front. Her breath caught in her chest. Using his control of teleportation gates, he had opened a rift just wide enough to cut through the bus seats and the children who occupied them. It was like a precision laser had sliced straight through them all like a knife through butter but stopping just before it reached the outside wall of the bus or the windows. In the time that passed, gravity had caused the top halves to sickeningly slide off the sides and splatter to the floor as intestines, blood and other organs seeped out. Some had fallen on top of others, mixing the carnage in an impossible mess. But the lower halves of the children sat exactly where they had been upon their deaths with blood that trickled down their legs and dripped into the pool of crimson below.

Two particular children caught her attention just as she was moving to get off the bus, and she found herself rooted on the spot. They were near the front, and both of the torsos of the girls had landed close together. One was a cute little black girl, her curly hair held back with a bright green ribbon turning brown from the blood soaking into it. The second was a small Asian with two yellow barrettes holding her hair out of her face. They were facing each other, their eyes wide in fear, and when they had fallen off their seats into the blood and organs below, their hands fell together, and there the little girls rested, holding hands in death.

Amanda tightened her grip on the strap of the bag she had on her back at the horrific scene and regretted that all she had taken from Gator was his hand. But she couldn't think about that. If she did it would have frozen her to that spot. She couldn't allow that. She had to get back to make sure Crow and the others were ok.

Chapter 24: Into the Lab

Sek placed the C4, and Crow and Shutters moved into the hall near the kitchen after Shutters was finished taking pictures of the scene. Crow made some of the power lines spark around the restaurant and charged the air, making it uncomfortable to come within a certain radius around the business. This seemed to keep the innocent bystanders at bay and they could already hear sirens starting to approach. She made sure that nothing she had done would harm any innocents.

"That should do it," Sek declared.

"Let 'er rip. Who knows when the police will get here," Crow called out to him from the far end of the dining room. She glanced just past him to the street outside and hoped that Amanda and James were watching out for each other against Gator.

"Yeah. Yeah. Don't get your panties in a twist." Sek waved her off dismissively as he stepped back. There was a muffled, controlled explosion, and when all three approached, there was a hole in the floor just large enough for them to lower themselves down one by one. Crow pulled some rope out from her bag and set to work fastening it to the unmoving host stand as Shutters clicked away. Then she dropped the rest of the rope into the hole, and all three stood on the edge looking down.

"Well, fearless leader," Sek said, looking at Crow. "Ninja go first. Isn't this your area of expertise?"

"Just make sure no one comes up behind us."

She knelt down and, after giving the rope a few rough tugs, swiftly lowered herself down into the depths. It took a minute for her eyes to adjust from the dimly lit dining room to the brightly lit florescent white lab she had descended into. Crow landed with a soft thud and looked around carefully, a throwing knife in one hand while lightning was charged in the other. It was smaller than she thought it would be, and she expected something else to jump out. Her eyes quickly honed in on the four large pods in each corner of the plain white room, and she saw the chords, wires, tubes and pipes running from each of them across the floor to a main terminal in the center of the room that she had landed close to. As she inspected it, she found medical data flashing across the screen, and beside the computer was a strange container-like mechanism that was likewise hooked up to everything. However, there was no one else inside that she could see, and it was eerily silent aside from the faint humming coming from the machines.

"How does it look?" Shutters called down nervously.

"It's safe. Aside from whatever is in these four pods, I'm the only one down here," Crow responded.

She began going through medical files. The records indicated that it was four people, who were only differentiated by the names subject one through four. After a little looking, she found a flash drive port in the computer and set to work on downloading all the data she could find on the terminal. Crow was so focused on the computer that she barely noticed Sek and Shutters sliding down the rope to join her. Sek walked over to the strange storage device and held his hand out to Shutters for the briefcase they had been given. Shutters was happy to get it out of his hands and placed it right beside the machine Sek was inspecting. Upon seeing that they were around the same size, he deduced that was where the artifact was being held and went about trying to find the best way to get it out with as little damage as possible. Neither spoke as they worked.

While they were so focused on the center console, Shutters went to each of the pods, taking pictures as he went. He was slightly disturbed to find that each pod held a person inside and each was in various stages of transformation into a Faceless. However, for the sake of Psion and their mission, he made sure to take one picture of each pod and the person who was inside. The first was a male who was almost completely finished in the conversion process. The second was a female partly converted with smooth skin grown over where her mouth had been. In door number three was a male whose face was mostly grown over except for one eye.

Shutters walked over to the last pod and froze upon looking inside. He quickly looked back over to Sek and Crow, who had not looked up from their work. He took a quick picture of the man inside and darted away as fast as he could, shivering as he walked back to them. It was around this time all three heard rustling above them and they tensed as they watched the rope. It wasn't until they recognized the figure sliding down as Amanda that they relaxed, and Crow and Sek went back to what they were doing.

"So, how'd it go?" Shutters asked, nervously shifting his thermos back and forth in his hands.

"We got the asshole. Some guys from Psion were taking care of him when I left," Amanda answered absently as she quickly looked each of them over to make sure they were ok. Amanda flittered over to Crow's side quietly for a moment and stood without speaking.

She seemed paler than usually but with no obvious physical injuries Shutters couldn't guess why. He glanced back at the rope again.

"Where is James? Is he ok?" Shutters asked.

"He got hurt, but he's fine."

"Is he on is way? Is he upstairs?" Shutters pressed in concern.

"I dunno," Amanda shrugged and walked around him to look at the first pod.

Shutters opened and closed his mouth, astounded at her apathy, but only shook his head in silence.

As she approached, the male inside began to move slightly, but she ignored him to inspect his physical transformation. Amanda leaned closer to the pod as she looked over the figure inside and found that he was naked. Instead of his genitals hanging between his legs, his skin was smooth, like a doll. His wrists had restraints fastened around them, and when she looked down, it seemed his ankles were likewise held in place. Amanda looked at his face and saw that it was just as smooth as the countless Faceless they had faced at the convention center.

The longer she stood in front of the pod, the more intense the creature's struggle became against its restraints, and it went so far as to start pulling away from the restraints that held it. Finally, the right-hand restraint snapped, and with a quick jerk, it made short work of the one holding the left hand back. The Faceless began pounding against the pod, and a large crack spread across the glass of the pod.

Amanda bounced back a few feet as she excitedly exclaimed, "Oh shit!"

"What did you do?" Crow hissed as she pocketed the flash drive.

The Faceless punched straight through the pod front and pushed it open to step out. While he freed himself, the second pod holding the female started to rattle as she too struggled to get out. She seemed just as determined as the male, and already had one of her arms free before the male straightened up and took his first steps toward the team.

"I didn't do anything! I swear I wasn't even touching it! This time it isn't my fault!" Amanda snapped back in her own defense.

"Uh, guys what's going on down there?" James called down from above.

"We're kinda busy at the moment! Shutters, go upstairs," Sek commanded.

He temporarily abandoned the artifact and pulled one of his throwing knives from his pocket. Shutters scrambled to do as he was told, and about halfway up, he heard the female breaking open the pod she had been held in. Sek came around to stand in front of the terminal and launched his throwing knife at the head of the male Faceless. The male was not fazed. His head snapped back from the impact of the blow, but he effortlessly ripped the knife from his flesh and dropped it on the ground as he focused his attention on Amanda, who was closest to him. In one fluid motion, the Faceless crossed the distance between them, picked Amanda up by her throat, and effortlessly hurled her across the lab like a doll the pod in the opposite corner. He turned his attention to Crow, and she drew herself up to face the creature. He seemed to tilt his head to the side as he froze in place. A few involuntary twitches and jerks broke over his form, but something in him refused to take another action.

The impact of Amanda's body slamming against the pod was enough to shatter the glass under her. The Faceless within reached out and locked Amanda in place with its arm wrapped tightly around her neck. She choked as it began crushing her windpipe, and Amanda kicked her feet wildly attempting to free herself. Sek cursed under his breath and rushed to her side to help while Crow faced off against the other two.

Shutters pulled himself so that he was sitting at the edge of the opening and could hear James arguing with an officer that the area was off limits and that it was classified information he did not have clearance to access. He had pulled a federal agent suit from one of his pictures. Even though the officer didn't notice it, Shutters saw the dripping blood coming from James' side. He keyed up on the collar-com for Tex to assist James in keeping the police out of the restaurant. As soon as there was confirmation they were on their way, Shutters slid back down the rope just enough to see what was going on. While Sek was working to free Amanda, the male Faceless that had turned to Crow still stood frozen and staring at her, twitching and jerking like it was fighting against some unknown order it had been given.

Crow watched the creature warily but turned her focus to the female who was trembling and shaking just as bad as her male counterpart. She, however, was moving a little easier and fixed her dark eyes on Crow as she tilted her head to the side. Crow was able to see a distinct birthmark on the side of her head that hadn't yet been covered by the smooth skin of the Faceless process. At the top of her left ear was a small crescent moon and Crow froze as she choked on sudden dread. It may have been two years since she had last seen it, and even then it was peeking out from a curtain of beautifully well-kept silk black hair, but there was no mistaking it. As she stared back into the eyes of the woman in front of her, Crow croaked out painfully, feeling her heart trying to rip itself out of her chest with every word she spoke, "M-Mom…not it can't be… No. No." She turned back to look at the male Faceless who hadn't moved and was facing her just as he had before. His face may have been completely covered, and she couldn't see his eyes, but Crow knew exactly who it was. Tears started to slip from the corners of her eyes as she whispered, "No… No… Dad…this can't be happening." Her adoptive mother gave Crow a twitching nod and then shakily walked over to her husband.

Sek reached out in an attempt to rip Amanda free from the chokehold the Faceless had on her but found that the creature was unusually strong. As he struggled against it, Sek could hear the fourth pod starting to shake. He cursed under his breath and looked to see Amanda's face starting to change colors from lack of oxygen as her own movements became weaker. Deciding that he had enough, Sek stepped back and freed his sword from its sheathe. It was at that moment Sek noticed that each of the arms had scars on them near the shoulders where it was like they had been sewn back to the torso. There was a similar scar on the neck as well. Realization dawned on him, but before he let it sink in, Sek leveled the sword and severed the arm holding his friend perfectly along the scar in one clean swipe.

The limb fell to the ground as Amanda pulled free and stumbled into Sek, who held out his free arm to stabilize her until she got her bearings. Amanda sputtered and coughed as oxygen flooded back into her lungs. She planted her feet as the room stopped spinning and pulled out the toy gun she had hidden on her hip. With another deep inhale she turned around and took aim at the Faceless who had been holding her. Amanda hesitated only long enough to make sure she was seeing straight before firing an energy bullet straight into the middle of its forehead. The Faceless fell back in the pod dead, and as its head lulled back, the same realization that had already dawned on Sek now struck Amanda. It was the Brit. It was Charles lying dead in that pod for the second time.

The final pod burst open with a beam of neon green energy shooting out from the one eye that had not been covered up with skin. Both Amanda and Sek had to duck out of the way to avoid a second one as the creature turned its gaze on them. Charles's lifeless body took more damage as the second beam bore a hole in the middle of his chest. It soon stopped, and when they both straightened up they found that it was having trouble getting free of its restraints. Instead of struggling against them, the Faceless turned its devastating gaze to the chains holding it in place.

"No, no, no, no, NO! No more of that!" Amanda cried. She took aim.

"Right there with you," Sek agreed as he pulled out another knife. Once again, with deadly precision, he launched the knife, and the blade planted itself cleanly into the middle of its forehead. Yet, just as with Crow's father, the creature acted like the injury was nothing and continued working on getting rid of the restraints that held it.

"I said no damn it!" Amanda exclaimed as she raised her gun and released another bolt of energy aimed at the knife. The Faceless was too focused on its restraints to notice, giving Amanda a clean shot. Her bullet flew true and slammed into the handle of the knife and pushed it even further into the skull. The creature snapped back at the force of the blow pushed the knife through its head to pin it against the back of the pod. Sek and Amanda looked from the now dead Faceless, to each other in relief and then over to Crow in concern.

Crow's adoptive mother had made her way to stand at her husband's side. For a moment, they took each other in, looked to their adoptive daughter, and then back at one another. Then she carefully reached up both of her hands to either side of his face and gently caressed his cheeks. That one gentle motion seemed to stir something in him and he reached one hand up to lovingly brush the side of her cheek with his knuckles. It was a simple display of affection Crow had seen them share so many times, and she shuddered as her chest went cold. It was so subtly them. Her heart ached. A strangled sound came from her mother, and the once frail women tightened her grip on her husband's face before snapping his neck with a quick turn of her wrists.

Crow's adoptive father crumbled to the ground in a heap, his head nearly twisted off, and her mother then turned her attention to Crow. There was a muffled groan as she tried to speak, but the skin grown over her mouth kept her silent. She slowly ran her finger over where her mouth should've been and began looking down at the ground. Crow stood in horror as she watched her mother fumble before picking up the knife her husband had pulled from his forehead. Her body was trembling more than before and it seemed to only get worse as time wore on. She turned her head away from her daughter as she brought the knife up to her face, and the sound of the blade cutting flesh chilled Crow.

"Mom...Dad...I...no," Crow choked as she could no longer keep the sobs at bay. Her body heaved with every breath she took and only succeeded in making her cries silent as she held her arms tightly around herself. Crow's mother turned around as she dropped the bloody knife to the floor and Crow cringed upon seeing the flayed skin sliced open over her mouth so she could talk as blood dripped down her chin.

"Not dad. Not anymore," she groaned in hoarse whisper. Each breathe came out as a gasp of pain. It echoed in her daughter's mind, and each shudder of pain rang through Crow's core. Finally, her mother was able to muster just enough strength to whisper through her gurgled gasp, "…Trust…Nakamura."

Her body gave out, and Crow's mother collapsed on top of her husband. Crow felt as though the wind had been ripped from her lungs, and she fell to her knees as she stared at their lifeless bodies. Tears were pouring down her cheeks, but no sound came from her. She crawled over to them and brushed her fingers across her mother's forearm. She didn't move. She looked to her father. He wasn't moving either. Crow sat there, slightly rocking back and forth without saying a word, but gasping quietly as though her heart was being ripped out of her chest.

Amanda approached her catatonic sister and placed a gentle hand on her shoulder. After a minute, she stepped to the side and looked over her sister's parents. With a careful look to Crow, Amanda carefully placed a bullet in the side of each of their heads, assuring that they would never be brought back in such a way ever again. Sek quietly went back to the middle of the room and set to work on removing the artifact from the machine.

Shutters crawled back up to the top of the rope and sat on the edge of the opening. He couldn't stop a few tears from slipping out the corners of his eyes as he reached into his bag and took out his thermos. He looked over to see Tex chest bumping some police sergeant and yelling about how they were imposing on federal matters. The officers around the restaurant were steadily being pushed out as more agents of Psion arrived. Shutters unscrewed the top from his thermos and took a long drink, finishing off the liquid film to recover from the many pictures he had been developing. He glanced down at the album he had been putting the photos into and turned away from the ones of Crow's parents. It was by far one of the saddest moments that he had ever had to photograph. He had never taken so many pictures before, and he wiped the sweat from his brow at the effort it had taken him. When he felt refreshed, he replaced everything in his bag and slid down the rope to rejoin the rest of the team below.

Sek was almost finished carefully opening the machine to get to the artifact as Shutters stepped away from the rope. Crow hadn't moved, and Amanda was standing dutifully at her side. Shutters respectfully stepped to the side and took a quick picture of her parents without anyone noticing. Then he turned back to the machine Sek had managed to get open and both leaned in as Sek removed the top.

The sight of the artifact caused both of them to pause and exhale in surprise. From the way Nakamura had talked about it, both were expecting some weird type of machinery, but instead they were met with something that looked more like a swollen brain that was radiating with a strange power. It was slightly larger than any normal brain they had seen and each faintly wondered what the Japanese Ambassador had planned for such an item. They looked between each other warily, and Shutters took a picture before stepping back out of Sek's way. Sek shuttered at the thought of touching the thing and, instead, raised it up with some of the metal around it and lowered it into the case as gently as he could. It took longer than it would have if someone had lowered it in by hand, but it was soon secured inside. Sek closed the case and locked it before handing it over to Shutters who started to make his way back up the rope.

"Alright, we've got the artifact. We're good to go."

Neither Crow nor Amanda moved. Amanda turned back to him, and it was clear that even she was at a loss for how she was going to get Crow moving. But after a minute more of silence, Crow mechanically rose and walked over to the computer terminal. She began typing away and said in a flat tone, "Everyone start heading up the rope. I saw a decontamination program when I was downloading the files. Once everyone is clear, I'll activate it and it'll destroy the lab for us."

"Crow," Amanda hedged warningly at her sister.

"Don't worry, Amanda. I can set a countdown on the program giving me enough time to safely get out of here. I'll be right behind you. I promise," Crow said looking at her and giving her a weak nod.

Amanda stared at her sister carefully before nodding back. Sek followed Shutters up the rope and Amanda lingered with her hand on the rope as she heard Crow quietly reciting a Japanese prayer. Amanda climbed halfway up the rope to give her some space but continued to watch to make sure that her sister would follow. Crow bowed her head as she finished the prayer and then gave one final look at her parents' bodies. She couldn't stop the tears and trembling in her voice as she whispered, "I'm so sorry. Mom, Dad, I love you."

She hit the button to initiate the decontamination sequence and then quickly scrambled up the rope after Amanda. Her sister was there at the top to help pull her clear, and once she had, Sek called some metal from the chairs and tables around them to create a cover over the hole in the floor. Shortly after, there was the sound of an explosion beneath them, and the team could feel heat rising from the floor. However, the program did as it was intended and kept the flames at bay.

There would be nothing left. No trace of what transpired. Only charred remains of metal and ash. But they had accomplished their first mission as a team, and it would be as a team that they would have to face the aftermath of it all.

Chapter 25: Debrief and Decompress

Crow moved to a nearby chair and carefully eased herself to sit down, staring at the floor blankly. James and Sek were messing with the artifact to watch her from afar while Amanda stood protectively close. Shutters shifted back and forth on his feet, glancing at the covered hole in the floor as though he was expecting it to collapse beneath them.

Tex walked up and cleared his throat to get their attention before he said, "Ok kids. Good work out here. We've got both of the Bayou Brothers taken care of and Ironhawk has already started on the cleanup and handling of the publicity. Let's get you kids home to rest."

At first, no one moved. Crow was still mentally checked out and staring at the floor, Amanda and James were glancing around the restaurant, Sek was checking on the briefcase and Shutters was standing there looking between the rest of junior team. Finally, Shutters moved over to Tex and leaned in close to whisper something to him as he gestured subtly in Crow's direction. Tex glanced over at her and then nodded carefully before telling them to stay inside while he went to get the limo for them.

The drive was silent, and the air in the car was solemn. Just as before, Ironhawk was standing on the front stairs waiting for them and gently ushered them inside to the conference room they had met in before. Nakamura was standing in the exact spot he had been when they met him, but where his expression had been superior and condescending before, now it was respectful and almost pained. The team began taking their seats around the table except for Crow, who lingered by the door looking as though she was ready to run at the slightest provocation.

"I've been made aware that things took an unexpected turn while you were on the mission, but despite that, I must commend each of you," Ironhawk said. "Not only did you successfully retrieve the artifact, but you were able to put an end to the threat of the Bayou Brothers. That in itself is a fantastic feat, and though killing is never easy, I'm aware that this time it came at quite a cost."

Sek placed the briefcase down on the table. Shutters stepped up to him and handed over the album of pictures he had taken while they were on the mission. Ironhawk glanced to Nakamura who was carefully inspecting the case, but also seemed to be glancing out of the corner of his eye at Crow. The young woman seemed to be an empty shell of what she had been before they left and was so pale it appeared as though she would pass out at any given moment.

"I apologize," Ironhawk continued, "but I need you to catch me up on a few things, and then I'll give each of you an hour to decompress. First, I'm aware that one of the brothers was killed in front of the public eye. What happened exactly?"

Amanda and James looked at each other and took turns explaining what happened. Sek was content to keep quiet and watch as Nakamura poured over the case like it was something precious. His attention even caught Nakamura murmuring under his breath and mentioning how it was perfect and things were going just as he planned. James picked up telling the events from the moment the fight began in the cooler and stopped as the brothers retreated with their teleportation. Amanda picked up as the fight spilled out into the street, killing Porter and then chasing Gator, not realizing what he had done to the kids on the bus until after he had been taken into custody.

"The asshole got lucky," she ended.

Ironhawk nodded. "Yes, the bus. Gator always was the more vicious of the two and took great enjoyment in killing children. However, now that he's in our custody, we can make sure no one else has to suffer at his hands."

The others didn't say a word. They didn't know what to say. Crow leaned against the wall. Tears fell from her eyes, but she didn't make a sound. Amanda was focused on how Nakamura gingerly picked up the artifact and placed it at his feet on the side away from Ironhawk. It did not set well with her.

"Is there anything else you need to know?" Shutters asked.

"Yes, the lab. I know what was inside, and I also know what was waiting for you. You recovered the artifact, and I was told there was an explosion underground before you left. What…how was the lab handled before you left it?" Ironhawk inquired.

"While I was going through the medical files on the subjects who were turned into Faceless, I found a total decontamination program. From what I understood, the protocols the program should have followed would've filled the room with flames intense enough to completely burn all organic and biological material to ash. All the machines should be damaged beyond any sort of repair and the data would have been purged from the system before the flames engulfed it. From what I understood, the protocols and machines were in perfect working order, and I doubt anything in that lab will be usable ever again." Crow spoke in a cold, flat tone that caused everyone but Amanda to flinch in shock. She looked up from where she had been staring to lock eyes with Ironhawk the entire time she was talking, and spoke in such a robotic tone it was clear that she only answered because she was the one who had a hand in doing it.

"I see. Thank you, Crow. In time, we may ask to look at the medical data you recovered from that terminal," Ironhawk said.

"I understand," she whispered.

"Very good. This mission has been a trying one. There are things on my end that I still need to take care of. Your team can take an hour to rest and collect yourselves. After that I will need to speak with you again, so please meet at the main doors in the back of the mess hall. There's something that I think will bring some comfort, even if it's only a little. I'll see you in an hour."

As soon as the last word left his mouth, Crow was gone. Amanda checked the hall to see what direction she had run, but found no trace of her. Before anyone else had a chance to move, Amanda placed herself in the middle of the doorway and jabbed her pointer finger in Nakamura's direction.

"I don't trust you and what the hell is with you fawning over that damn artifact. You were practically jizzing all over yourself with that damn box instead of listening to the hell we had to go through to bring the damn thing here. Does no one else see this?"

Nakamura growled and snapped in disdain, "Your vulgarity is revolting and unbecoming in a young woman your age. You remind me of someone I used to know."

"I don't give a damn what you think. Ironhawk, are you really just going to ignore how he was drooling over that thing?"

"Amanda please calm down, Ironhawk said. "Nakamura has worked closely with us for years and has gotten us out of some very tough situations in the past. He has used his own money to build a special vault that will safeguard parahuman artifacts such as this and keep them from falling into the wrong hands."

"Wrong hands? His are the wrong hands! The only things he's not doing is petting a cat or steepling his fingers saying 'excellent!' How are you not seeing this?" Amanda exclaimed in exasperation.

"Her wild imagination tends to run away with her, Ironhawk," Nakamura said. "You may want to pay attention to that. As for myself, I have more important matters."

He took the artifact case in his hand and with a simple nod to Ironhawk, disappeared right before their very eyes. Amanda growled something under her breath that would have caused the Japanese Ambassador to cringe had he heard it.

"I can't blame you kids for not trusting. You each have had enough experience in your past to know that things are not always as they seem, but as much as you may not trust people here, I assure you, we have known one another and worked together for longer than you can imagine. Each of us has our own way of handling the trials and tribulations we have faced in our time, and Nakamura has always been there to back us up even if he thought we were fools for it. Now, you all have an hour. Go relax and recover some."

As they filed into the hall, Shutters suggested that coffee might do them all some good. When they looked at him incredulously, he explained that there was always fresh coffee on standby for situations like theirs. He led them toward the mess hall, but paused as he looked around the halls.

"I just hope Crow will be ok," he muttered under his breath.

"She'll be fine," Amanda answered simply.

She spoke with confidence but seemed distracted as she looked toward the front entrance as they stepped into the mess hall. They found Tex and Nurse already by the coffee station preparing mugs for each of the team. The old woman looked up and smiled as she wrapped her fingers around the neck of a container of apple juice. She motioned for Amanda to come over and sit beside her and put the container in her hands.

"Hey! Good to see you made it back in one piece, Specs! Figured you were done for!" a voice called out from behind them, and Shutters spun around.

Walking up was a rather tall figure who looked to be around the same age as the rest of them. He had the build of a toned athlete who continually worked to keep himself in his peak condition, with short, dirty blonde hair and a perfectly sculpted face with handsome, youthful features. He was dressed in what appeared to be a modified jogging suit with the sleeves rolled up to his elbows. His bright blue eyes looked out from bangs, and he clasped Shutters in a rough one armed hug.

"I'm fine, Jock," Shutters said. "These guys are everything we heard about and more."

"I wasn't worried about them," Jock said with a smile. "I figured you'd do something stupid and screw it up."

"Thanks, asshole," Shutters answered.

Nurse motioned for James to come over to where she was sitting beside Amanda, and set to work on getting his wound taken care of. When that was finished, he returned to his seat beside Tex.

"You kids pulled off one heckuva mission today," Tex said with a smile. "Y'all should be proud."

"We got a busload of innocent kids killed because we let Gator get away from us," James muttered darkly under his breath.

"Honey, you don't realize just how good you did," Nurse added with a smile as she pat Amanda's head absently. "Usually when the Bayou Brothers are concerned, they run into crowded areas and start fights using the civilians for shields or distractions. All confrontations with them in the past have led to dozens of casualties. You babies made it so that won't be happenin' anymore."

"Besides, you were able to limit the damage they did and took control of the situation fairly quickly," Tex said. "The casualties in this mission are the lowest for a first deployment of a junior team we've ever had."

James was somehow comforted and horrified at the same time. Amanda was kicking her feet while drinking her juice, only seeming to partly pay attention to the conversation at hand. Sek, however, was carefully sipping from his mug as he kept a close eye on Shutters and Jock, who were talking just out of earshot.

"It sure sounds like you newbies did some amazing fighting out there," a new voice chimed in from the entrance of the cafeteria. They all looked to see a man walking over to them with a gun hanging on each hip.

"Well, look at what the cat dragged in. Good to see you Billy, I take it y'all are back from the mission?" Tex greeted the new arrival and handed off a mug to him as he plopped down in a chair to prop his feet up on the table.

"That we are, and it went as usual, Medic is patching up the others. But enough of that, I've to come see our new junior team. Especially since I heard how good of a shot some of them are."

"Kids, meet Billy the Kid. He's one of the best shots around and our own fire combat instructor," Tex said.

"Yeah, yeah, but I ain't a kid anymore, am I? Anyway, it sounds like you kids have some potential, and I'd be happy to teach you a thing or two," Billy said as he looked between Amanda and James. "You have some things to learn, but you got the skills to get there. And you, little lady, those are some pretty interesting energy bullets you have there. I'd love to see those in person."

"Ok, but if you can't do it you can't blame me," Amanda said warily.

Billy laughed before telling her that those were fair terms.

"So, is this going to be our new normal? All of this?" James sighed and shook his head.

"Well, everyone has different definitions of normal, son," Tex said. "But listen. We all have our rough days and missions that leave us wondering why we do any of it, but you're still here. We're all still here, and we've got a job to do. And if we ain't the ones to do it, no one else will." Then he smiled and winked at them as he said, "Besides, for a first mission, your team did pretty damn good."

"Indeed you did," Ironhawk said, seeming to appear out of nowhere. He made his own cup of coffee and stood beside the station as he took a sip.

"Well, it seems like there wasn't much for you to clean up if you're already joining us for coffee," Billy whooped with a hard laugh. "It usually takes you hours before you can get away when you're dealing with the aftermath of one of our missions."

"I can neither confirm nor deny that statement," Ironhawk replied with a small smirk and took another drink of his coffee. "Although junior team took two very vicious and dangerous mercenaries off the streets. We won't be seeing any more reports of the Bayou Brothers killing kids. Also, the information collected from Legion's base will aid us greatly in our future efforts to take him down. You have all made your mark on Psion."

"But how is Crow?" Shutters asked.

Amanda glanced at the clock on the wall to see that they had half an hour left before they had to meet. She finished off the juice she had been drinking and slipped out of the chair she was sitting in. While the others were too busy staring at Ironhawk, she silently made her way out the front entrance of the mess hall and began tracking where her friend had disappeared to, but she did manage to catch Ironhawk's response before she left the scene.

"Someone is with her now. She will be fine."

"We'll, we've still got some time before we're all supposed to meet up for this debriefin'. So why don't we regale these young'ins with some stories of our earlier missions. Hoohee, we had some setbacks in our day," Tex yipped.

Billy shook his head with a smile.

"The early days, when everything we touched seemed to either explode or end up getting set on fire," Ironhawk said with a small chuckle.

"Speakin' of fire, lemme tell you about the time we had to go driving down the side of a volcano that was supposed to be dormant, but turned out to be a little more active than we thought it was," Tex started, but Billy kicked his feet off the table and sat up.

"Well, it wouldn't have been active if that short-tempered chick hadn't been there. Then again, you didn't have to drive us there in the first place. You could've flown us in!"

"Now, you wait a minute. One, I'm the one a-tellin' the story now, ya hear. And two, that woulda given up our element of surprise!

Besides, those paths weren't anything to be worried 'bout see. I had everything under control."

"That's why the car was out of commission for six months when we got back! I still don't know how it held together as long as it did!" Billy shot back with a hoot.

"Because I had everything under control, like I said. Now can I please tell the story?"

Chapter 26: The Prayer Garden

The evening air was cool, and the setting sun had taken away most of the early spring heat from the day. Crow rushed outside as soon as Ironhawk had given her the chance and tore across the grounds of the compound. Consciously, she wasn't paying attention to where she was going. Her only goal was to get as far away from people as she possibly could. When her legs had reached their limits, she stopped to rest beside a tree and looked around to find that she was only a few yards from the wall that surrounded Psion's grounds. The sound of running water drew her, and she found a small creek a few feet away. She sat down on a rock beside it and absently grazed the tips of her fingers across the surface of the water.

For a while, it seemed as though she was in shock and this was all she was capable of doing. Then she leaned over the creek and cupped some water in her hand to bring up to her face. Crow set to work rinsing her face and scrubbing away the makeup she used to hide her scar. All the while, she was completely unaware of the figure that had tracked her down and was watching her, though it would've been difficult to spot him even if she had been paying attention to her surroundings. There were no sounds as he leapt from branch to branch among the trees, and he timed his shifts in perfect harmony with the wind rustling through the leaves. Cloaked in the long shadows of twilight, Nakamura was able to keep tabs on her. Without a sound, he stepped off the branch and landed on the ground behind her with a gentle thud.

He watched her a few moments more before clearing his throat and asking, "Were you injured, child?"

Crow nearly jumped out of her skin and attempted to get to her feet, but her left foot slipped on the very rock she had been sitting on. She would have fallen into the water if Nakamura had not reached out and firmly grabbed her arm.

"What are you doing out here?"

"Ironhawk was concerned for you," Nakamura answered. "You did not answer my question. Are you hurt?" He gestured at her forehead as the scar was now visible in the dim light.

"Oh, that. No. I was just washing away the makeup hiding it. I got this when I was sixteen. I was mugged in an alley. They took all my stuff and left me for dead. Amanda found me and took me to the hospital that my dad worked at. He saved my life…both mom and dad…died two years ago…someone set our house on fire. Well, it was more like someone firebombed it. I thought they were dead…" Crow's voice fell to a whisper as she looked back at the creek. Tears were starting to burn her eyes. "No matter how horrible I was, they always loved me. All I have left is a few pictures of them. Someone blew up my apartment like their house."

"Your parents would be disappointed in you, Crow."

She winced. "Why do you say that?"

"I knew your parents. They were agents of Psion. They were proud and honorable people who wanted you to grow up with the same strength you valued in them."

"You knew them?"

"Yes. Your father was a skilled healer – one of the best. Your mother was quite skilled, not only in mind, but also in body. Her telepathy was incredible, but her talent with Ninjutsu was even more spectacular. I can see some of her in the way you move."

Both fell silent.

"Will you teach me?"

The question caught him off guard and he stiffened involuntarily. Nakamura turned his attention back on the young woman. Makeup-free, red and puffy eyes, broken: she looked entirely different from the girl who had challenged him before, but there was a fire in her eyes he had not seen before. It was so strong that he could not deny her potential. "Teach you what?"

"Will you teach me Ninjutsu?" She straightened up and bowed to him. "I have a lot to learn, and I can only get so far on my own."

Neither moved. The inscrutable man closed his eyes after a moment and took a deep breath. "I was a pupil of a strict master. Like my master before me, I do not coddle the weak. If you wish for me to teach you, you must understand what I expect. You will learn discipline, strength, confidence, and power. You will know yourself, and each time you train with me there will be no second guessing, of either of us. When you go into battle, you cannot afford to second guess anything. You must act swiftly and definitively. A ninja must push themselves to their absolute limit and prove that they are willing to do whatever it takes to accomplish the mission at hand. Do you understand?"

"Yes, I understand."

"Very well. Due to my position as ambassador I cannot be at Psion as often as the other trainers. That means the days I am able to be here, we will train, regardless of what else is going on. When I am gone, I expect you meditate and perfect what I have taught you. Am I clear?" Nakamura raised his brow.

"Crystal," she responded, still maintaining her respectful tone.

"Very well."

Though she was still heartbroken from the mission and tears were still in the corner of her eyes, Nakamura noticed that some life had been breathed back into her. He looked over to the main house and caught sight of Amanda making her way toward them and grimaced. "It would seem your friend Amanda is on her way to check on you. I will leave her to it."

He leapt straight up to the tree branch above and stepped back to disappear into the shadows cast by the leaves. Amanda made the scene mere minutes later.

"I saw him over here. Where the hell did the Jap-bastard go?"

Crow shook her head with a slight sigh, "Amanda, I'm a Jap-bastard too."

"There's a difference. You're MY Jap-bastard. You're my sister. I love and trust you. I don't like or trust him. Did he do anything to you? I will kick his ass. You say the word I will shoot him right. in. his. ass!"

"He agreed to train me in Ninjutsu," Crow replied using her sleeve to wipe away the rest of the makeup on her face, unable to stop the smile creeping across her lips.

"Why him? Can't we find someone else?" she huffed in annoyance.

"No, Amanda. He's the only one."

"Nu-uh! You could go to any of those places we passed in D.C."

"Amanda, that would be like taking you to the Y.M.C.A. for boxing."

The dark-skinned girl narrowed her eyes on her sister for a moment and then begrudgingly said, "Fine, but I don't like it."

"Noted. Shall we get back to see what Ironhawk has to say?" Crow suggested.

"Sure, but uh, Crow..." Amanda danced around what she should say before finally pointing at the scar on her forehead.

"I know. I'm not gonna hide it anymore."

"Oh. Ok."

Amanda held her sister's hand as they walked back inside and stepped into the cafeteria to join everyone else. As soon as everyone sensed Crow's presence, they immediately quieted down, and she noticed that they seemed red in the face from laughter. They all stared at her, and there was a moment of tense silence.

Crow tried to put them at ease with a small smile and said, "I'm ok now."

"Here, take some coffee, little lady," Tex said as he stood and got her a mug of coffee. She thanked him and took a sip as Ironhawk cleared his throat.

"I've asked everyone to meet here because I know this mission wasn't an easy one, and it struck close to home. However, the discoveries your team made and the things you recovered made some developments for us possible. I will bring you up to speed on that later. Right now, we have losses to mourn, and it's important to do so properly. If you will follow me to our special little prayer garden, I will show you how we pay respect to those we have lost."

There was a quiet murmur as they got to their feet and filed out after him. Amanda pulled Crow along with her as she walked up to Nurse, and the old woman smiled as she wrapped a loving arm around each of them. Sek, James, Shutters and Jock followed close behind them while Tex and Billy brought up the rear.

The night air had a little bite as the wind had picked up. Ironhawk led them back toward a rather large, lush looking garden that had waist-high hedges all along the outside of it. As the group stepped inside, they were met with beautiful assortments of colorful flowers and bushes as well as strong, healthy trees. There were a few fountains and benches where people could sit and look over the beauty around them. As they looked around, junior team noticed there were strips of paper secured to branches of trees and bushes, and sturdy stems of beautiful flowers were tied with brightly colored bits of string. When inspected, there were names written on them. Junior Team took a closer look around and saw that there were so many papers they couldn't count them all.

"This is our Prayer Garden. Each slip of paper holds the name of someone we've lost. No one is forgotten. They are honored every day as—" Ironhawk began to explain, but stopped as a strange crackling sound boomed across the grounds and interrupted him. The static sound rippled out of the main speakers and then went quiet for a moment before coming to life again.

A song began to play. Amanda stiffened up as she recognized the tune, and Crow flashed back two years ago when Amanda had run out of her apartment before it burst into flames. It was the Battle Hymn of the Republic being whistled. Amanda began to hyperventilate as Nurse pulled her in close and the present members of senior team tensed and began to carefully spread out through the garden.

Sek reached for his knives and muttered, "What the hell is this?"

"Nothin' good, son. Nothin' good," Tex muttered quietly as the rest began to prepare their weapons.

Chapter 27: The Whistling Man

    No one could see the lean figure standing on the hill three miles out from Psion. He was just over six feet and was dressed in a worn, dark trench coat with dozens of pockets lining it. Shoulder-length black hair peaked out from his hunting hat, and his dark brown with a hint of hazel eyes stared out upon Psion as he rolled a toothpick between his teeth. There was a long, heavily customized rifle slung over his shoulder in one hand, and the other held a strange button that he triggered with his thumb. The sun-tanned man counted quietly under his breath for a few seconds before he shifted on his right leg and pocketed the small remote. A strange squeaking sound came from his right arm as he moved, and after a few more seconds, he began whistling.

    His expression was unreadable as he looked down the sight of the rifle. He watched as Amanda went rigid and pushed away from Nurse before taking off out of the garden at top speed.

    He clicked the toothpick to the other side of his mouth and shifted his sight to Crow, who was stunned for a second before rushing after Amanda, struggling to keep up. She was just as predictable as she had been two years ago. Both of them were. He continued whistling.

Agents were starting to spill out of the building. Ironhawk meticulously moved across the grounds as he held his sunglasses at his side and scanned the world around him. The gunman followed him until Ironhawk stepped just behind a structure that he could not see past from his current vantage point.

"That's right asshole. You've always been good at hiding."

He lowered his gun and opened the chamber as he pulled a special bullet from one of his inside pockets. A small slip of paper was wrapped around the casing that would leave the message undamaged after the bullet met its target. He quickly checked to make sure that, as per his signature, the name of his target was etched into the bullet. Satisfied, he loaded it into the chamber and prepared his gun before looking down the sight one final time. With a flex of his power, he grinned and mentally marked the exact place his bullet would land. The gunman exhaled and squeezed the trigger. His shot echoed in the silence around him.

"That's one."

Made in the USA
Lexington, KY
14 December 2019